P9-CBJ-804

"Stay back, Devlin!

"You're an international criminal and I'm going to bring you in!"

He stood his ground. The look of bemusement was gone. "Good Lord, what have they told you about me?"

"You're a killer, Devlin."

"And just who am I supposed to have killed?" He tossed the revolver onto the bed and seized her wrists.

"Those doctors and nurses who gave you a new face...with them out of the way there'd be no one to identify you."

He stepped in close, so close she could see her reflection in his dark blue eyes. "Except you, Tally. Now you can identify me. If you're right about me, that means I'll have to kill you, too...."

ABOUT THE AUTHOR

Fran Earley, who comes from a newspaper family, had her first article printed at age eighteen and since then has been nominated twice for the Pulitzer Prize in journalism. Fran first developed an interest in Latin America when she was sent to Mexico on an investigative assignment for the *Denver Post*. That trip has led to a continuing interest in the area, and Fran has now traveled extensively throughout Central America. She makes her home in Texas.

Books by Fran Earley

HARLEQUIN INTRIGUE
52–CANDIDATE FOR MURDER
69–RANSOM IN JADE
76–MOVING TARGET
79–SETUP

Don't miss any of our special offers. Write to us at the following address for information on our newest releases.

Harlequin Reader Service
901 Fuhrmann Blvd., P.O. Box 1397, Buffalo, NY 14240
Canadian address: P.O. Box 603,
Fort Erie, Ont. L2A 5X3

Hot Pursuit

Fran Earley

Harlequin Books

**TORONTO • NEW YORK • LONDON
AMSTERDAM • PARIS • SYDNEY • HAMBURG
STOCKHOLM • ATHENS • TOKYO • MILAN**

To the women of the United States Border Patrol

Harlequin Intrigue edition published September 1988

ISBN 0-373-22098-7

Copyright © 1988 Fran Earley. All rights reserved.
Except for use in any review, the reproduction or utilization of
this work in whole or in part in any form by any electronic,
mechanical or other means, now known or hereafter invented,
including xerography, photocopying and recording, or in any
information storage or retrieval system, is forbidden without
the permission of the publisher, Harlequin Enterprises Limited,
225 Duncan Mill Road, Don Mills, Ontario, Canada M3B 3K9, or
Harlequin Books, P.O. Box 958, North Sydney, Australia 2060.

All the characters in this book have no existence outside the
imagination of the author and have no relation whatsoever to
anyone bearing the same name or names. They are not even
distantly inspired by any individual known or unknown to the
author, and all incidents are pure invention.

® are Trademarks registered in the United States Patent and
Trademark Office and in other countries.

Printed in U.S.A.

CAST OF CHARACTERS

Tally Gordon—She was torn between her duty and her conscience.

Raul Devlin—There were many sides to the man, and an enemy on every one.

Nate Abrahamson—He meant to find Devlin, by fair means or foul.

Blaine Murchison—He had more to do in this investigation than anyone had planned.

Simon Ybarra—His polished manners failed to disguise the killer within.

Hans Uhlmann—He had a personal score to settle.

Federico Fuentes—His vision could result in unity, or devastation.

Chapter One

Tally Gordon first laid eyes on Raul Devlin shortly after eleven on a howlingly bitter night in mid-December when he popped up in the sights of her Star-Tron scope, one of two pale green images zigzagging across the north bank of the Rio Grande. Tally and other Border Patrol officers had been warned that Devlin was a dangerous and desperate man, and from what she could see in the scope he was obviously that and more: fleet, furtive and cunningly elusive as he darted from hillock to gully, like a jungle cat closing in on its prey, pausing from time to time to scan the darkness and listen, quietly sure of himself, but wary and ever alert.

At first, Devlin and his guide were little more than shimmering suggestions of movement among the dry brush and the harsh, jutting slopes where the river bottoms ended and the vast desolation of the West Texas range began. Slowly, shimmer became shape, and shape acquired embryonic characteristics of identity and personality as the figures in Tally's night-vision scope moved stealthily toward her.

The guide, thick and squat, halted occasionally to point the way, but then, as they moved on, he fell behind with a lurching, clumsy gait that Tally had come to know all too well during her five years on Patrol duty.

Most of the time, his client, who was far trimmer and much more agile, actually seemed to be leading the way. Everything about him—at least everything Tally could make

out through the darkness-dissolving lens of the Star-Tron—
bore the unmistakable stamp of leadership.

The guide, or *coyote*, was named Jaime Guerrero, and he
did business out of a bar in Juarez, hanging about day in,
day out, waiting for customers to come his way. His business was smuggling undocumented aliens across the border
and into the United States, at fees that ranged from a few
hundred dollars to a thousand or more, whatever the market would bear. The client paid cash up front and took his
chances. It didn't matter to Guerrero whether the client
made it to his destination, or got busted along the way, or
even died trying, as so many had. Guerrero always got his
money.

But don't stop too long this side of the border to count it,
Tally reflected as she knelt at the tripod that the heavy scope
was mounted on and observed the two men. *Someday,
somehow, I'll find a way to put you out of business—you
and all the other trash who prey on human misery.*

Maybe not this time, though, she realized. This time,
Jaime Guerrero was low on the list of the priorities. The
Border Patrol brass—and that fellow from Washington
who'd been closeted for two hours that afternoon with the
sector chief—were far more interested in the second man,
the one Guerrero had just shepherded across the river.

So was Tally.

Why? she wondered. Why should she be so fascinated
with this single individual, one of perhaps a million who try
to slip past the Patrol each year on the Texas border? All she
knew about Raul Devlin was his name and the fact somebody high up wanted him taken into custody, alive and
kicking and presumably talking about something important.

Tally didn't even know what her quarry looked like, and
apparently the man from Washington didn't, either, or he
would have given the Patrol at least a partial description, not
simply a name. Who was he and what had he done, or what
was he about to do, that made him the focus of such high-

level interest? Was he an international criminal of some sort, perhaps a spy or a terrorist? Whatever he was, Tally sensed that Devlin was an adversary to reckon with, bold and determined, all too willing to brave a black unknown to achieve an end she couldn't even begin to imagine.

She unclipped the walkie-talkie radio from the back of her equipment belt, held it to her lips and spoke into it—softly so that her voice wouldn't carry on the blue norther whistling down from the Llano Estacado of eastern New Mexico. "Delta One, this is Delta Four. I think I've got him."

The radio crackled to life. "This is Delta One. Is the *coyote* still with him?" Delta One would be Nate Abrahamson, she knew, the man from Washington who was in command of this special assignment. One of the Patrol's night supervisors who'd just been transferred from the east coast said he thought Abrahamson worked for the State Department, but he wasn't sure. All he knew—all anybody at sector headquarters seemed to know—was that Abrahamson carried a lot of clout, and when he said "jump," you jumped.

"Delta One, affirmative." Tally's gloved right hand came down off the Star-Tron and groped for the safety strap securing the hammer of the heavy Smith & Wesson revolver holstered on her hip. "Do you want me to take him?"

Blaine Murchison broke into the conversation, and there was a note of urgency in his husky, West Texas drawl. "Delta Four, this is Delta Two. You're there to observe and report. I repeat, observe and report. We'll make the collar."

Yes, sir! Tally reflected angrily. *You want to swagger in like John Wayne and grab all the credit. I'm just a helpless little girl playing big-boy games, and you're big and strong and so-o-o superior. Blaine Murchison, I wish you'd get off my back!*

"Delta Four? Do you copy?"

"I copy, Delta Two."

Blaine's tone softened. "Look, Tally, it's been a long night, and it's colder than a well-digger's hind end out here. We've had a half dozen reports of sightings all the way from here to Fort Hancock. You probably spotted a couple of stray cows—"

"I tell you, I saw them, Delta Two!"

"Sure you did, Tally. Just hang in there and give us a chance to check out all these other reports. I'll get back to you." Pause. "You read me?"

You don't know how well I read you! Tally thought. By ignoring radio discipline and using her first name, Blaine made it clear that he considered her a child in need of mature guidance. "Delta Two, I want some backup just in case those 'stray cows' start shooting," she said stiffly. *And while you're at it, listen up, Inspector: you're talking to Delta Four, not Talia Gordon. On duty, as far as you're concerned, Tally Gordon doesn't exist. It's Agent Gordon, who's assigned to an observation post code-named Delta Four, and the sooner you accept that, the better off we'll both be.*

"Now look, Tally..."

It hadn't gotten through to him. Damn him! He wasn't a bad sort—just insensitive. They'd known each other all their lives, had even dated for a while. But that was behind them, well behind them as far as she was concerned, yet he persistently seemed to refuse to see her as a professional. He allowed their former familiarity to color the way he treated her now, and at times tried to smother her under the force of his own personality. She needed space. She needed room to breathe, room to make her mistakes.

"...just keep your head down and observe. We'll be in your zone in five or ten minutes. Acknowledge."

Tally's thumb hovered over the on-off switch of the radio. "Delta One—" she'd talk to Nate Abrahamson, not Blaine. She had nothing more to say to Blaine, even if he was the Patrol Intelligence officer assigned to the case

"—I'll be off the air for a while. They're getting close and they might hear."

"Tally, you—"

Tally flicked the switch and refastened the radio to the belt where her gun holster, handcuff case, ammunition pouch, five-cell flashlight, chemical-mace canister, nightstick and keys hung. It was no time for chatter. Voices carried on the wind. If anyone was going to blow this stakeout, it wasn't going to be *her*.

She guessed the two men were less than thirty yards away now, moving directly toward her.

Loosening the knurled set screw that locked the Star-Tron scope in position on its tripod, she panned the bulky lens across the area on either side of the two men, covering a full ninety degrees.

Her pulse quickened. Was that movement of some sort off to the right?

She squinted into the eyepiece.

No, nothing to worry about, just a clump of tumbleweed that had blown free from the tangles of a mesquite tree. The two men seemed to be alone.

And then she heard it: the throaty sputter of an engine, from somewhere on or near the dirt road that paralleled Interstate 10. Glancing over her shoulder, she peered into the gritty darkness and saw the blocky outline of a van, lights out, moving slowly along the dirt road, as if the driver were looking for something.

She drew in a deep breath, feeling both relieved and irritated. It was reassuring to have backup, but why in God's name hadn't Blaine told her he'd stationed another agent just down the road? Why'd he let her think she'd been abandoned out here?

She could hear voices now, speaking hushed Spanish, and she turned back and sighted along the barrel of the Star-Tron, trying to get another fix on the two men approaching her outpost.

"*¿Cuan lejos?*" Tally heard one of them say. How far?

"Unos pocos metros, amigo." A few more meters, friend. *"No se preocupe."*

Tally's lips tightened in a determined smile. Guerrero was sadly mistaken. He had *plenty* to worry about. Maybe they wouldn't let her lock him up this time around, but she could make sure he had one less satisfied customer to write testimonials for him.

Unholstering her revolver and reaching for her flashlight, she straightened up from behind the Star-Tron, the stiff leather of her gunbelt creaking. *"¡Alto!"* she shouted, switching on the flashlight. *"¡Levanten los manos!"* Stop! Put up your hands!

She aimed the flashlight beam first at the scowling Guerrero, then at his companion, both of whom held their forearms in front of their faces to shield their eyes from the sudden glare. She knew the *coyote* and paid little attention to him. It was Devlin she was interested in. The latter was in his mid-to-late-thirties, lean and of medium height, and the quick glimpse Tally caught of him before he raised his arms revealed a man with clean-cut good looks and penetrating, dark blue eyes, which for a moment, made her wonder who was the hunter and who was the hunted. He was wearing jeans, a heavy black jacket and a black knit watch cap pulled down over his ears and forehead, and he had a small canvas carryall slung over his left shoulder.

Tally edged off to her right, so that by just shifting her eyes, she could watch both her prisoners and the van that had stopped on the road. *"Estamos ir a—"*

Guerrero grunted. "Please, *señorita,* you need not practice your high school Spanish on us. We are both fluent in English." He started to lower his hands.

Tally motioned with her gun, holding it so that the blue steel barrel caught the beam of her flashlight. "Get those hands on top of your head and stay put!" she said sharply. "The two of you are in violation of United States immigration laws, and it's my duty to tell you that you have the right to—"

"We're both well aware of our rights," Raul Devlin spoke up in a deep, cultured voice that was without a trace of accent. "Now would you be good enough to stop shining that light in our eyes? You're blinding us."

So pleasantly civilized was his tone that Tally started to lower the beam, then caught herself. Raul Devlin wasn't giving the orders; she was. Besides, she wanted the two men at a disadvantage. She shifted the beam of the flashlight until it was playing full against Devlin's upraised arms. "You listen to me, both of you. You're going to put your hands behind your necks and then we'll walk over to that van. *¿Entienden?*"

"We understand," Devlin said affably. He made no move to lower his arms, and all she could see of his face were those dark eyes squinting over the top of one sleeve.

"Then march!"

Half turning, but without taking her eyes off her prisoners, she directed the flashlight beam at the van and blinked the light on and off several times to signal the driver that it was safe to approach the outpost.

Again, Guerrero lowered his hands. "This was not part of the deal, *señorita,*" he complained sullenly. "You have the man you seek, eh? I can be of no further service, so..."

The *coyote* turned and began sauntering toward the riverbank.

Tally trained both the beam of her flashlight and the muzzle of her revolver at the retreating Guerrero. He still had some questions to answer and she didn't intend to let him walk away just yet. "One more step and I'll shoot!"

"I don't think you will," the *coyote* called back over his shoulder in mocking nonchalance. "I'm sure you know what would happen to you if you did." He kept moving.

Tally sighted down the barrel of the gun, watching him walk away. His bulk and his leisurely stride made him an easy target. One squeeze of the trigger—that's all it would take. One squeeze, and there'd be no more Jaime Guerrero. Shooting a man like Guerrero might even be considered striking a blow for human dignity.

But it didn't work that way, Tally knew. She was a cop, and a good one. It was a struggle sometimes when you ran up against a fellow like Guerrero, but good cops always managed to resist the temptation to become a law unto themselves. Pop had taught her that.

She raised the gun, and there was a deafening roar in the night as she fired a warning shot over the smuggler's head.

Guerrero stopped dead in his tracks, turned and stared wide-eyed at her.

Tally could hear the engine of the van rev, and from the corner of her eye, she could see the vehicle spurt forward, heading straight toward them, sending up a shower of loose gravel from its rear wheels.

It's about time, she thought. *Where were you when I needed you?*

Wishing the driver would switch on his headlights so she could see better, she trotted off after Guerrero.

All at once, there was a sharp rat-a-tat and puffs of dust mushroomed up from the ground around her feet. She whirled about and saw the darkened van barreling down upon her, its gears whining, little tongues of flame spitting out at her from the passenger-side front window.

She froze, gun at her side, paralyzed by an icy wave of panic. *Oh, my God!* she thought, momentarily powerless to move a single muscle. *It's not my backup. It's one of them! They've got a machine gun and they're trying to kill me.*

Bouncing and rattling as it tore across the prairie, the van bore down upon her, its boxy black shape becoming larger and deadlier by the second.

Move! a voice inside Tally's brain screamed. *Don't just stand there—do something!*

Closer and closer the van came. Thirty yards, twenty yards, ten yards . . .

And then, as suddenly as it had seized her, the panic was gone, replaced by an icy determination to fight back, to defend herself.

Raising her gun, she took careful aim at the windshield of the onrushing vehicle and started to squeeze off a shot.

Suddenly she was slammed to the ground, hard, and for a few seconds she thought the van had struck her. Shaking her head, blinking, she twisted about and saw that Devlin had thrown himself at her, knocking her out of the path of the vehicle. His cheek was pressed against hers, his breath warm against her neck, his powerful arms tight around her waist, pinning her to the ground.

Before she fully realized what was happening, Devlin pried the gun from her hand. Raising himself to a crouch, he trained the muzzle on the van as it rumbled past them, his left hand clutching his right wrist, holding the gun rock steady, waiting for a clear shot.

Tally saw the taillights of the van glow as the vehicle braked to an abrupt halt. And then it began to back up, and the red glow changed to white. Another burst of machine-gun fire sent a hail of bullets whistling around her and Devlin.

Devlin didn't budge. Still crouching, he fired two more quick shots, and almost immediately there was a howl of pain from the open window on the passenger side of the van.

The van's back-up lights went out as the driver hurriedly shifted gears and spun around, pointing the vehicle back toward the road.

Devlin casually tossed the gun to one side and rose to his feet, reaching for Tally as he did so. Trying to take charge of the situation again, she slammed her flashlight into his cheek, and he drew back, dazed. As the flashlight beam flickered and died, she saw Guerrero rush in and grab her gun. Quickly she scrambled to her feet, groping for her nightstick, but it was too late. Guerrero jabbed the muzzle of the gun against the small of her back and clamped a beefy hand over her mouth.

"A deal is a deal," the *coyote* hissed. Taking his hand off her mouth, he jerked her around and slapped her viciously with the back of one hand, sending her reeling backward. He moved in and grabbed her by the mop of tawny hair that had spilled down across her neck when her broad-brimmed Smokey hat came flying off. "*Señorita,* I'm afraid I'm going to have to teach you a lesson about not interfering." He drew back the hand holding the gun as if to club her with the barrel.

Suddenly Guerrero toppled backward. Devlin's right arm was locked around his neck. Devlin stripped the gun from the *coyote*'s hand and sent him sprawling forward on his hands and knees.

Still dazed, tasting blood on her lips from the blow she'd taken, Tally lunged at Devlin, but he sidestepped and gave her a playful pat on the rump as she went sailing by. "You are quite the wildcat," he chuckled as he deftly extracted the cartridges from her revolver and tossed the weapon to her.

Tally caught the revolver with one hand and grabbed for the ammunition pouch on her gunbelt.

"Please don't do that until I'm gone," he cautioned her. "I have no quarrel with you."

Guerrero had gotten to his feet and was moving toward them, sputtering with rage. Wheeling about, Devlin kicked the *coyote*'s feet out from under him, and sliced the heel of his left hand against the side of his neck. Guerrero crumpled.

In the few seconds in which Devlin's attention was diverted, Tally managed to slip two cartridges into the magazine of her revolver. She snapped the cylinder into place, then took a step back and pointed the weapon at the two men. "Hold it right there!" she ordered. "Neither of you is going anywhere."

"Quite the wildcat, indeed," she heard Devlin say. "But you sound like a very attractive one. What a shame I can't see your face. I'd like to stay and get acquainted, but I think we're about to have company."

Out of the corner of her eye, Tally saw that two cars and a truck were racing toward them along the dirt road paralleling the interstate. The van was nowhere in sight. "Don't move," she said, keeping her gun trained on Devlin.

The driver of the first vehicle to approach turned on his headlights and rooftop emergency flashers, and the sudden glare caused Tally to blink.

Still, she didn't waver, didn't take her eyes off Devlin.

The other car and the truck now had their headlights on, and the range was aglow with the criss-crossing of high beams, the red and blue emergency flashers adding an almost surrealistic touch.

Keep coming, Tally thought. *I've done my job, and now it's up to you.*

A few feet behind Devlin, she could see the *coyote* stir, then bring himself to his hands and knees, muttering and breathing heavily. One hand went to his hip pocket, and came away with something. She heard a metallic click, then saw Guerrero lunge at Devlin. There was something long and pointed and shiny in Guerrero's right hand.

"He's got a knife!" Tally shouted at Devlin, moving to one side to get a clear shot at the smuggler.

Spinning about on the balls of his feet, Devlin grabbed Guerrero's outstretched arm and then, in a single, fluid motion, twisted and ducked, sending his attacker tumbling head over heels.

The *coyote* landed at Tally's feet, knocking her backward and causing her to lose her balance. She fell hard, with Guerrero on top of her.

She worked her way out from under the dazed smuggler and looked around for Devlin.

He was gone, swallowed up in the darkness of the riverbank.

HIS CANVAS CARRYALL balanced on one shoulder to keep it dry, Devlin waded ashore on the Mexican side of the river and paused for a moment to look back. Close, he thought.

Almost too close. The immigration people were a lot sharper than that treacherous Guerrero had indicated. The young woman he'd encountered was perhaps a bit too fearless for her own good, but he had to admire her. It took real dedication to stand up to the enemy on a darkened riverbank when it was coming at you from all directions.

Devlin could see other headlights appear on the slope across the river, and he counted at least seven vehicles. He'd been set up. The Border Patrol had been waiting for him, and it probably was a good thing. If he'd gotten into that van...

He refused to think about it. Failure could be a self-fulfilling prophecy, and Raul Devlin had no intention of failing, not again. He'd failed once, and he knew the pain and the humiliation would haunt him until he managed to set things straight.

"Hasta la proxima vez," he murmured, turning and setting out for the city. Until next time. And there would be a next time, and a time after that, and a time after that if need be. He'd keep trying until he made it safely across the border and did what he had to do.

Striding along briskly, ignoring the numbing cold of his wet clothes, he considered going back to Monterrey and trying the airport again.

No, that wouldn't work, he decided. The Protectors were everywhere. They were almost certain to have at least one team at the Monterrey airport. He knew they had Mexico City and Guadalajara covered—Acapulco, too. They had money and they had contacts. They'd passed the word, greased the right palms. Every hoodlum, every corrupt official, would be watching for him.

He could try one of the other, lesser-traveled border crossings—Piedras Negras or Ciudad Acuña, perhaps. But each of them lay opposite smaller Texas cities: Eagle Pass and Del Rio, respectively. In a smaller city, it would be difficult to make the kind of connections he had to make if his mission was to be successful. In any case, the *norteameri-canos* weren't fools. He knew them, had fought alongside them, respected them.

But he had to do something. Time was running out.

Chapter Two

"It was the lousiest piece of police work I've ever seen!" Nate Abrahamson thundered, pacing the floor, hands clenched behind his back. "What idiot gave the order to turn on the lights and go charging in there like a herd of elephants?"

"I did," Blaine Murchison said laconically. "We heard shots and we knew an officer was in trouble and needed help. That's the way we do things around here, Mr. Abrahamson."

Abrahamson stopped pacing and stared contemptuously at Blaine. "It's damn well not the way *I* do things! In my book, the mission comes before any personal considerations. If your people can't look out for themselves, they shouldn't be wearing a badge."

"Just a minute," the chief spoke up from behind his memo-cluttered desk. "Agent Gordon did everything in her power to—"

"Devlin still got away," Abrahamson reminded him.

Tally could see the chief's cheeks flush. He was as angry as Tally ever had seen him, angry at everyone in the office—probably most of all at Abrahamson, who'd breezed into town on an Air Force jet and had taken over the entire El Paso sector.

Tally had been kept standing rigidly at attention ever since she'd entered the chief's office ten minutes before, while

Abrahamson paced and the chief and Blaine sat stiffly, largely ignoring her, as they discussed the case. Also seated in the office were the two men who'd arrived in El Paso with Abrahamson. Abrahamson hadn't introduced them—had in fact made it a point to keep them out of the discussion—but their icy presence was still felt. Both were thin, dark and prosperous-looking, with eyes like ferrets.

"What's done is done," the chief growled. "The end result is that Devlin made it back across the river, and the van just up and disappeared." He gave Abrahamson an accusing look. "If only we'd had a little more information, maybe this wouldn't have happened. But no, you people in Washington have to play this one close to the vest."

"There was no other way," the balding, middle-aged Abrahamson said in his clipped, New England accent. He seemed out of place here in El Paso sector headquarters, Tally thought. It wasn't just the accent or the pallor of his pinched face, it was everything about him: the gray pinstriped suit, the blue oxford-cloth shirt and striped tie, the always sour, sometimes holier-than-thou attitude.

"What do you mean?" the chief demanded. "You send my people out on a job where they can get themselves wasted by some trigger-happy hoodlum with a machine gun, and you tell me there was no other way. What the hell kind of an explanation is that?"

Abrahamson frowned. "It's a matter of national security. We need to get our hands on Devlin, and we can't broadcast our reasons. All right?" He glanced at the taller of his two companions, as if seeking approval. The other man just sat there patiently, his heavily lidded eyes half-closed, hands folded in his lap, as if he were an old-time hanging judge waiting to pronounce sentence.

"Just what's so all-fired important about this Devlin?" Blaine asked. Blaine, who was wearing a rumpled corduroy sport coat, jeans and cowboy boots, was a former football player, blond, freckled and thick-necked, and just brimming over with good-ol'-boy macho charm. Most of the time. Not now, though.

"Don't ask," Tally said caustically. "It's a matter of national security."

The chief shot her a withering glance. "Keep it up, Gordon, and you'll find yourself on the railroad graveyard shift so fast you won't know what hit you."

"Yes, sir," a subdued Tally murmured, squaring her shoulders and staring straight ahead. The railroad detail was the pits, not just dangerous, but ugly, nasty dangerous. It wasn't so much the undocumented aliens, but the psychopaths and drunks whose anger a Border Patrol officer faced when rousting them from boxcars. These non-paying passengers often came up kicking and cursing, sometimes slashing out with switchblades and broken bottles.

"Look," Abrahamson said, fatigue and exasperation showing in the lines around his eyes, "I'd like to clue you in, but I can't. You'll just have to accept what I say. Devlin is a hot item and we want him—fast." He glanced again at the taller of his mysterious companions.

"Why haven't you requested cooperation from the *federales*?" the chief asked.

Abrahamson snorted. "The Mexican authorities won't get involved, not unless we tell them exactly why we want Devlin picked up, and that we won't do. They've reluctantly agreed to look the other way when our people go nosing around in Juarez. But that's *all* they'll do."

"Hey, wait a minute," Blaine said, half rising from his chair. "Intelligence is *my* business. I've got sources on the other side of the river who—"

Abrahamson cut him off with a scowl. "If you object to the way I do things, Inspector, I suggest you get on the horn to the Commissioner of Immigration and Naturalization. If he's out, try the attorney general. You want direct orders from the White House, I can arrange that, too. All right?"

"We could have a go at sweating Guerrero," Blaine persisted. "We've got him dead to rights on a smuggling case, not to mention felonious assault. After all, he tried to pistol-whip Tally, and then he pulled a switchblade on Devlin. Given the right sort of deal, Guerrero might be persuaded to help us find your boy."

"Guerrero's already back in Juarez," the chief said.

"He's what!" Murchison jumped up, and both he and Tally stared open-mouthed at their boss.

"You heard me. We cut him loose."

"Why?" Tally ventured.

Abrahamson spoke up. "Because I ordered him released, that's why. Guerrero knows nothing more than he's already told us, and he can't do us any good sitting in one of your detention cells."

"So what do you want us to do now?" the chief asked, his tone heavy with grudging resignation.

Abrahamson brought out a pipe and tobacco, and glanced appraisingly at Tally. "It's just possible we can salvage something out of this." He packed coarsely cut tobacco into the bowl of the pipe, tamped it and then examined his handiwork. "You," he said, returning his attention to Tally, "are the only one who's actually seen Devlin in the flesh."

Tally wondered what he was getting at.

"The *coyote*'s seen him," Blaine corrected him. "And so has whoever put Devlin in touch with him."

"That's not what I mean," Abrahamson said. "Guerrero isn't on our team. *She* is. Besides, Guerrero's only met the man once, and that was in the dark with Devlin taking pains to keep his face covered. All the rest of their contact was by phone." He pointed a finger at Tally. "For God's sake, sit down, Gordon. You make me nervous standing there."

Tally glanced at the chief, who waved her to a seat.

"You got a good look at him," Abrahamson said. "Describe him for us."

"Again?"

"That's right—again." He flicked his head in the direction of his companions. "I want them to hear it."

Why? Tally wondered. *Just who are they and what business do they have here?*

"We're waiting, Gordon."

"Yes, sir." Tally tried to be as precise as she could. "He appeared to be in his mid-thirties, no more than forty. Height about six feet, I'd say, and leaner than average in build, but wiry in an athletic sort of way. He has very intense, dark blue eyes, the kind that make you think he's looking right into you. He's got a squarish chin, rather ordinary features—someone who'd be difficult to pick out of a crowd. He has sort of an energy about him—quick mind, fast reflexes, that sort of thing. His cap was down over his ears so I couldn't tell what color his hair is." She paused, trying to collect her thoughts. "No visible scars, but I got the impression..." What was it about him? Why couldn't she quite put her finger on it?

"You got what impression, Gordon?" Abrahamson prompted.

Tally hesitated, wondering whether she should say what she was thinking. She'd tried her best to be objective, confining her remarks to a straightforward presentation of the facts. But there was something about Devlin that defied any attempt at pat categorization. She shrugged and decided to forge ahead. "Looking at him, even for a few seconds, I sensed he was a person who'd known a lot of suffering. It was as if he didn't really care if he got hurt. He'd go on doing what he had to do. He had...well, an air of determination, I suppose."

One of the mystery men, the shorter of the two, gave a little grunt that might have passed for a laugh. Tally couldn't tell.

"Devlin has determination all right," Abrahamson admitted. "Then again, as one of only a handful of women in the Border Patrol, you may just be a hopeless romantic."

"Not really," Tally said defensively. "I consider myself quite practical."

"Do you, Gordon?"

Blaine laughed and winked at Tally. "'Fess up, girl. Tell the man that you're a dyed-in-the-wool do-gooder."

Tally glared at him.

"What's this do-gooder business?" Abrahamson asked.

"Tally's been a part-time law student at the University of Texas in El Paso for the past few years. She says that someday she wants to run for Congress and help rewrite our immigration laws. To paraphrase Will Rogers, she's never met a wetback she didn't like."

Why don't you drop dead, Blaine? Tally thought. *For your information, I'm not a part-time law student anymore. I've taken the bar exams and now I'm just waiting for the results. When I find out I passed, I'll hand in my badge and get on with my life. And none of that has anything to do with Raul Devlin anyway.*

Abrahamson stuffed his tobacco pouch and unlighted pipe into his coat pocket. He got up, walked to the door and opened it, then turned and looked at his two companions and at Blaine. "You people mind waiting outside?"

The two mystery men got up and left the office. Blaine hesitated long enough to give the chief a do-I-have-to? glance, then shrugged and left.

Abrahamson closed the door and confronted Tally. "Tell me, Gordon, did Devlin get a good look at you?"

"No."

"You sure?"

"As sure as I can be. You know how it is when you're in a dark room and the lights come on. It takes a while for your eyes to adjust. That's how it was when I shined my flashlight on them. Both of them were blinded for a minute."

"You'd recognize him if you saw him again?"

"I think so. Yes, I'm sure of it."

Abrahamson resumed his pacing, momentarily lost in his own thoughts. Suddenly he stopped directly in front of Tally, studied her, and then looked at the chief. "I'd like to borrow Gordon for a few days. She's the only one this side of the Rio Grande who's ever set eyes on the new Raul

Devlin. I want to take her across to Juarez and see if we can't pick up his trail.''

The chief wasn't happy with the idea. "You're aware we have no authority whatsoever on the Mexican side?"

"I am."

"She'd go over as a tourist. No uniform, no weapon."

Abrahamson grunted. "I don't anticipate another gun-fight at the OK Corral. If I did..." He let the sentence dangle.

The chief settled back in his swivel chair and folded his hands across his chest. "Even so, there's an element of danger. The *coyotes* are downright ticked off with our people, what with the way we've been putting the screws to them lately. Who's to say Guerrero wouldn't try to get even with Gordon if he had the chance?"

"Our people will keep him in line, chief. Don't worry about it."

Tally spoke up. "Mr. Abrahamson, what did Guerrero mean when he told me 'a deal is a deal'?"

"He was paid money to deliver Devlin—five thousand dollars, plus whatever Devlin gave him. Guerrero obviously got upset when he found out you were trying to run him in. I assume he figured we were trying to cheat him out of the money."

"Who paid him?" Tally demanded.

"Our people, of course."

Tally shook her head slowly. "I don't understand."

"I'll spell it out for you, Gordon. We put out the word in Juarez that Devlin was going to try to cross the river in this sector. We don't know what he looks like nowadays, but we do know the names and addresses of some of his contacts in Juarez. When one of those contacts got in touch with Guerrero, Guerrero came to us and we waved some money under his nose. Guerrero agreed to deliver Devlin."

"You seem to be going to an awful lot of trouble just to grab one undocumented alien."

"Devlin is no ordinary illegal alien—believe me."

"So I gather." Tally hesitated. "Who are those two other men you brought with you?"

Abrahamson eyed her coldly. "Why do you ask?"

Tally shrugged. "I'd like to know who I'll be working with, that's all."

"I've got news for you, Gordon. You won't be working with them—I will be. You stay away from them. Understand?"

Tally resented the way he was treating her, but she was in no position to argue. "Yes, sir," she said crisply.

"Any more questions?"

Lots of them, Tally thought. *And I'm sure you've got a put-down for each and every one.*

But there was something she had to know...

"You indicated Devlin has had his features altered. Why has he gone to so much trouble to keep from being recognized?"

Abrahamson stopped pacing and addressed himself to the chief, pointedly ignoring the question. "It's agreed then? I can borrow Gordon for a few days?"

The chief threw up his hands. "If she's willing to take the risk."

"Well, Gordon, how about it?"

Tally thought about it. She'd been shot at, beaten and nearly run down by a van, all this in an effort to arrest a man she still knew absolutely nothing about. She had to know why Devlin was wanted and there was only one way to find out. "When do we start?"

"First thing in the morning. I'll pick you up."

"Exactly what will I be doing?"

"You have reservations about this, Gordon?"

"No, not really. I was just wondering how to dress."

"Like a lady, if you don't mind. Think you can manage that?"

"I'll do my best," Tally said dryly. *What a hateful man!* she thought.

IT WAS ALMOST DAYLIGHT when Raul Devlin got back to his hotel near the center of Juarez. The tiny, tiled lobby was empty, and for that he was grateful. The fewer people who saw him, the better. Nodding affably to the night clerk, he skipped up the stairs to his second-floor room. He'd tried to brush off the worst of the riverbank mud from his jeans and shoes, but he was sure the clerk had noticed his appearance and had mentally filed away the information for future use and possible profit. The clerk had a hungry look, as had so many of the people he'd encountered in Juarez.

Raul hadn't wanted to return to the hotel, but he'd planned for the possibility. He always made it a point to maintain a fallback position. Basic military strategy: they'd drilled that into him at West Point, and he'd passed on the lesson to the troops who'd served under him.

Stripping off his damp clothes, he got under the shower and let the tepid water soothe his hard-muscled body. In cold weather such as this, the thin scar that angled from collarbone to right hip ached, reminding him of a time and a place he'd just as soon forget.

He'd almost made it, he told himself as he tilted his face toward the spray. Almost, but not quite.

He'd thought about it on the long walk back from the crossing point. That Border Patrol woman—*la migra*—hadn't been there by chance. She'd obviously been waiting for him, and that meant Guerrero had tipped off immigration authorities. What was it Guerrero had said? "This was not part of the deal, *señorita*." What deal?

Raul stepped out of the shower stall and toweled himself dry.

He couldn't blame the woman. She was just doing her job. It was Guerrero who'd betrayed him. He'd have a talk with Guerrero, see how much the *coyote* had told them. Then he had to be on his way north.

He thought again of the woman he'd encountered in the dark, on the other side of the river. *La migra*. He'd had only a fleeting impression of what she looked like, an impression gleaned from the sweep of a flashlight beam as her heavy flashlight thudded against his cheekbone.

She was very much a woman, he sensed. Very much a woman trying to act tough and masculine. No, that wasn't it. Not tough and masculine, but serious about her job, wanting to prove something. Perhaps she wanted to show that she considered herself every bit the equal of a man. He liked people who stood up for themselves. He smiled. I'll never see you again, *migra,* and more's the pity.

Changing into slacks and a sweater and dry shoes, he set out to look for Jaime Guerrero.

DRESS LIKE A LADY, Abrahamson had said. You bet, Tally said to herself as she paused by the full-length mirror mounted to the back of her bedroom door and gazed at the reflection of the olive-green uniforms hanging on one side of the closet. The uniforms were reminders of what she was, as opposed to what she'd like to be, and the circular yellow patches sewn just below the shoulder seams on the left sleeves said it all: U.S. Border Patrol. In other words, you're just another federal cop, with rules and regulations coming out your ears, unbecomingly cynical after five years on the job.

Who am I? she wondered, staring at the stranger in the white bikini panties and strapless bra. She wanted to be a woman, but even more than that she wanted to be somebody, wanted to do something with her life, something significant. Because of her wants, she seemed to have developed a talent for frightening off people—men people, that is—who might otherwise have been attracted to her.

Blaine Murchison? No, not Blaine. Not ordinary men, with ordinary egos. Blaine might be a family friend, but never anything else—not again. They were two different kinds, and always would be.

What men, then?

Oh, come off it, Gordon. At twenty-eight, you're too old for adolescent games.

Aren't you?

She stared at the figure she saw reflected in the mirror. It wasn't a great figure, but it wasn't all that bad, either—certainly not voluptuous, but not fashion-model skinny, either. She was tanned, vibrant, reasonably pretty, with brownish yellow hair and oval eyes and a pleasant smile, when she chose to smile.

"I just want to be me," she told herself aloud. "I want to put this phase of my life behind me and set up a law practice and do my thing, and then we'll see what happens."

I want to be me. Wasn't that the theme song of a generation, her generation? Then why was she a federal cop, waltzing around with a gun on her hip, a badge on her shirt, acting like a textbook tomboy?

She promised. That was why. She made a promise.

Pop had been a Border Patrol agent. He was a gruff, no-nonsense sort, but with the heart of a real softy, and he'd desperately wanted a boy to bounce on his knee and play catch with and take hunting and rafting and do all those father-son things with. Pop had wanted a boy, and he got her, Talia, a girl who could never give him what he wanted: someone to follow in his footsteps, do all the things he did, live the life he led.

Pop had been aboard a Border Patrol helicopter that crashed in the Franklin Mountains one night when the wind went crazy and the desert skies crackled with lightning. He lingered on in intensive care for a week, and before he died she'd told him not to worry, that she'd carry on, make him proud.

She meant one thing; he understood something else. And Pop died pressing his silver shield against the palm of her hand, telling her she was his kid and he knew he could count on her. Always had, always would.

Always. How long was always?

Five years, Tally had told herself. Five years should do it. Five years on the job and she would have kept faith with Pop, would have done all that he could possibly expect her to do. After five years, she had her law degree, and any day now, when the official notification came from the state Bar, she could turn in her resignation from the Patrol and start practicing law. It might not be quite the life Pop had in mind for the son he never had, but it was the compromise she had to make to be at peace with herself and with Pop's memory.

She looked in the closet and examined her civilian wardrobe. Exactly what were "ladies" wearing this season? She had no idea, never bothered to keep tabs on such things. If ladies were wearing sweaters and skirts, or jeans and sweatshirts, she'd make the best-dressed list for sure, she decided. That was all she really needed for what little she had of a private life after putting in her eight hours on line watch and four or five hours in the classroom, listening to lectures on torts and writs and rules of evidence.

She chose a khaki-colored wool skirt, a blue cotton shirt and a white wool cardigan. A bit preppy, perhaps, but ladylike. If Abrahamson didn't like it, too bad. When it came to identifying Devlin, she was the only game in town.

Pulling on knee-high argyle socks, she slipped her feet into an old pair of cordovan loafers—just the thing for negotiating the cracked sidewalks across the river in Juarez, for roaming the crowded markets and bar-hopping, pretending to drink while she studied the crowds in search of one special face, a face she'd seen only once in the beam of a flashlight.

She examined herself in the mirror. Too casual? She didn't want Abrahamson going back to Washington telling the State Department or whoever else he worked for that some bubble-headed little college girl had let the big one get away. Perhaps she ought to put on hose. And heels. And maybe...

Twenty minutes later, wearing her only suit, of dark blue wool with a tailored skirt, a ruffled white blouse, and black leather pumps with two-and-a-half-inch heels, she opened the door and greeted Abrahamson.

And her mouth dropped open.

He stood there, his attaché case at his side, a complete transformation from the man she'd been introduced to the day before. Oh, he was still very much the stuffed shirt—always would be, she was sure—but the somber three-piece suit had given way to cotton slacks, tan herringbone jacket and open-necked checked shirt. Very casual, very Ivy League.

"Where's the funeral?" Abrahamson grumbled, brushing past her into the living room.

Tally restrained an urge to give him a swift kick. "You told me to dress like a lady. If you want me to change, I'll change. But I'd like to have some idea just what it is you expect of me."

Abrahamson thumped his attaché case down on the maple coffee table in front of the couch. "I expect you to help me find Devlin. You want to tramp the streets looking like an undertaker, that's up to you."

"Mr. Abrahamson, if you . . ."

"If I what?"

"Nothing," Tally sighed, biting back the words she wanted to speak. "Excuse me, I'll be right back."

She ducked into the tiny bedroom, slammed the door and changed back into skirt, shirt, sweater, argyle socks and loafers. Slinging her purse over her shoulder, she returned to the living room. "All right," she said, "lead on, Mr. Abrahamson."

Giving her a puzzled frown, he sat down and opened his attaché case. "No, Gordon, I want you to lead on." He scanned the topmost file, then closed the case and spun the combination lock securing it. "It's all up to you from here on out."

Tally studied him. "You want to find Raul Devlin."

"That's the general idea."

"All right, tell me who he is."

"I can't do that."

"Then I can't be of much help. Juarez is huge. It has a population of upwards of a million people. It has sprawling slums, a few high-rent districts, zillions of shops, hotels and restaurants of every description. Unless you tell me something about Devlin—who he is and what he's like and exactly what it is you want him for—I won't have the foggiest idea where to begin looking."

Abrahamson thought about it, then made his decision, but it was clearly a decision he was not at all happy about. "All right, Gordon, tell me what you need to know, and I'll give you what answers I can—within the limitations of security naturally."

"Naturally. First off, is he a Mexican?"

"No."

"With a name like Devlin, I assume he's part Irish. Just what is his nationality?"

"Sorry, I can't tell you."

"Can you specify what planet he's from?"

Abrahamson pursed his lips. "He's from Latin America. That's all I can tell you."

"That narrows it down to a third of a billion people, give or take a few million."

"Gordon, your flippancy isn't helping things. If you knew the pressure we're under, you'd understand."

Tally smiled sweetly. "Tell me about the pressure."

"I can't do that."

She tried another tack. "What can you tell me about the man? What sort of work does he do?"

"He's a poet."

"A what?"

"You heard me—a poet. Until a year ago, he was living in Brussels, making his living writing poetry."

Tally thought of the man she'd seen in the glare of her flashlight. "He didn't look like a poet."

"What did he look like to you?"

"You've seen those World War II movies about commandos dressed in black, slipping through enemy lines? That's what he reminded me of."

"Not surprising, Gordon. Raul Devlin is a graduate of the United States Military Academy at West Point and he went through airborne ranger training at Fort Benning. In addition to being a poet, he's a soldier—that is, he was a soldier, and a first-rate one, at that."

Tally brought coffee and mugs from the kitchenette. The diversion gave her time to look for holes in the bits and pieces Abrahamson was reluctantly sharing. "If Devlin went to West Point, surely there are photos of him. Yearbooks, ID cards, that sort of thing."

Abrahamson shook his head. "That was almost twenty years ago."

"You said he was a soldier. Surely you could turn up a more recent photo of him from that part of his life."

Abrahamson reopened his attaché case. He dipped into the file he'd consulted earlier and held up a glossy photo. It was a head-and-shoulders portrait of a dashingly handsome man wearing a dark tunic with touches of gold braid and several rows of ribbons pinned above the left breast pocket. Although Abrahamson didn't let the photo out of his hands, he allowed Tally to get a quick glimpse at it. "Recognize him?"

Tally shook her head.

"I didn't think you would. This—" he tapped the portrait with a blunt forefinger, then slipped it back into his file "—is the most recent photograph we have. It was taken six years ago when Devlin was promoted to major."

"He doesn't look a thing like the man I saw. What did he do? Have plastic surgery?"

Abrahamson nodded. "Yes, but not by choice. He was badly wounded in a scrape in northern Guatemala, and he was flown to a hospital in Mexico City—more dead than alive, I might add. One of the finest cosmetic surgeons in the hemisphere completely rebuilt his face, and we have no idea what the new face looks like. No one does, for that matter."

"Have you tried talking to the surgeon?"

"Impossible, Gordon. The surgeon, his assistant and the two nurses who worked with them were murdered shortly after Devlin checked out of the hospital."

Tally's jaw dropped, and she stared wide-eyed at the man from Washington. "He killed them?"

"Possibly. The Mexico City police tell us that just a day or so before the murders, someone broke into the surgeon's office and stole the case files and photos showing Devlin's reconstructed face."

Tally shook her head slowly. "But if he had the photos, why did he return and murder those four people?"

"Maybe under that suave exterior you described to us, the man's a vicious killer."

CIUDAD JUAREZ, which hugs the south bank of the Rio Grande, directly across from El Paso, is a major gateway to Mexico and, sadly, little more than an untidy inconvenience for motorists headed south to Chihuahua, Durango and other more picturesque destinations in the interior. The Mexican government has tried its best to make Juarez more inviting. The city has a modern shopping center, Centro ProNaF, where tourists unschooled in the fine art of haggling can buy fixed-price curios with the reasonable assurance their purchases are authentic. The best restaurants are clean, the food first-rate. Townspeople generally are friendly, and local police have even been known to go out of their way to assist strangers. There are well-kept bullrings, museums and parks, and while the streets remain in a constant state of pothole-pocked chaos, signs with international symbols make it difficult to get hopelessly lost. On the debit side, Juarez still makes a shoddy first impression with its persistent sidewalk hustlers, the bustle of crowds, the glare of neon over portals leading to seedy saloons that thump with Tex-Mex rhythms and woebegone wailings and, over it all, an odor of overripe produce and general decay.

"You people in the Border Patrol certainly have your work cut out for you," Abrahamson observed as he and Tally sat at a table in La Fogota, a few blocks from the ProNaF, eating a late lunch.

Tally looked up from her *carne asada*. "How's that?"

"All these people we've seen this morning, they all want to come to the United States, and there are so few of you to keep them out. I wonder if you don't sometimes feel like the Dutch boy who stuck his thumb in the dike."

Tally put down her knife and fork. "How long have you been in government service, Mr. Abrahamson?"

"Almost thirty years. Why?"

"What do you do?"

"Security."

"What kind of security?"

Abrahamson's eyes narrowed. "Just what are you getting at, Gordon?"

Tally refused to be intimidated. "Simply this. You seem to have a way of jumping to conclusions, and I hope your attitude isn't typical of Washington. You talk about Mexicans as if they were some lower-life form. They don't all want to come to the United States. Most of them would rather stay in Mexico. They love their country, just as we love ours—perhaps even more so, because their revolution wasn't all that long ago and they're that much closer to their history. I'll grant you, a lot of them try to slip across the river to find jobs in the United States, but it's simple survival. The *mojados*, as we call them, have families to feed and clothe, and there isn't enough work in Mexico. I'm aware the labor market on either side of the river can take only so many workers, but we've got to remember that undocumented aliens are still human beings, and we have to keep trying to find solutions."

A thin smile played at the corners of Abrahamson's lips. "I see what Murchison meant when he said you were a do-gooder."

Tally winced. She'd been trying not to think about Blaine. They hadn't dated in some time, but now he wanted to get together again. No way. He was good-hearted, and he'd been there for her when Pop died, but their relationship never could go anywhere. They worked for the same agency, but that was all they had in common. Although he'd proposed, he'd made it clear he didn't want to be married to a woman who had a mind of her own. He wanted a quiet little homebody who'd devote her every waking moment to stroking his ego.

"Inspector Murchison sometimes takes a shortsighted view of things," Tally said cautiously. "Anybody with an ounce of intelligence has to realize that we have to do more than—how did you put it?—keep a thumb in the dike. We have to do something about the underlying problems."

"That's why you want to become a lawyer, Gordon?"

"That's right, Mr. Abrahamson. That's why I want to become a lawyer."

"Very well, now that I've heard your little lecture, let me tell you something. You people in the Border Patrol could let a million illegals slip into the United States, and collectively, they couldn't do as much damage to our national interests as a single Raul Devlin. From here on, Gordon, spare me your bleeding-heart dissertations and help me find the man. Time is of the essence."

Tally pushed aside her plate. The *carne asada* was delicious, but she'd lost her appetite. "What are you going to do with Devlin when you do get your hands on him?"

Abrahamson smiled grimly. "We're going to see that he gets across the river—one way or another."

"I thought you wanted to keep him out of the United States?"

"On the contrary, Gordon. There are those at the highest level in Washington who are most eager to have him come visit us. On our terms, of course."

"In other words you want him for interrogation? You want him to tell you something, right?"

Abrahamson looked at her strangely, as if Tally had stumbled upon a great truth and he wasn't at all sure she was to be trusted with it. "You might say that."

"And after you question him—what then?"

The man from Washington stared at her, but didn't answer.

She was beginning to get the picture, and she didn't like what she saw. She didn't like it at all. "You're going to kill him," Tally said in a low voice. "Isn't that right, Mr. Abrahamson?"

His laugh didn't quite come off. "You've been reading too many spy novels, Gordon."

Tally knew then and there she had to do everything in her power to keep Raul Devlin alive. All her training in law and police work, all her instincts, told her she could do no less. And Nate Abrahamson be damned.

JAIME GUERRERO STARED wide-eyed at the whirring drill. He couldn't move. Raul Devlin and his white-jacketed friend had strapped his wrists to the arm of the chair, and a firm hand was on his forehead, pressing him back.

Raul stood alongside his friend, his eyes hidden behind dark glasses, the brim of a gray, tweed slouch hat pulled low over his face. "Scream if it makes you feel better," he said cheerfully. "This is a dentist's office. No one will pay the slightest attention."

Guerrero's round eyes rolled from side to side. "Why are you doing this? I tried to help you. I tried to be your friend, provide a service, and this is how you treat me?"

"You betrayed me, Señor Guerrero. I trusted you, and you took my money and then betrayed me. Not only that, you attacked me with that pig-sticker of yours."

It was chilly in the office, but Guerrero was sweating profusely. "I didn't! I swear it! I was trying to save you from that woman—that's all!"

"I don't believe you."

"It's true!"

"Then why have you been hiding from me?"

"I wasn't hiding! I've . . . I've been sick in bed."

"Then you must take better care of your health, *señor*. Tell me, how much did they pay you?"

"I don't know what you're talking about, hombre!"

Raul nodded, and the man in the white jacket pulled down Guerrero's thick lower lip and moved the drill closer. "Shame on you," the man in the white jacket said, clucking his tongue. "You haven't been brushing regularly, and as a result you have many cavities. Filling them is apt to be painful. I might even have to do some root-canal work."

"No!"

Fingers tightened on the *coyote*'s chin and his lower lip was pinned down by knuckles. The tip of the drill was only an inch away from his upper incisors.

"How much did they pay you?" Raul repeated.

"I don't—" Guerrero stared at the drill, then at Raul. "Make him stop! I am not your enemy."

The drill remained where it was, still whirring.

"How much?"

"A . . . a thousand dollars."

"How much, *señor*?"

"A thousand dollars."

Raul sighed. "You disappoint me. I disappoint myself. I'd hoped I was worth more than that. Let me ask you again, *señor*. How much did they pay you?"

Guerrero ran the tip of his tongue over his upper lip. "Five thousand dollars."

"Who gave you the money?"

"I don't know—some gringo I never saw before."

"What was his name?"

"Abrahamson."

"Was he alone?"

"He . . . he had two men with him."

"Describe these men."

"They were well dressed, middle-aged, important looking. Dark suits, white shirts, ties. Obviously businessmen."

"What were their names?"

"I forget."

Again Raul nodded to the man in the white jacket.

"Ybarra—that was one of them!" Guerrero screamed. "The other was Uhlmeyer or Ulbar, something like that!"

"Could it have been Uhlmann?" Raul asked.

"Yes, yes! That was it. Uhlmann! Hans Uhlmann!"

"Who else was with them?"

"No one that I know of."

"You're sure? You'd stake your life on it?"

Guerrero made a visible effort to remember. "There may have been two other men waiting for them in a car across the street. Yes, there were two other men. I remember now. All four of them, they . . . they . . ."

"They what?"

"They had the look of death about them. You know, like they were going to a funeral."

Raul signaled to the man in the white jacket, who stepped back and turned off the drill. "I hope you've told me everything, *señor*. If you haven't, we'll have another chat, you and I."

"I've told you all I know, hombre! Believe me!"

Raul shrugged. "We'll see. In a moment I'm going to lead you outside. Under no circumstances will you come back here, nor tell anyone about this place nor about that gentleman you see there." He pointed to the man in the white jacket. "If you do, I promise you'll be visited by other men who have the look of death about them. And those men won't wait outside in a car."

"You have my word!" Guerrero said quickly.

"One other thing, *señor* . . ."

"Yes?" the *coyote* said, now eager to please.

"You tried to hurt that young woman we encountered across the river. Try that again, and you'll be in serious trouble. I shall not be here to deal with you, but I have friends who will be keeping watch on you. *¿Entiende?*"

"Yes, yes! I understand!"

"Good."

The man in the white jacket set aside his drill. "You really should visit your dentist more often, my friend. Your teeth are in deplorable shape..."

Chapter Three

Tally spotted him purely by accident late in the afternoon of the second day, a Saturday. She was in the doorway of a pharmacy at Avenida Juarez and Insurgentes, waiting for Abrahamson to finish making a call from a phone inside the shop, when she saw Devlin come hurriedly down the stairs of a tired old building with gilt-and-black signs advertising not one but three cut-rate dental clinics. He was wearing a dark blazer, gray wool slacks and an open-collared, white shirt, and he was much better looking than Tally remembered from their brief encounter on the riverbank. She was technically on duty, undercover, but she still wanted to kick herself for setting out that day in scruffy jeans and a college warm-up jacket.

She and Abrahamson had looked everywhere, and Abrahamson had even called in reinforcements to flash copies of a rough sketch an artist had done based on Tally's description. Tally had described Devlin as best she could, but the likeness was far from adequate. There was no way an artist could capture the style and personality, the magnetism, that set the man apart.

At the foot of the stairs, Devlin glanced up and down the avenue, as if checking faces in the crowd, and then set out for Insurgentes, where he turned east.

Peering into the plate-glass window of the drugstore, Tally saw that Abrahamson was still on the phone. She rapped on the window and waved, but couldn't get his attention.

Devlin was already almost out of sight and Tally started after him, with not even a vague idea of what she might do if she caught up with him. Perhaps if she came right out and told him it would be dangerous for him to try to slip across the border again . . . Didn't she owe him that much? Hadn't he shoved her out of the path of the van, then saved her from a beating at the hands of Guerrero? More than that, she was sworn to uphold the law, and the law could never countenance murder.

Ducking around a car double-parked in the middle of the block, she crossed the street, head low to prevent Devlin from getting a good look at her.

No, she couldn't warn him—at least not until she had more to go on than her own private suspicions. She was under orders to help apprehend Raul Devlin, and on the surface, those orders were clear-cut and lawful.

Still, if he didn't cross the border, he wouldn't be much of a threat to the national security, would he?

No, she decided, she had to help apprehend him.

The seemingly irreconcilable conflict gnawed at her conscience. Apprehend? Kidnap was a better word. Why did Washington want Devlin? What had he done, or what was he about to do, that made him so important?

Maybe she shouldn't ask. Maybe she didn't want to know. In any case, the law was the law.

Temporizing didn't help. She knew the answer even before she'd framed the question clearly in her own mind. U.S. statutes might not apply to Raul Devlin here on the Mexican side of the Rio Grande, but they certainly applied to her. Like it or not, she was expected to follow orders.

Devlin walked unhurriedly, not looking back, as if he didn't have a care in the world. Tally stayed half a block behind him, keeping other pedestrians between them.

And then she lost him.

Tally stepped up her pace, came to a narrow side street and saw Devlin striding along, faster now. The side street was a corridor of barred-window adobe, and there were no other pedestrians in sight—just a few mangy dogs meandering listlessly in the late-afternoon sun. If she went after him, he was sure to spot her. Did he suspect someone was tailing him? Perhaps this was his way of getting them to show their hand.

She had to take the chance.

She waited until he was a block away, crossing Vicente Guerrero, and then she started after him, the heels of her penny loafers clicking briskly against the cobblestones.

Halfway between Vicente Guerrero and Avenida 16 de Septiembre, Devlin stopped, half turned and took a map from his jacket pocket. As he opened up the map, did he glance back at her out of the corner of his eye? Tally couldn't be sure. She kept on walking and, nodding pleasantly as she passed by him, said, *"Buenas tardes."*

"Good afternoon to you, too, miss," Devlin said in unaccented English. He smiled. "Say, do you have a minute? I'd like to ask you something."

Ask her what? Tally wondered, turning to face her quarry. Ask her why she was following him? She looked at Devlin, said nothing. But she confirmed her initial impression that his eyes were dark blue, not brown like most Latins.

He held out the folded map. "I'm trying to find the city market. Could you direct me?"

Tally stared at him. He didn't look a bit like the man in the photo that Abrahamson had shown her. The man in the photo was cool, aloof, aristocratic. The Raul Devlin who stood before her was warm and apparently guileless. His closely trimmed hair was a soft brown, and the golden cast of his taut skin might be attributed to a tan acquired on a golf course. He had a look of strength, but strength without bulk, for he was lean and on the short side of six feet. His lack of accent was remarkable. Could it have been the result of four years at West Point, mixing daily with a cross-section of American youth? Probably. Or else Devlin was a quick study and a brilliant actor, so brilliant that surely he could have slipped into the United States by some other means—by jetliner from one of the Mexican resorts, maybe; he wouldn't even have needed a passport, just some easily forged identification, if that. She'd mentioned this to Abrahamson, but the man from Washington just shrugged and said that Devlin had his reasons.

"According to the map, the market is supposed to be along here somewhere," Devlin said. He laughed and stuffed the map into his pocket. "You know, I never could learn how to read these things."

Tally almost said, *I thought map-reading was a required course at West Point.* Instead, she smiled sympathetically. "What you want is called El Mercado. Go down to Avenida 16 de Septiembre and turn right. You can't miss it. I'm going there myself."

"Hey, mind if I tag along? I'm a stranger in Juarez and I don't speak Spanish."

Am I crazy? Tally asked herself. A second ago, I was melting when I saw those blue eyes, and now he's looking straight at me, lying through his teeth! "Sure. Come on along."

"You must live in El Paso," Devlin said, falling into step beside her as she started walking again. "Do you get over here to Mexico very often?"

"Now and then."

"What brings you over today?"

"I had a day off, so I thought I'd do some Christmas shopping." She could lie, too. It wasn't all that hard.

"Same here. I've been in El Paso on business and I came over to pick up a few souvenirs before going home."

She glanced at him. "Oh? And where's that?"

"Colorado."

"Where in Colorado?"

"Denver. I'm in the insurance business."

"It must be nice living in Denver," Tally said, thinking quickly. "I've never been there, but they tell me it's surrounded by mountains and I just love mountains." *What do you say to that, Raul Devlin?*

Again he laughed. "They told you wrong. The mountains are some distance west of the city. You have to drive an hour to get to the closest ski area. The fact of the matter is, Denver is known as the Queen City of the Plains."

"I didn't realize that—about the mountains, I mean," Tally said lamely. Maybe she'd been right all the time, she decided. Maybe she couldn't lie to Raul Devlin, not successfully at least. She'd visited Denver and knew the city well. In fact, her closest friend, Karen Yarborough, lived there. She'd tried to trap him with her remark about the mountains, but he hadn't fallen for it.

Devlin put one arm around her waist to steer her around a muddy puddle where the side street intersected Avenida 16 de Septiembre, and Tally flinched. She didn't want him to get close enough to sense her uncertainty.

"We go right here," she announced. "It's not far."

"What do you do in El Paso?" he asked, his arm still around her as they left the puddle behind them.

"I'm a student," she said, hoping a measure of truth would allay any suspicions he might have.

"You seem a bit too old to still be in school."

"Actually it's law school. There are a lot of other senior citizens in my class—one of them almost forty. I suppose it's our way of warding off creeping senility."

"Touché," Devlin said, giving her a one-arm hug. "I didn't mean to suggest that you looked old. Actually, you're a very attractive young woman and I simply assumed you were well launched on a career by now."

"Oh, I work, too."

"What do you do?"

Tally pushed his arm away. "I'm a legal secretary."

"That must be interesting."

"It pays for tuition." They were approaching a camera shop, and an idea occurred to Tally. "Let's stop in here. I want to see what sort of a buy I can make on a Polaroid."

"Polaroid is an American product. You could probably pick up one cheaper in El Paso."

"I suppose, but I'd like to check it out now while it's on my mind." Slipping her arm through his, she guided him inside the shop.

For the next few minutes, she examined an assortment of instant cameras, even buying a pack of film and a flash bar so she could test the various models.

"See anything you like?" Devlin inquired, after unobtrusively glancing at his watch.

"I'm not sure. This one is kind of nice. Stand over by the doorway and let me try it out."

"I'd rather you—" He blinked as Tally fired off first one exposure and then a second. The startled look in his eyes reminded her of the first time she saw him: on guard, wary.

The prints spurted out of the base of the camera one after another. With a quick glance at them to assure herself that she had what she wanted, she leaned across the counter and pretended to drop the prints into a wastebasket.

She turned to face Devlin. "Not a very good likeness," she explained as she palmed the prints and slipped them into the pocket of her warm-up jacket. "They were both fuzzy."

She handed the camera back to the clerk. "I don't know," she said dubiously. "Let me think about it and come back later." She led Devlin back out onto the sidewalk. "You were right," she said under her breath. "They wanted too much money for their Polaroids. I'll look around El Paso."

He made a face. "You might at least have let me look at the prints."

Tally smiled. "Take my word for it. They didn't do you justice." She stopped and pointed. "See that big old building up the street? That's El Mercado."

They spent the next hour wandering through the market, taking in the sights and sounds and smells of the various stalls. Now and then, Tally sensed that Devlin knew he was being followed and was trying to throw the hounds off the track. He knew the Americans were after him, but could there be someone else on his tail, too?

Acting out the role of tourist, Tally bought a huge, red-and-white papier-mâché piñata in the shape of a burro and made a show of going through the pockets of her jacket, looking for money, while she gave the piñata to Devlin to hold. She wanted to make sure the Polaroid prints were still tucked away safely. When she finally reached into her purse for her billfold, Devlin was already paying the vendor in pesos.

She frowned. "You don't have to do that."

"Consider it your guide's fee, Miss, ah—"

"Tally."

"—Miss Tally. My name is Shannon, but I'd rather you call me Kevin so we can get this onto a first-name basis." He winked at her. He actually winked at her. Men just didn't do that anymore, she thought.

"Tally is my first name," she informed him, taking the piñata out of his hands. "Come on, there's a little café just up the street that serves the best Mexican chocolate you'll find anywhere. I'll buy." She had to stall Devlin until Abrahamson could catch up. As soon as he discovered she was missing, he'd probably called for reinforcements.

Devlin tagged along after her. "Sure you wouldn't rather have a drink? A margarita perhaps? I found a place that makes some wickedly good ones."

No way, Tally thought. She intended to keep her wits about her. She wasn't going to lose Raul Devlin now. "No, just hot chocolate."

"You don't drink?"

"Once in a while. Not now."

She led him to a table by the front window of the café, in full view of the street. She still had mixed feelings about helping capture Devlin, but if Abrahamson should happen to come by the café and see them sitting there, it would be out of her hands.

Dammit, she thought angrily, that was a cop-out and she knew it. It was her job to hand him over. But hand him over to what? That was the thing that troubled her. She was all but certain Abrahamson intended to have Devlin killed. And she couldn't sit still for that.

"You've been very kind to show me around, Tally," Devlin said. "I'd like to repay you."

"You bought the piñata. That's payment enough."

"It really isn't. Look, why don't I see you home and then perhaps we could have dinner?"

"See me home?"

"Back across the border."

"I...I don't know." Prospective prisoners weren't supposed to ask their captors for dates.

"Please, it would mean a great deal to me."

You don't know how much it would mean, she wanted to tell him. *You saved my life and now I'm going to repay you by turning you over to Abrahamson and his people so they can put a bullet in your brain.*

"How about it, Tally?"

She hesitated. She had the photos. She could see that one of them got to the El Paso newspapers. If the story were published—keeping her out of it, of course—perhaps it would bring enough pressure on Abrahamson to force him to handle Devlin with kid gloves. It was worth a try. "All right," she said at last, looking around and spotting a pay phone mounted to the wall back by the kitchen door. "But I'll have to break a date. Be right back...." She got up and headed for the phone, looking over her shoulder to make sure he didn't leave.

A minute later, she was talking to the Patrol dispatcher in El Paso, giving him instructions to have other undercover agents track down Abrahamson and bring him to the border station at the foot of Santa Fe in downtown El Paso. As she talked to the dispatcher, she smiled across the room at

Devlin and waved. He smiled and waved back, then looked away and ordered two more hot chocolates from the waiter.

"What if I can't locate Abrahamson?" the dispatcher asked. "You want me to send Blaine? He just checked in."

Tally turned her back on Devlin and cupped her right hand around the mouthpiece. "Leave Inspector Murchison out of this. If you can't find Abrahamson, I'll handle it myself." She hung up. One thing she didn't need now was Blaine Murchison telling her how to handle things.

When Tally returned to the table, Devlin was sipping a second cup of chocolate. He rose and held out her chair for her. "I hope your gentleman friend wasn't too upset."

Gentleman friend. That was an expression she hadn't heard for years. It sounded like something out of an old Noel Coward play.

She sat down and tasted her second cup of Mexican chocolate. It was sweeter than the first, but oh so good—thick and dark and smooth, with a blob of whipped cream on top. "We didn't have anything special planned," she said.

Devlin clinked his cup against hers in a toast. "Then your friend has to be a complete fool, Tally," he said softly. "Any time spent with you—a minute, an hour, whatever—would be special. You're the type of woman who makes anything special." His eyes sparkled as he spoke.

"That sounds very much like a line, Kevin." Kevin. That wasn't his name, and she knew it wasn't his name. His name was Raul Devlin, and he was a fugitive. She'd have to keep that in mind.

He chuckled. "Certainly it's a line. I'm sure you'd be disappointed in me if it wasn't. You see, Tally, being with you brings out the poet in me."

Poet. She swallowed some more hot chocolate and dabbed at her lips with a paper napkin. Raul Devlin was a poet. But who was Raul Devlin anyway? She had trouble remembering. Everything seemed so fuzzy and disjointed. She yawned. "Suddenly I'm exhausted."

"It's all the walking we've done. Finish your hot chocolate. It'll wake you up."

Tally reached for the cup she'd just replaced in its saucer and nearly upset it. Her fingers didn't seem to be functioning. Neither was her brain. What was wrong with her?

Devlin placed his hand over hers, steadying it, and guided the cup to her lips. "Drink up and I'll take you home," he said softly.

"All right," she said, emptying her cup.

Devlin paid the bill despite her earlier offer to do so, got up and held her chair for her. As she stood up she felt lightheaded and giddy. She shook her head to clear it, but it didn't help.

"Is anything wrong?" he asked solicitously.

"No, I just need some air."

"All right." He put one arm around her shoulders and guided her toward the door. "We'll head back across the border. I'm sure you'll feel better soon."

"I'm sure," Tally murmured sleepily, leaning her head on his shoulder. She closed her eyes and let him lead the way, floating dreamy-eyed out the door, to the busy sidewalk.

A chilly dusk was settling in as they walked back along Avenida 16 de Septiembre and turned north on Avenida Juarez and crossed the International Bridge. Most of the traffic was coming in the opposite direction, the bulk of it consisting of "green card" Mexicans who worked in El Paso during the day and were returning home.

Midway across the bridge, when they'd technically entered the United States, it vaguely occurred to Tally that all bets were off. She hadn't encouraged Devlin to cross the Rio Grande, but since he had, he was now fair game.

And then the thought was gone. She could barely keep her eyes open, much less think coherently.

Who was Raul Devlin anyway? She didn't know any Raul Devlin, only Kevin Shannon....

Raul Devlin. Yawn. If only she could be sure no harm would come to him...

Cars and trucks were lined up at the inspection points outside the customs station, and pedestrian traffic was routed inside the building where uniformed officers waited to check identification. As Tally stood in line, her mind drifted in and out of reality. She vaguely recognized some of the officers, but somehow she didn't care. All she wanted to do was sleep.

Devlin took the piñata from her and stepped up to the first vacant check station. "Back again," he announced cheerfully.

To Tally, the voice sounded as if it were coming from a deep well, far away.

The customs officer squinted at Devlin, as if wondering if he should recognize him. He nodded. "A little light Christmas shopping, eh?"

"It's that time of year."

"Where were you born, sir?"

"Des Moines, Iowa."

"What did you buy in Mexico?"

"Just this—what do you call it?" He held up the papier-mâché burro.

"That's a piñata, sir. You're supposed to fill 'em with candy and hang 'em up from the ceiling. You blindfold the kids and give 'em sticks and they try to break open the piñata to get at the candy. It's an old Mexican custom."

Devlin formed the word silently with his lips before speaking it aloud. "Peen-yata. I must remember that."

"You buy any liquor in Mexico?"

Devlin shook his head. "No. Don't you remember? I'd brought back a fifth of Kahlua when I came through here last night, and you told me that was all I was allowed."

"That's right, sir—one bottle every thirty days." The customs officer nodded dismissal. "Have a nice evening. Next."

Tally stepped up to the counter and sucked in a deep breath, hoping a fresh surge of oxygen would clear away the cobwebs. The customs official was a new man and she didn't recognize him. She wondered what he'd say if she told him she was a Border Patrol agent who'd just brought in an internationally wanted fugitive. He'd faint.

"Place of birth?"

Tally yawned. All she had to do was blurt out her story, and it would be all over for Raul Devlin. He'd be off to...to where? She didn't know. She didn't even know Raul Devlin. She only knew Kevin Shannon. Nice man, Kevin Shannon....

"El Paso," she said.

"Do you have anything to declare?"

Tally glanced groggily at Devlin, who was standing patiently at the exit, holding the piñata. No, his name was Shannon, Kevin Shannon. He was seeing her home. "Nothing," she said sleepily. "Nothing at all."

And then she passed out in Devlin's arms.

IT HAD BEEN almost too easy, Raul thought as he loaded Tally into a cab. He'd known who she was the minute she'd palmed those photos. She was prettier than he'd remembered, quick-witted, too. He liked that in an adversary. It heightened the challenge, and the challenge was what made life interesting. A man could get lazy if all he had to deal with were clods like Jaime Guerrero. When a man got lazy, he got careless, and Raul couldn't afford to get careless.

The cabdriver was staring at them. "What's the matter with the little lady, mister?"

Raul sighed. "A few too many margaritas. I told the poor thing to taper off, but she wouldn't listen."

Tally opened her eyes. "Wha' happened?"

"You passed out, my dear," Raul said, putting his arm around her and giving her an affectionate pat. "You were showing the customs officer how you'd learned to do the Mexican hat dance, and all of a sudden you just keeled over."

"Oh." Tally settled back, her cheek against his shoulder and closed her eyes again.

"Where to?" the cabdriver inquired.

Raul laughed. "I knew you were going to ask. We just moved into a new apartment, and I can't for the life of me remember the address. But wait...." He took Tally's billfold from her purse, removed her driver's license and studied it under the dome light. He gave the address to the driver.

The cabbie was no dummy. "If you folks just moved, how come the lady's already got a driver's license with the new address on it? Those things take months."

"The little lady works for the state. They take care of their own, you know."

"Yeah," the driver nodded, "they sure as hell do."

Raul opened both rear windows, hoping the brisk air would revive Tally before they got to her apartment. He wanted to talk to her, find out how much she knew, and she couldn't be very helpful if she were fast asleep.

He leaned forward. "Tell you what," he told the cabbie, "just drive around for a while. The air will do her good."

Raul looked down at Tally. *I'm not going to hurt you, migra, I promise you. I just need information.*

His dentist friend had given him the knockout drops, a form of thiopental that was often used in truth serum. The effects wouldn't last long, he knew.

Raul considered his strategy. That business at the border had been a calculated risk, a ploy that occurred to him as they sat talking in the café. Since Tally was the only government agent in El Paso who could identify him, she'd obviously been sent to look for him. It was strange the Americans hadn't assigned anyone to work with her. Several times during their stroll through Juarez, Raul had checked to see if they were being followed. They'd ducked through arcades, melted into crowds, doubled back, done all the standard evasion exercises. They weren't being followed. So what was her game plan?

He tried to put himself in her position. Tally was a Border Patrol officer with orders to track him down. She had no jurisdiction on the Mexican side of the river. That meant she'd intended to lure him across to El Paso, where she would have jurisdiction. She was probably working alone because she wanted all the credit for apprehending him. His arrest would look good on her record.

All he'd had to do was go along with her, up to a point. Tally's superiors were looking for a lone man, not for a couple, certainly not for a carefree couple coming back from a pleasant afternoon south of the border.

She'd been the best cover he could possibly have, and he'd enjoyed her company, but now it was time to get on with his business, with her.

EYES CLOSED, letting the night air splash across her face, Tally tried to organize her thoughts, tried to figure out what had happened. One minute, she'd been fine. The next minute—zap! she was a wobbly-legged zombie, unable to put one word after another.

Think.

Raul Devlin must have drugged her—that had to have been it. All this time she'd been wrestling with her conscience, trying to devise a way to prevent him from being killed by Abrahamson, and he'd slipped her some knockout drops.

But when? She hadn't taken her eyes off him for a minute.

Except . . .

That was it! She'd gone to the phone in the café to call in, and he'd put something in her hot chocolate!

The bastard!

She felt the cab come to a stop, and she opened her eyes. The cab was parked in front of her apartment complex just off Hawthorne, near the campus of the University of Texas in El Paso.

"It looks like we're here," she murmured groggily, wondering what to do now.

Devlin reached across her and opened the door. "Are you sure you're all right?" he asked in a tone that suggested genuine concern. "You gave me a scare when you passed out back there."

Tally shook her head, trying to clear the cobwebs. "I'll be all right," she said. "Just hitting the books too hard, I guess." She eased herself out of the back seat and stepped out onto the curb, then turned to block his way. She needed time—time to think, time to act. "I'll go up and change. You wait here."

He looked up at her from the back seat. "Are you sure you can make it?"

"Quite sure. I'll just be a minute."

He laughed. "Very well, then, I'll hold the piñata as hostage."

"Fair enough." A plan was beginning to take shape in her mind, and she wondered if she'd have enough time to carry it out. "Don't go away."

Tally hurried into the courtyard and ran up the iron-railed staircase to her apartment, her head clearing as the exertion forced the blood to circulate faster.

Did he know who she was? He had to have gone through her billfold to get her home address, she realized, but she'd taken pains to leave behind her Border Patrol ID. Chances were that as far as he was concerned she was just a woman who'd strayed across his path and whom he could easily dupe into providing him with the cover he needed. Well, guess again, Raul Devlin!

Inside her apartment, Tally went straight to the window and looked down at the street. Devlin had gotten out of the cab and was leaning against it, the piñata in one hand, gazing up at her. He gave a cheerful little wave.

She'd have to move fast or he'd get suspicious.

She went to her desk, phoned Border Patrol sector headquarters and asked if Abrahamson had checked in.

"Not for a while," the dispatcher informed her. "He said if we heard from you, we were to find out where you are and tell you to stay put."

Tally lowered her voice. "I'm at home. In El Paso. I need some assistance."

"What's the problem, Tally?"

"I've got—"

She had what? There was no time to explain, but she certainly didn't want people rushing in here with guns blazing.

"Murchison's in service," the dispatcher said. "You want me to have him come by your place?"

Anybody but Blaine! "That won't be necessary. Just send in whoever's closest. No red lights and sirens, please. It's not that big a deal." No, only the biggest arrest she'd ever made, or ever would make, that's all.

She hung up and returned to the window. The cab was still at the curb, but Devlin was nowhere in sight. She decided he'd probably gotten back inside the cab.

She returned to the desk and brought out the photos she'd taken in Juarez. She slipped one of the prints into an envelope and put the other in her purse. Looking up the listing for the *El Paso Times*, she addressed the envelope, then reached again for the phone. She'd make an anonymous call to the newspaper and say that the Border Patrol had just nabbed a big-time crook named Devlin. Abrahamson wouldn't dare do anything to Devlin if Devlin suddenly was in the headlines. Abrahamson couldn't risk it. The phone call would furnish Devlin with at least *some* life insurance—which was more than he deserved after drugging her.

Before she could finish punching out the number, there was a knock on the door. "Hey, the piñata is getting cold!" Devlin called out. "Can't we come in?"

Tally slammed down the receiver and jumped up from her desk. "I'm not dressed!"

"I'll close my eyes."

"Wait!" She scurried into the bedroom and slipped a long, white bathrobe over her clothes.

He knocked again.

She started to leave the bedroom, then noticed the open closet. If he started snooping around, he might see her uniforms.

"Just a minute!" she yelled, doubling back and whipping the uniforms off their hangers. She stuffed them into a corner of her closet, then removed her revolver from her gunbelt holster and slipped it into the waistband of her jeans. She stacked the gunbelt and two Smokey hats on top of the uniforms and covered the heap with a raincoat.

Better play it safe, she told herself, checking to see that the gun was adequately concealed under the thick robe. Devlin had saved her neck once, but he'd also drugged her. Why take chances?

After one more darting glance around the bedroom, she went to the front door and unlocked it.

"I was in the bathroom freshening up," she said as Devlin stepped inside, the piñata under one arm.

He glanced around. "Nice place you've got here, Tally. Do you live alone?"

"No," she lied. "I have a roommate."

"Is that him?" He was looking at her desk and at the framed photo of Pop in full uniform.

"No," she said quickly. "That's—" there was no use lying about it; Devlin wasn't stupid "—my father."

"Oh? A military man, I see."

Tally shook her head. "He was in the Border Patrol. He's dead now." She loosened the belt of the robe around her waist, satisfying herself that her service revolver was readily accessible. "Sit down. I won't be long."

She tried to step past him, but he caught her arm. "Tally."

She looked at him. Was she just imagining the accusation in his eyes? "Please," she said softly.

Pulling her into his arms, he searched for her lips and found them, his mouth open, his breath warm and sweet.

No! a voice inside her screamed. *You're not going to sucker me again, Devlin!*

She pushed herself away from him.

And then she saw the revolver in his hand. Her revolver. He wasn't pointing it at her. He was just holding it, hefting its weight, looking back and forth from it to her in smiling bemusement. He chuckled. "My, you certainly carry heavy armament for a law student."

Angrily Tally grabbed for the gun, but he hid it behind his back.

"I'm not going to hurt you, *migra*," he said soothingly. "But I don't want you to hurt me, either. Give me those photos you took and I'll be on my way."

He'd called her *migra,* Mexican slang for immigration officer. He'd known all along who she was, Tally realized. She'd tried to do what she could for him, but it simply wasn't to be.

"You're under arrest for violation of United States immigration laws," she announced in a businesslike tone, pulling off her robe and tossing it aside to give her freedom of movement. "You have the right to remain silent. You have the right to an attorney. If you—"

"You're rather confused, *migra*. I have the gun."

Tally glared at him. "By now, this building is surrounded. I called my office the minute I came in."

"I know you called somebody." He flicked his head in the direction of the entryway. "I must say, your front door isn't very thick. I could hear you talking." He brought the revolver around in front of his body and extracted the shells, exactly as he had done the night they'd met. This time, he didn't toss the pistol aside, but held onto it. "You were very quick the way you reloaded the other night. I don't want to take any more chances with you. Now, may I have the photos you took?" He slipped the shells into his jacket pocket and waited.

Tally edged to her right, positioning herself between Devlin and the bedroom door. If she could get to the bedroom, maybe she could find another weapon—perhaps the tear-gas canister clipped to her gunbelt. "They're over there," she said, glancing beyond him at the desk.

He turned and Tally barreled past him and into the bedroom. She slammed the door behind her and punched the button that locked the knob. It wasn't much of a lock, she knew, but it would give her a few extra seconds.

Snatching the gunbelt out from under the raincoat-covered heap on the floor of the closet, she fumbled for the tear-gas canister.

She wasn't fast enough. Before she could reach the canister, he'd kicked open the door and had lunged into the room, still holding the gun.

"Stay back!" she shouted, straightening to face him, empty-handed.

Devlin sighed, tossed the revolver onto the bed and seized her wrists. "I must say, *migra*, you certainly don't make a visitor to your country feel very welcome."

"Damn you, Devlin! You're an international criminal and I'm going to bring you in!"

He released his grip on her wrists, but stood his ground. The look of amusement was gone, and in its place was an expression of hurt surprise. "Good Lord, what have they told you about me?"

"Go to hell, Devlin!"

"I undoubtedly shall, someday. Look, I'm aware Guerrero tipped off the Border Patrol. He's hardly a reliable sort. I paid him, your people paid him, and I'm sure—" He stopped in midsentence.

"You're sure of what?"

"I'm sure he's laughing all the way to the bank." There was a glint of bitterness in his eyes.

Tally wasn't satisfied. "You started to say somebody else paid him, too, didn't you?" she prodded. "Who else is trying to track you down?"

"Why don't you ask your friend Abrahamson?"

"What do you mean?"

"You know what I'm talking about, *migra*—those two fellows he has in tow. Simon Ybarra and Hans Uhlmann."

The names meant nothing to Tally, but it was clear he was referring to the mystery men who'd flown in from Washington with Abrahamson. Abrahamson had refused to tell her who they were, but perhaps Devlin would. "Ybarra and Uhlmann don't say much."

"Their kind seldom do." Grabbing her by the wrists, he pulled her toward the door.

Tally knew she had to keep him talking, had to delay him until her call for assistance was answered. How long had it been since she phoned in? It seemed like hours, but it was only minutes.

She dug in her heels. "I assume they're policemen," she said.

He frowned. "Ybarra and Uhlmann? Hardly. They're professional killers, *migra*. Ruthless, sadistic killers."

"I don't believe you."

"Believe what you like." He dragged her out into the living room, nimbly dodging her kicks.

"You're the killer, Devlin."

"Am I? And just who am I supposed to have killed?"

"Those doctors and nurses who treated you in the hospital." *Would her backup never come?*

"Who told you that? Abrahamson?"

"Not in so many words, but it's obvious. The doctors gave you a new face, and with them out of the way there'd be no one to identify you."

He stopped tugging at her and stepped close, so close she could see her reflection in his dark blue eyes. "Except you, Tally. Now you can identify me. If you're right about me, that means I have to kill you . . ."

Chapter Four

Blaine was livid as he paced the floor, hands clenched behind his back, gray Stetson shoved back off his forehead. He'd arrived at the apartment only minutes after the uniformed officers had gotten there, and he'd insisted on calling in the chief. "You mind telling us just what the devil you were trying to pull, Tally?" he demanded after the chief had shooed everyone else out of the apartment.

Tally massaged the pale welts on her wrists where the handcuffs had held her prisoner on the bathroom floor, chained to a water pipe under the washbasin, waiting for help. She was embarrassed rather than physically hurt, and she was angry—angry at herself, at Devlin, at everybody who had the slightest connection with her humiliation. "I was trying to make an arrest," she said, struggling to keep her voice under control. "That's what I was trying to pull."

"Dammit, you should have asked for backup sooner, girl!"

Tally glared at him. "Don't call me girl!"

Blaine plopped himself down on the couch, pushing aside the unloaded revolver that Devlin had left there, and planted his dusty cowboy boots on the coffee table. Leaning back, he tipped the brim of his hat down over his eyes, then laced his fingers behind his thick neck. "Your daddy would have a conniption fit if he knew how you let the big one get away."

"Leave him out of this, inspector!" She snatched up the pistol and slammed it down on the dinette table, alongside her gunbelt. "I'm sorry you don't like the way I handled things, but I did my best."

"Did you? Are you sure you didn't start feeling sorry for that clown, Devlin?"

The chief glanced sharply at Blaine. "That's enough, Murchison. Tally's an experienced agent. She knows better than to let emotions get in the way of doing her job."

Did she? Tally wondered. "All right, I screwed up and I'm sorry. What more do you want me to say?"

Before Blaine could answer, Abrahamson stomped into the apartment. "I've been looking all over Juarez for you," he said peevishly, looking at Tally. "What happened?"

"I've already made a full report," Tally said.

Abrahamson sat down beside Blaine. "I don't care. Go over it again. Start with where you spotted Devlin."

Tally took a deep breath. Was he hoping he'd catch her in a lie? Maybe he thought Devlin had bribed her to help him. She sank into a seat at the dinette table and gave a blow-by-blow recitation.

Blaine excused himself and left the room, taking her equipment belt and gun to have them dusted for prints by the police lab team at work in the bathroom.

She'd just finished her story when Blaine returned. Abrahamson was on his feet, scowling at Tally. "I still want to know why you didn't take him at the border," he said. "One word from you and the customs people could have grabbed him on the spot."

"I told you I was drugged," Tally reminded him. "When I got here, I tried to reach you."

"You should have been more careful, Gordon." He paused. "What about the photos?"

"They're gone. One of them was in my purse, the other—" she couldn't tell him she planned to mail one print to the newspaper "—was in an envelope, on the desk."

"In an envelope?"

"I didn't want to keep them together," Tally said quickly. "It was a matter of insurance."

"An insurance policy isn't much good if it doesn't pay off when you need it." He glanced around at the apartment. "Let me get this straight, Gordon. You came here, went to the phone and called in. That was all you did?"

Tally nodded.

"You hung up the phone and rushed straight to the door as soon as he knocked?"

"I went into the bedroom and got my gun." She motioned to the gunbelt on the dinette table.

Abrahamson walked up to the counter separating the kitchen from the living room. He peered into the kitchen. "Nice and neat, a place for everything and everything in its place. You seem to be a good housekeeper."

Tally wondered what he was getting at.

"Exceptionally neat," Abrahamson went on, "and yet you carelessly threw that garment aside." He cocked his thumb at the robe that lay in a heap on the floor by her desk. Tally remembered removing the robe after Devlin had pretended to kiss her and had found the pistol in her waistband. "Just tossed it, as if..."

Tally knew immediately what he was hinting at, and she was infuriated. She got up and crossed to Abrahamson, who was eyeing her coldly. "I don't have to take this!" she snapped.

"Take what, Gordon?"

"You're suggesting I took off my clothes and tried to seduce Devlin! I've got news for you, Mr. Abrahamson! There are some things I will not do for my country!"

His eyes narrowed. "I wasn't suggesting you were doing anything for your *country*," he said in a low voice.

Tally resisted an almost overpowering urge to slap him. Instead, she leaned in close, her stare matching his, icicle for icicle. "You're a dirty old man, you know that? I mean, you're sick!"

"All right, Gordon, settle down!" the chief barked. He looked at Abrahamson. "I think you owe her an apology, mister."

"It would appear the young lady is a bit sensitive," Abrahamson grumbled. "It's too bad her effectiveness as an officer doesn't match that sensitivity."

"Get out of here!" Tally growled in a throaty voice quivering with rage. "Get out or, I swear, I'll throw you out!"

"That's enough, Gordon!" the chief said. "No one's accusing you of doing anything wrong. You might be guilty of poor judgment, but it's easy to be critical after the fact. The question is, what do we do now?"

Abrahamson tried to recover the remnants of his bruised dignity. "We'll talk about it later, chief. Right now, let's go on back to your office." He shot a warning glance at Tally. "You stay here, young lady."

"Don't call me young lady," Tally shot back. "I'm a United States Border Patrol officer, dammit, and I'm supposed to report for duty in a couple of hours. I'll go wherever the Border Patrol wants me to go. I don't take orders from you."

The chief gestured placatingly with his hands. "Look, Gordon, Devlin got the drop on you. I'm not blaming you. It could have happened to anybody. You did what you thought was right, and it didn't work. Devlin is a man who's been around. He knows all the tricks. Don't worry, we'll get him."

Abrahamson flashed a scowl of annoyance. "This is a matter for my department. It's out of your hands."

The chief wheeled on Abrahamson. "Hold it, mister! Devlin is an illegal alien, and illegal aliens come under our jurisdiction. I've already alerted our checkpoints on the principal highways leading out of El Paso, as well as our details at the airport, bus stations and railroad yards."

Abrahamson snorted. "You're not going to find him. He probably stole a car and is a hundred miles away from here by now."

"What direction is he headed in?"

"If I knew that, I wouldn't be wasting my time standing here talking to you people."

The chief's ruddy cheeks darkened, and Tally sensed he was near boiling point. She didn't blame him. Abrahamson might work for the State Department, but he didn't know a thing about everyday diplomacy.

The chief managed to hold his temper in check. "Albuquerque's the nearest big city, and it's a good five-hour drive. Of course, if he made it to the airport and got past our teams there, he could be halfway to Dallas or Los Angeles by now. My guess is that he—"

Abrahamson held up one hand to cut him off. He turned to Tally. "You own a car, Gordon?"

Tally nodded. "A seven-year-old Volvo wagon."

"Where do you keep it?"

"In the lot in back of this building."

"Check and see if you still have the keys."

Tally went to the desk and picked up her handbag. She methodically ticked off the contents: billfold with ID and money—some thirty dollars—intact; notebook, ballpoint pen, comb, lipstick, tissues, and . . . no keys.

"They're gone," she said.

"Find out if the car is still parked in the lot."

Tally went down to check. Her orange Volvo wagon was gone.

MANUEL BENAVIDEZ WASN'T in the habit of going by the office on Sunday mornings. But his wife's sister's family—nine of them, headed by that Bible-thumping patriarch Lorenzo Velasquez—had driven in from Silver City the night before to ruin his weekend. The youngsters were scurrying all over the place, wrestling, laughing, chattering, tying up the telephone and the bathroom, eating him out of house and home. If that wasn't bad enough, he just knew Lorenzo was going to try to haul him off to church for the ten o'clock service. Benavidez had to get out of there.

Mumbling his excuses, Benavidez had fled to the battered old trailer from which he sold used cars. Benavidez Motors was on the south side of Socorro, just off the access road that ran parallel to the interstate, and while the trailer might not be luxurious, it provided a quiet refuge this Sunday morning.

At least, it should have been quiet. Now, though, there were immigration people all over the place, along with sheriff's deputies and state policemen and a number of important-looking civilians wearing suits and ties and expressions as briskly unpleasant as the morning.

Benavidez didn't understand what all the fuss was about. "It is not as if he stole the car," he told Nate Abrahamson. "I mean, he left me this money under the visor of the Volvo he left behind." He held up ten crisp hundred-dollar bills. "If he was stealing the Ford of mine he took, why would he leave the money? A thousand dollars is a fair price."

Abrahamson reached for the money, but Benavidez stuffed the bills into the pocket of his scuffed leather jacket. "That's evidence, Mr. Benavidez," Abrahamson said sternly. "Hand it over."

"I think I talk to my lawyer first."

"Fine. Have him meet you at the Socorro County Jail." Abrahamson signaled to one of the sheriff's deputies. "Take Mr. Benavidez in and lock him up. Give him a receipt for whatever he's got in his possession, and we'll be along to look it over. Now get moving."

Benavidez handed over the money.

"That's better," Abrahamson grunted. He gave the bills to one of the civilians. "Try to run a trace on the serial numbers. I doubt if the money is stolen, but we might be able to backtrack on how it was circulated. That could give us a clue as to who's helping Devlin." He turned to Tally. "Anything missing from your car?"

"He took a couple of road maps, but that was all."

"Road maps for what states?"

"New Mexico and Colorado."

"It figures," Abrahamson said. "Anything else?"

"Just this." Tally handed over the hundred-dollar bill and the note she'd found tucked away in the glove box with her car-registration papers.

Abrahamson examined the note, penned in blockish, black script on the back of a postcard advertising Hotel el Presidente in Juarez. It read:

> My dear Tally—Sorry to inconvenience you, but it was necessary to borrow your car. Someday, perhaps, you'll understand—R.D.

The chief looked over his shoulder and read the note. "I think it's time we got out a federal warrant."

"On what grounds?" Abrahamson asked.

"Let's start with assaulting a federal officer, interstate transportation of a stolen vehicle—"

"No warrant!" Abrahamson snapped, pocketing the postcard and the hundred-dollar bill. "No warrant, no press releases, no anything unless I say so. Now find Murchison and tell him I want him to hold the fort for me in El Paso." He cocked his thumb at Tally. "Until further notice, Gordon here is assigned to me. Now let's get cracking."

THEY WEREN'T ALONE in their pursuit. Tally was sure of it. Somewhere along the line, they'd picked up a tail: a black Mercury sedan that kept them in sight as they headed north, the high mountains lost in the low clouds to the west, the Cibola Indian reservation nesting on the buff tablelands of the Manzanos to the east. Tally, still in the uniform she'd worn for the helicopter flight from El Paso to Socorro, was driving an unmarked Border Patrol car, with Abrahamson sitting beside her in sullen silence.

"Who are Simon Ybarra and Hans Uhlmann?" she asked as they entered the outskirts of Albuquerque.

"I told you before, they're none of your business."

"They are if they're interfering in an official investigation, Mr. Abrahamson." She glanced up at the rearview mirror. "I think they're following us."

Abrahamson swiveled in his seat and looked out the back window. "You're imagining things, Gordon."

"I wasn't trained to imagine things, Mr. Abrahamson. I was trained to be observant. I want to know about Ybarra and Uhlmann. Devlin said they were professional killers."

"You believe Devlin?"

"Frankly, I don't know what to believe. You told me—that is, you suggested—that Devlin killed those doctors and nurses in Mexico City to keep them from identifying him after they gave him a new face. If that's true, why didn't he kill me when he had the chance? He knows I can identify him. Apparently I'm the only one who can." Again, she checked the rearview mirror. "I want to know about Ybarra and Uhlmann."

"They don't concern you," Abrahamson replied.

"They most certainly do! I'm trying to do a job, and you won't give me a clue as to what we're up against. They're following us—at least, somebody's following us—and I want to know why."

Abrahamson sniffed. "I'll tell you this much, Gordon. Some people want Devlin dead, and some people want him alive. Sort out who's who and I'll happily pin a medal on you."

Tally slowed for a truck lumbering onto the interstate from an entrance ramp. "The Border Patrol is devoting a lot of resources to a search for one individual. What is it that Washington wants with Devlin? Why is he such a threat to our national security?"

Abrahamson said nothing for several minutes, and then, "You know the difference between a terrorist and a freedom fighter, Gordon?"

Tally nodded. "There's a textbook answer for that. It has to do with perspective."

Abrahamson nodded slowly. "Exactly. Is he one of ours, or is he one of theirs? That's it in a nutshell. Trouble is, Devlin doesn't fit into that nutshell. So we have to cancel him out of the equation."

"Cancel him out?" Tally looked at him out of the corner of her eye. "Is that a euphemism for murder?"

Abrahamson made a deep, rumbling noise in his throat that might have been interpreted as a laugh. "Whatever you may have heard, Gordon, our government does not sanction murder. Perhaps I should have said neutralize. That's a far less-ominous word."

"I still don't know what it means."

"When one neutralizes, one removes a specific factor from active involvement in a situation—that is, the factor is made ineffective. Surely you've encountered the word in one or another of your classes?"

Tally was tempted to tell him he was a patronizing boor. Maybe he didn't like having a woman do what he considered a man's job. Maybe he didn't like anybody.

"Are you familiar with Albuquerque?" Abrahamson asked.

"More or less."

"Good. Drop me off at the federal courthouse and then swing back and get us rooms at that Howard Johnson's." He nodded toward the orange-roofed motor hotel coming up on their right. "You have any money?"

"A little."

"Do you carry any credit cards?"

"MasterCard."

"All right. Use it to buy some civilian clothes—enough to last you several days—then go on back to the motel. I'll meet you later."

Tally swung onto the ramp that would take them to downtown Albuquerque. "If I'd known, I could have brought some things from El Paso. Buying clothes seems like an unnecessary expense."

"The government will pick up the tab. Just don't go overboard."

"Going overboard on clothes isn't one of my failings, Mr. Abrahamson. I've got other things to spend my money on—books and tuition, for example."

"I'm sure you're a model of frugality."

And I'm sure I'd like nothing better than to give you a good swift kick you know where, Tally thought.

She checked the mirror. The black sedan was still following them.

FRUGAL ENOUGH, Mr. Abrahamson? Tally wondered as she spread out her purchases on the bed. She'd bought a brown-and-green plaid wool skirt, a dark brown turtleneck sweater, a blouse, a pair of jeans, a pair of low-heeled brown leather boots, a matching handbag large enough to accommodate her service revolver, a trench coat with a zip-out lining, two changes of underwear, toiletries and a small canvas carryall. The total came to just over three hundred dollars. She hoped her expense voucher would come through before her MasterCard statement arrived.

She showered and changed into skirt, sweater and boots, then packed away the other clothing. Everything fit easily into the carryall—everything but her stiff-brimmed Smokey hat. She wrapped the hat carefully in a plastic bag and made a mental note to leave it in the trunk of the car.

Now all she had to do was wait.

Wait, and ask herself the same questions, over and over again.

Who was Raul Devlin? What did he want in the United States? Why did Nate Abrahamson, who obviously had clout at the highest levels of government, want to stop him from doing whatever he was intent upon doing? And who were Simon Ybarra and Hans Uhlmann, and why were they tagging along with Abrahamson?

Questions, all sorts of questions. And no answers.

She switched on the television set and watched the Chicago Bears maul the Green Bay Packers. She didn't care that much for football, but it was a way to pass the time.

What was taking Abrahamson so long? She imagined that the man from Washington had all but taken over the local FBI office, shouting orders, deploying his forces, directing that roadblocks be set up, bringing in the Albuquerque police to search for the gray, Ford two-door Devlin had taken from the used-car lot in Socorro.

From the television speaker came the roar of the crowd as someone intercepted a pass and scored a touchdown.

Tally didn't even glance at the screen. She was lost in her thoughts.

Was Devlin really a murderer? How far did he hope to get? Even though he'd left money at Benavidez Motors, the car he was driving was technically stolen. He must know that the police had a full description of it by now, right down to the last scratch, the last little dent. Maybe Devlin had figured that the car wouldn't be missed until Monday morning, that by then he'd have done what he set out to do.

The phone rang at five-fifteen, just as it was getting dark. Tally turned off the TV and answered it.

"We've got the Ford," Abrahamson informed her. "It was parked on the street down by Old Town."

Tally knew the district. A commercial area not far from downtown, it had been restored to look much as it might have in the early nineteenth century when New Mexico was still part of New Spain. There were all sorts of little shops and hideaways where Devlin could disappear and, what's more, Old Town would be busy with Christmas shoppers this time of year.

"Do you want me to come down and help you look for him?" Tally asked. She wanted to get out of the motel room. She was beginning to feel the walls closing in.

No such luck. "You stay put, Gordon. I've told the front desk there at the motel that if they get any calls for me, they're to ring your room."

Great, Tally thought. *A law degree and five years on the job, and I get to play clerk.* She said nothing.

"I've asked the people at the university to try to run down a Professor Olivera for me," Abrahamson went on. "He just moved into a new apartment and he hasn't had a phone put in yet. If he calls, find out where he can be reached."

"I could interview him for you," Tally suggested.

"Forget it. It'd probably just be a waste of time. I've got more important things for you to do."

"May I ask what sort of important things, Mr. Abrahamson?"

"Later, Gordon. Now let's leave this line open."

"Yes, sir." *No, sir!* she wanted to scream. There was too much happening, and she wanted to be part of it. "Who is this Olivera?" she asked aloud, knowing that Abrahamson would probably refuse to give her a direct answer.

He surprised her. "He's one of Devlin's fellow countrymen—an authority on Latin American politics."

"Do you think Devlin might get in touch with him?"

"Not likely, Gordon. It's just a shot in the dark."

"It still might be worthwhile talking to him. If you're busy, I could—"

"I told you. Just stay put. That's an order."

IT WAS ALMOST SEVEN and Tally was getting worried about Abrahamson. She wondered if he'd come in and gone to his room without telling her. It would have been just like him. Leaving her door ajar, she walked down the hall to his room, failed to get an answer to her knock and returned to her own room.

Waiting for her when she got back, his cold eyes taking in everything, was one of Abrahamson's mysterious companions. When she stepped into her room, he thrust his hands into the pockets of his black overcoat and peered at her coldly from beneath the narrow, turned-down brim of his black fedora. Her visitor was the taller of the two men who'd apparently come with Abrahamson from Washington. He was thin and fiftyish, and his pinched, clean-shaven face reminded Tally of a cadaver.

"I must talk to Abrahamson," he announced. "Where is he?" It was the first time she'd heard either of the two mystery men speak, and his deep, rumbling voice seemed every bit as malevolent as his face. He had only the faintest trace of an accent.

"I have no idea," Tally lied. She had no use for Abrahamson, and instinctively even less for his companions. Still, there was a difference in her dislike of the three men. Abrahamson was rude and overbearing, but this man and his companion were more than that, somehow evil. They frightened her.

"You must know where to find him. You work for him, do you not?"

"I work with him, not for him," Tally corrected her visitor.

The man glanced past her, obviously trying to see if there was anyone else in the room. Instinctively, Tally shifted to one side to block his view.

"I must talk to him." Her visitor stepped forward.

Tally stood her ground. "I told you he's not here. If you want to leave a message—"

"Tell him it is imperative that he get in touch with me at once."

"May I ask why?"

The man glowered at her. "*Señorita,* my business is with Abrahamson."

"He'll want to know why it's so important."

He thought about it. "Tell him I have located a witness who might be persuaded to assist us."

"What's the name of this witness?"

"Abrahamson will know who I mean," her visitor said impatiently.

Not good enough, Tally thought. Not nearly good enough. "He has a lot on his mind. It would help if I passed along the name."

"I assure you, the name would mean nothing to you, *señorita.*"

"It wouldn't be—" Tally caught herself before she came out with the name Olivera. If her visitor didn't yet know about the professor, she wasn't going to be the one to tell him. She nodded. "All right, I'll pass that along. And your name is..."

His hands came out of his pockets to unbutton his overcoat. He reached inside his suit jacket for a black leather wallet. As he did so, Tally caught a glimpse of a shoulder holster. He opened the wallet and extracted a business card, which he handed to her. The card read, Simon Ybarra, Coffee Broker, and it listed an address and telephone number in San Salvador.

Another question to add to her growing list, Tally thought: Why did a visiting coffee broker need to carry a pistol? There were too many questions and not enough answers. She had to see if she couldn't change that.

"Why are you looking for Devlin?" she asked point-blank.

Ybarra didn't hesitate. "Major Devlin has something I want."

"What?"

"Information." He rebuttoned his overcoat. "Be good enough to pass along my message to Mr. Abrahamson. He knows how to reach me."

Information. She had the answer, at least a partial answer, to one question, but it raised still other questions. What sort of information? Why was Abrahamson cooperating with Ybarra? Most of all, what did they intend to do with Raul Devlin once they got the information they sought?

"Why did you follow us from El Paso?" Tally asked.

Ignoring the question, Ybarra pushed past her and strode off down the hall.

What if the witness *was* Professor Olivera? Tally asked herself as she stood in the doorway and watched Ybarra disappear through the outside door at the end of the corridor. She couldn't let Ybarra and Uhlmann get to him first.

Closing the door, Tally went to the phone and put in a call for Abrahamson at the FBI office.

He was unavailable, she was told. He'd left the office, and had radioed in a short time later to say he'd be out of reach for a while.

Damn!

Tally hung up. Abrahamson would be furious, she knew, but she had no choice. By the time Abrahamson got the message from Ybarra, it might be too late.

She had to find Olivera herself.

She went to work. Her first few phone calls were routine: the University of New Mexico security office, the phone company, the city utilities people. None had a new address for the professor, whose first name, she learned from her initial call, was Anastacio. Professor Olivera's former landlord was out of town and his records were locked up, so no forwarding address was immediately available. She tried several of Olivera's fellow faculty members. One of them remembered the professor's mentioning that he was moving to an older complex near the University Boulevard and Lomas, but, sorry, they didn't know the exact address.

Time for some plain, old-fashioned legwork, she decided.

Taking along her carryall so that her uniform would be handy if she needed it, she went out to the car. She put the carryall in the trunk, then drove to the neighborhood where Olivera was thought to have moved. She found that there were too many apartment complexes to check rapidly. Circling the area, she spotted a cluster of campus hangouts. On a hunch, she parked and started checking them out.

She hit pay dirt on her third stop, a pizza parlor frequented by students. Yes, a young man told her, he'd seen Professor Olivera at a reception that very evening, at the

Sheraton Hotel over by Old Town. Olivera might even still be there, he suggested helpfully.

And he was.

"I've got to talk to you," Tally said when she got Olivera on the phone. "Stay right where you are and I'll be along in just—"

"I am sorry," the professor said, "but I have a ten o'clock flight to Los Angeles, and I do not wish to miss my plane. I'm scheduled to speak at a seminar at UCLA in the morning. Can this wait until my return later in the week?"

"I'm afraid not, sir. Mr. Abrahamson and I are just passing through Albuquerque, and—" She stopped, wondering if she'd made a mistake mentioning Abrahamson by name.

The professor had seemed pleasant enough at the outset, but now his tone became chilly. "Out of the question," he said. "I do not have the time."

"It's very important," Tally pressed. "I can't explain it over the phone."

"Are you Mr. Abrahamson's secretary?"

"I am *not*," Tally said emphatically. "I'm a United States Border Patrol agent."

Olivera's tone thawed. "I am quite sure my papers are in order, Miss Gordon, if that is what this is all about. I have been in this country eight years now."

"This has nothing to do with your immigration status."

"Then what does it have to do with?"

"I'll let Mr. Abrahamson tell you. Please, wait there at the Sheraton."

The professor sighed. "Impossible. I have to go straight home and pack my bags." He paused. "However, if you and Mr. Abrahamson wish to stop by there, I can perhaps spare a few minutes." He gave her the address.

"We'll be there," Tally promised.

She tried the FBI office again. Abrahamson still wasn't available. Tally passed along Olivera's address and asked the clerk to get the message to Abrahamson as soon as possible.

She then called Border Patrol headquarters in El Paso, on the chance Abrahamson had talked to someone there—Blaine possibly.

Blaine wasn't there, and the dispatcher hadn't heard from Abrahamson.

It was almost eight o'clock. Olivera had said he couldn't wait. Couldn't or wouldn't? Maybe Olivera was hiding Devlin.

Tally left the pizza parlor and returned to her car, looking around carefully. No sign of the black sedan. There was no reason Ybarra and Uhlmann should tail her. Abrahamson was directing the pursuit of Devlin. She was just a small cog in a very large wheel.

Still, she couldn't be too careful.

She drove out of the parking lot and headed for Interstate 25. It was Sunday night and traffic was light, but she kept her speed well under the limit, checking the rearview mirror every few seconds.

The few cars within view behind her had been there on the interstate when she came off the entrance ramp. There was no way they could have followed her from the motel or the pizza parlor—unless someone watching the gray-and-green Border Patrol car had seen it and had radioed to an accomplice....

She was getting paranoid, she chided herself. She'd been around Abrahamson too long.

But there was no point taking chances.

Approaching the interchange where Interstate 25 joined Interstate 40, she made sure she was a safe distance ahead of the nearest car behind her, and then braked suddenly and swerved from the inside lane to the exit leading eastbound on Interstate 40.

One car turned off after her, she noticed. She couldn't tell its make.

I don't know who you are, she thought, *but if you want to play games, we'll play games.*

Checking to make sure her seat belt was securely fastened, she reached down to the floor and brought up a red, plastic-domed light. Then she rolled down her window and secured the light to the rooftop by its magnet. She switched on the light and tromped down on the gas pedal, sending the car hurtling forward, pressing her back in her seat as she groped for the siren switch.

Traffic was heavier on Interstate 40—heavier, but well behaved. As cars and trucks slowed and pulled to the right to give her room, she went screaming by at high speed, still keeping a close eye on the mirror.

Swinging off the interstate at San Mateo Boulevard, she turned into the first side street and killed both emergency light and siren. She made a quick U-turn, switched off the headlights and parked facing San Mateo.

None of the cross traffic seemed at all in a hurry.

At last, Tally put away the emergency light, pulled out onto San Mateo, then doubled back on Lomas toward town.

She had no trouble finding Olivera's address: an older, two-story adobe structure built around a courtyard. It was only a few blocks from the main campus of the university.

There was no place to park on the block, so she drove around the corner and pulled into a darkened alley. Before getting out of the car, she made one last attempt to locate Abrahamson via radio.

"Sorry," said the same voice she'd heard on the phone earlier, "I still haven't been able to raise your man."

"You'll keep trying?"

"Affirmative."

Well, she'd tried. That was all she could do.

She locked the car and walked around the corner to the front of the apartment building, where a bank of free-standing mailboxes stood under a lamp at the side of the walkway leading to the courtyard entryway. She paused and looked at number seventeen. Professor Olivera hadn't taped his name to the box the way his neighbors had, but then he'd just moved in that weekend.

As she turned away from the mailboxes, a late-model sedan cruised past the building, and the yellow glow of the streetlight allowed Tally a fleeting glimpse of the driver before the car was swallowed up by the night.

Was it her imagination, or did the driver look an awful lot like Raul Devlin?

Chapter Five

Raul smiled. Not the nervous, twitching smile of a hounded fugitive who was beginning to doubt his invulnerability, but the satisfied smile of a man who sensed that, in spite of all obstacles, things were going his way.

Somehow I knew that our paths would cross again, he thought. *It's destiny, of course. You do believe in destiny, don't you,* migra? *Of course you do! The two of us are cut from the same cloth, cast from the same mold. You know what you want, just as I know what I want, and neither of us is afraid to risk all we possess, our very lives, to attain our goals.*

Destiny or not, he kept on driving. Raul Devlin the poet might be an incurable romantic, but Raul Devlin the man was no fool. He knew Tally Gordon would be very much on guard—thus even more of a threat to his mission—when next they came face-to-face. He was well aware the Border Patrol eventually would pick up his trail, but he'd hoped for more lead time—with luck, a full day, considering that this was Sunday. His luck had been short-lived. His pursuers must have found Tally's Volvo abandoned in the lot in Socorro, and now they knew he was headed north.

Raul had no fear Anastacio Olivera would betray him. The professor had been a friend of the Movement for too long, and when they'd gotten together earlier that day in Old Town he'd been most helpful. The professor had even lined up transportation for him to help him on his trek north. Raul had been quite candid and had told him about Abrahamson, about how the federal government had joined forces with the Protectors. Olivera knew the risks, and he still wanted to help.

Now *la migra* was closing in, just as Raul was arriving to pay another, final, call on the professor.

Driving on a few blocks, Raul pulled up in front of a phone booth outside a convenience store six blocks from the apartment complex. And then he remembered: shortly after he'd arrived in Juarez, he'd called Olivera at the university, and the professor had mentioned he was moving and had no home phone.

"When can I expect you?" Olivera had asked.

"As soon as I can get there," Raul had replied.

"Good. Contact Gabriel at his shop in Old Town. He will arrange a rendezvous. There is much to be done...."

That had been four days ago. Time was running out, and Devlin knew he ought to be on the road north. It would have been so much simpler to fly, but that was out of the question. He'd be captured the minute he stepped up to an airline ticket counter anywhere in this part of the country. Nor could he risk renting a small airplane here in New Mexico. That fellow Abrahamson undoubtedly had been informed he was a pilot and would have covered the charter services.

Since Tally had already found the professor and was on her way to interview him, that meant other Border Patrol officers and Abrahamson weren't far behind. And if Abrahamson was in Albuquerque, so were the Protectors.

He had no choice. He had to consult Olivera again before leaving Albuquerque and he didn't have much time. Maybe he'd even run into Tally herself. He rather hoped he would.

SITTING PRIMLY ON THE EDGE of a well-worn, dark leather couch that was all but buried under a jumble of books and research papers, Tally peered intently at the tall, gray-bearded man seated at the rolltop oak desk against the opposite wall. His swivel chair was turned so that he was only half facing her. He'd been polite enough, but Tally sensed he resented her intrusion, and that he wished she'd leave—soon. She had no intention of doing so until she got some answers. "Just who is Raul Devlin?" she asked.

Anastacio Olivera continued sorting papers into the partitioned depths of the battered, old-fashioned briefcase balanced on his lap. The briefcase was already stuffed beyond capacity, but Olivera didn't seem to notice. He was at least seventy, thin and fragile looking, with a scholar's clear eyes and an intensity that said he was always willing to learn new things. "You do not know?"

Tally shook her head. "All I know is that he's managed to slip into the United States and that we're making an all-out effort to find him."

Olivera scrutinized a folder, then tossed it onto the clutter of his desk top. "You will not find him, Miss Gordon. Mark my words. No one will find Raul Devlin until he wants to be found." He sifted through the papers on his desk as if he'd misplaced something, then looked across at the couch Tally was sitting on. "Would you hand me that blue folder—the one there on top of those journals?"

Tally looked down and saw a thick, plastic-bound booklet labeled *Cyclical Aspects of Nationalism*. She passed it to Olivera, who wedged it into the briefcase. "I still have to try," she said. "It's important."

"To whom?"

I wish I had a good answer for you, but I don't, Tally thought. "I know you're on a tight schedule, professor, so I'll try not to take up too much of your time, but I'm not here to play games. I'm here to get some answers. Why has Raul Devlin slipped across the border into the United States?"

"I suggest you ask your Mr. Abrahamson that question."

"I'm asking *you*."

The professor just looked at her, saying nothing.

Tally tried again. "Have you ever met Devlin?"

He shrugged. "I may have."

"Where? When?"

He didn't answer.

Tally was getting impatient. "Look, professor, there's a lot at stake here."

"I know," he said, nodding slowly. "How well I know."

"If you're a friend of Devlin's—"

"I did not say that, Miss Gordon."

"Have it your way. But if you are, you should know that his life is in danger."

Olivera smiled wearily. "Raul Devlin was born to a life of danger, Miss Gordon. He knows how to protect himself."

"Then you admit that you do know him!"

He stared at her.

Tally tried another approach. "Have you ever heard of two men named Simon Ybarra and Hans Uhlmann?"

There was a flicker of hatred in Olivera's eyes. "I have."

"They're trying to find Devlin, too, you know."

"I told you. He won't be found until he wants to be found."

"Who are Ybarra and Uhlmann?" Tally persisted.

"Ask Mr. Abrahamson. The three of them are—" He stopped, looked away, as if realizing he'd said something he shouldn't have said.

Tally leaned forward, her resolve strengthened by the professor's unwitting admission. "If you know Ybarra and Uhlmann are working with Abrahamson, you've obviously been in touch with Devlin. Don't deny it."

"I deny nothing, Miss Gordon. And I admit nothing. Now if you'll excuse me..." He started to get up from his chair.

"Tell me about Raul Devlin."

Olivera looked at his wristwatch. "I have to get to the airport."

"You know, professor, I could arrest you as a material witness. I don't want to have to do that. So tell me about Devlin and you can be on your way."

Olivera sighed and settled back in his chair. "What can I say? He is a very complex man. A soldier, a poet, a dreamer, but also a doer—one of those rare individuals blessed with the innate ability to be whatever he wishes to be and to excel at it, and yet at the same time cursed with a strong sense of morality."

"Go on," Tally prodded.

Olivera used both hands to compress the sides of the bulging briefcase, and then cinched it shut and lowered it to the floor at his feet. "You would do just as well at the public library. Try *The New York Times* or *The Washington Post*. They both—"

"I don't have time, professor."

Again, Olivera started to stand up. "As you know, I am a bit rushed myself, Miss Gordon. I must get to the airport, check in—"

"I'll run you out to the airport. You won't miss your plane. I need to know more about Raul Devlin."

"Why? Do you want to make an honest effort to understand the man, or are you just trying to cut some corners in your investigation? What do you propose to do if you do find him?"

"That's not up to me, professor."

"Who *is* it up to?"

Tally sensed that Olivera was testing her. "To Mr. Abrahamson, of course—and the people he reports to in Washington."

"Well, then, what do Mr. Abrahamson and his people intend to do?"

Tally hesitated. She couldn't very well say that she suspected Devlin was marked for execution. "Deport him."

"Deport him? Deport him to what country?"

"Argentina, I suppose."

Olivera shook his head slowly. "Argentina was merely a way station on his road to self-fulfillment. If ever a man was truly a citizen of the world, it is Raul Devlin."

Tally cocked her head. "I don't understand."

Again Olivera made a show of consulting his watch. "I shall be brief, Miss Gordon. Devlin comes from one of the most powerful families in Argentina, a family that made a fortune in cattle and textiles. He's Irish on his father's side, Spanish on his mother's. He grew up in England and Spain, was educated at West Point—a courtesy your government extends to certain allies—and served in the Argentine Army, rising to the command of a parachute battalion. A few years ago, he was sent to Honduras as a military attaché in the Argentine Embassy. It was an assignment that changed his life." He paused. "How much do you know about Central American history?"

"I'm certainly not an expert, but I've read quite a bit about the region."

"Then you will recall that early in the nineteenth century, there was a movement to bring the five newly independent nations of the region under the umbrella of a single government known as Provincias Unidas del Centro de America—the Central American Federation. It was a grand notion, but one that was far ahead of its time. Regional jealousies and inevitable self-interest got in the way, and after fifteen years the experiment was abandoned."

"What does this have to do with Devlin?"

"As a military attaché, Devlin saw firsthand the tragedy that had befallen Central America—the revolutions and counterrevolutions, the terror and the violence. And then one day, while on a tour of El Salvador, he heard Dr. Fuentes speak, and he was impressed. He—"

"Who is Dr. Fuentes?" Tally broke in.

Olivera frowned, as if annoyed she didn't recognize the name. "Federico Fuentes is the leader of the modern federation movement. He is a Nicaraguan by birth, but a man who has divorced himself from the partisan wranglings that have torn that country in order to concentrate on loftier goals. As a result, he enjoys wide respect throughout Central America. He has come up with a plan that resolves the problems of the past and makes federation a viable alternative for the five republics—Guatemala, Honduras, El Salvador, Costa Rica and Nicaragua, his own country. As I started to say, Devlin was so impressed that he resigned his commission and stayed in the region to work with Fuentes for a year, after which he moved to Brussels to write poetry. Why poetry I have no idea—I suppose it was his way of completing the renunciation of his military career." The professor stood up. "I am sorry, Miss Gordon, but I really must insist you leave now."

"Finish your story, professor. Please."

Olivera sighed. "Fuentes attracted some powerful enemies after Devlin left Central America, including a group of well-organized, hired thugs called the Protectors, who are controlled by a faction dedicated to preserving the status quo. The Protectors were ordered to kill Fuentes, because their masters saw him as a threat to their privileged status—"

Tally interrupted him. "Is that where Ybarra and Uhlmann fit in? They're members of the Protectors?"

The professor nodded. "Knowing Devlin's military background, and his training in counter-terrorism techniques, Fuentes's friends asked Devlin to return to Central America to organize security for Fuentes—specifically, to protect him from the Protectors. Devlin did so. Then, some months later, both Devlin and Fuentes were gravely wounded in an ambush. Devlin dropped from sight, and Fuentes, using an assumed name, came to this country to recuperate. Without the steadying hand of its founder, the Movement is struggling as it prepares for elections in February."

Tally saw the lead she'd been looking for. "Where can I find this Federico Fuentes?"

"I have no idea, Miss Gordon."

"I think you do."

Olivera glanced sharply at her. "I will not be called a liar. Good evening, Miss Gordon." Olivera moved toward the front door.

Tally made a last attempt to regain her foothold. "I don't know anything about your movement, professor, but I can tell you this. If you're counting on Devlin to accomplish anything in its behalf, you better tell me the truth. I've seen Ybarra and Uhlmann. They—"

Olivera held up his hand to stop her. "I do not want to hear those names again. Ybarra, personally, has executed some of my closest friends. Now, I suggest you go on back to El Paso and forget you ever met Raul Devlin. If you keep looking, you may learn things about him you don't wish to know."

"What sort of things?"

Olivera studied her. When he spoke again, he weighed his words carefully. "There are those in the Movement who suspect that Devlin sold out to the Protectors, that he actually arranged that last attempt on Dr. Fuentes's life."

"Then why would Ybarra and Uhlmann be after him now?"

Olivera shrugged. "Perhaps to silence him, perhaps to force him to lead them to Fuentes. I really can't say."

"Do you think he sold out, professor?"

"I know only what my instinct tells me. And my instinct tells me Raul Devlin is an honorable and decent man. Still, Dr. Fuentes knew him best, and only he can say for sure."

"Where can I find Fuentes?"

Olivera opened the front door and stood there, looking troubled. "I can't say."

"Can't, or won't? I gather from what you say that the Protectors still want to get their hands on Fuentes. Tell me where he is and we can help him."

The professor started to say something, then changed his mind. "I shall have to think about it, Miss Gordon. I must talk to other people before I decide . . ."

"I have to know now, professor."

"I can't tell you now, Miss Gordon!"

Tally softened her tone. "When can you tell me?"

"Let me think about it on the flight to California. Give me your phone number. I shall call you from Los Angeles."

"Do I have your word on that, Professor Olivera?" Tally asked, scribbling her hotel number on a piece of paper and handing it to him.

"You have my word. Now, Miss Gordon . . ."

Tally stepped up to the open door. "I'll take you to the airport. We can talk some more on the way."

"That is not necessary, thank you. I have a few things yet to do."

"I'm in no hurry, professor. I can wait."

"No, no, I shall manage." He reached out to shake hands, and as he did so, he steered her out through the door. "I will call you later this evening."

"I'll be waiting to hear from you," Tally said.

But she was talking to a closed door.

PRESSED CLOSE TO THE WALL, to one side of a window that opened onto a uniquely New Mexican atrium filled with cactus and decorative rocks, Raul had listened in on part of the conversation between Tally and the professor. And as he listened, he knew he had problems. Tally was asking some very pointed questions, and while Olivera was sharp, he'd given away too much, not the least of which was the bit about Federico Fuentes. If Tally kept on putting two and two together at this rate—and she was a bright woman—she couldn't help but come up with some answers.

He had to do something about that.

But what?

As Tally and the professor moved to the door of the apartment, their voices fading, Raul reviewed his options.

One, he could do nothing, just keep on running, looking back over his shoulder every step of the way, deferring the inevitable next confrontation with his determined and very attractive pursuer.

Well, he thought, better her than Simon Ybarra and his friends, including that fellow Abrahamson. Much better.

No good. He had to know what the other side was doing. As it was now, he was flying blind, without instruments, and he was likely to crash any moment. He smiled grimly.

Two, he could go to her, spell it all out, tell her how important his mission was, appeal to her sense of decency and fair play—qualities he knew she had. They'd been indicated several times during their brief acquaintance. By the things she'd said, the questions she'd asked, she'd made it clear she had her doubts about her assignment and about Abrahamson.

Now that Olivera had told her about Federico Fuentes, she had to realize that he must not allow her or anyone else to interfere. What was it the professor had told her? *No one will find Raul Devlin until he wants to be found.* Now if only he himself could believe that . . .

He thought about it. The second option presented certain risks. He could be wrong about Tally. He'd been wrong before, and those past mistakes had nearly cost him his life.

He could hear Olivera saying something about calling Tally later, and he knew he had to make a decision soon.

A third option crossed his mind as he slipped out of the atrium, toward a rear passageway leading out of the complex.

He could dispose of Tally Gordon once and for all.

LISTEN, POP USED TO SAY. You'll always learn more by listening than talking. Listen not only to what people have to say, but to how they say it. Everybody tends to be nervous dealing with the law, but when they're too nervous, or too glib, be on your guard. Maintain eye contact and try not to blink, because blinking is a sign of uncertainty. Stay cool, detached, alert. And above all, listen.

The interview with Anastacio Olivera hadn't gone all that well, Tally decided as she walked to her parked car. An experienced investigator like Pop or even Blaine Murchison would have gotten more out of him. The professor had told her only what he wanted to tell her, and then he'd sent her on her way with a vague promise that he'd get back to her later. It was the classic runaround: don't call me, I'll call you.

Sure he will, Tally thought. When hell freezes over.

Listen, Pop used to say.

She hadn't been listening well enough. She'd been too busy asking dumb questions.

Tally stopped dead in her tracks, just outside the main entrance to the apartment complex. Olivera had told her something important, and it hadn't registered at the time. She tried to remember Olivera's exact words. It was something about El Paso. What was it?

"I suggest you go on back to El Paso and forget you ever met Raul Devlin," he'd said.

How did he know she was stationed in El Paso? And how did he know she'd actually met Devlin? She certainly hadn't told him. Only one person could have told him, and that person was Devlin. Obviously, the two *had* been in contact.

Tally turned and started to reenter the apartment complex. She had every right to haul Olivera off to jail as a material witness. Let him try to stand up to a few hours of interrogation by Abrahamson!

But what about Ybarra and Uhlmann? Wherever Abrahamson went, they went. If Ybarra and Uhlmann knew about the professor, they were sure to resort to strong-arm tactics, and she'd be powerless to stop them—not with Abrahamson backing them up.

Who could she turn to?

She went into the complex and walked down the hallway to Olivera's apartment. Her finger hovered over the buzzer. Then she hesitated.

What good would it do to press Olivera? If her hunch was correct, it would only spook Devlin, and there was a chance Devlin might get in touch with the professor again.

She headed back to her car, got in and drove off.

A parking spot had opened up down the street, half a block west of the main entrance to Olivera's apartment building, and Tally eased her car into it and turned off the lights. She had a clear view of the mailboxes, but she knew there was an alley entrance that should be covered, as well.

She picked up the microphone and identified herself. "Has Mr. Abrahamson checked in yet?"

"Negative," came the reply.

Great. What was she supposed to do now? She was working mostly on intuition—too much intuition, maybe, and too little time. It would take forever to explain the situation to someone coming in cold. She couldn't risk doing that over the air, and she certainly didn't want to attract attention by having a face-to-face huddle out here on the street.

She couldn't watch both entrances to the apartment building. So she was taking a risk, but it was a better risk than the alternatives.

"I'll be on the air," she informed the dispatcher. "Please have Mr. Abrahamson contact me as soon as he can." He'd be furious with her for disobeying orders, but he'd get over it when she told him what she'd learned.

Pulling her coat collar up around her ears to keep warm, she settled back to wait.

Olivera had to be holding back to protect Devlin. From the way he had talked, he was clearly on Devlin's side—even if some of Fuentes's friends did believe Devlin was a traitor to the cause. Tally still didn't know a great deal about Devlin, but based on what she did know, and what she sensed, it was impossible to think of him as a man who'd sell out a friend. He was dangerous, true. A man capable of killing, growing ever more desperate as his pursuers closed in on him. But a traitor? It didn't seem possible.

Was it really Devlin she'd seen drive by just before she'd gone into the apartment building? If so, he must have recognized her and kept on going. The question was, would he return now that she'd left the apartment? There wasn't much time. Olivera would be setting out for the airport any minute.

Again she wished she had someone covering the rear entrance to the apartment complex.

It was eight forty-five, and she felt as if she'd been sitting there in the car for hours instead of minutes, waiting for something to happen.

Tally had turned off the engine when she parked, to prevent the Plymouth from sending up an exhaust plume from the tailpipe, which would have been a dead giveaway on a cold night such as this. She'd left the ignition on, though, so that the radio would continue to function. Now she was beginning to worry that she might run down the battery, and then where would she be if she had to take out after Devlin in a hurry?

She hadn't spoken to Abrahamson since midafternoon, and she wondered if Ybarra and Uhlmann had caught up with him. Perhaps she should have tailed Ybarra when he left the motel, to see if he'd lead her to the witness he'd mentioned. For all she knew, someone else was in danger from the Protectors. But who?

And Abrahamson...what was he up to? He'd never tell her. That was for sure.

Was the occasional crackle and sputter of the radio getting weaker, or was it just her imagination?

She couldn't take a chance.

She turned the key in the ignition and held her breath as the engine turned over slowly, reluctantly, several times, before catching.

Breathing a sigh of relief, she swiveled about in her seat to see how noticeable the exhaust was. Not too bad, she decided. You'd see it if you were looking for it, but...

Raul Devlin would be looking. He'd be looking for everything. He was an expert in counter-terrorism techniques, Olivera had said, and people like that had to be observant because their lives depended on it. Now he was a man on the run, and he knew all the tricks.

But she'd have to chance it.

And then she saw him. At least, she thought it was him. She was just turning back around in her seat when she detected movement to one side of the lighted area around the bank of mailboxes just outside the main entrance to the complex.

She switched off the engine, dropped the keys into her purse and checked her service revolver. She slipped the revolver into a side pocket of her trench coat. Devlin wasn't going to get away *this* time.

She started to ease open the curbside door, then quickly pulled it shut when the dome light came to life. Reaching up, she switched off the light, and then opened the door again and slipped out of the car.

She scanned the shrubbery around the mailboxes.

There he was: back in the bushes, moving away from the entrance to the complex.

Crouching for cover behind the line of parked cars, Tally moved parallel to the street, keeping pace with the figure in the bushes.

At the corner of the block, her quarry disappeared up the side street that served as the western perimeter of the apartment property.

Tally knew she had to cross the street. She'd have to gamble on not being seen, watching for the first opportunity to confront him.

Retracing her steps by three car lengths to minimize the risk of being seen in the full glare of the corner streetlight, she darted across the street and ducked into the bushes bordering the apartment house.

She'd lost sight of him, but he couldn't be too far ahead of her, she knew. Did he realize he was being followed?

There were no lights anywhere on the street running alongside the apartment house, and it took a minute for her eyes to become accustomed to the darkness. Very appropriate, she mused. The first time she'd seen Raul Devlin, it had been pitch black and she had to use a Star-Tron scope to get a close glimpse of him. She wished she had the scope with her tonight.

Removing her revolver from her pocket, she checked to make sure it was on safety, and then, gun in hand, edged along the windowless adobe wall of the building. She halted every dozen paces to peer into the darkness and listen.

No sign of him.

She thought again about calling in help. Her explanations might be weak and lengthy, but they'd do.

She heard the car before she saw it. A powerful engine surged to life and the dark bulk of a sedan swung away from the curb and out into the side street.

Oh, no! she thought. *He's getting away—again!*

As the driver switched on his lights, Tally ran out from behind the bushes, across the sidewalk and into the middle of the street, clutching her gun in both hands as she faced the onrushing vehicle.

"Halt!" she shouted at the top of her lungs.

The car was headed straight for her, and the driver showed no intention of pulling up.

Tally was about to fire and jump aside when something large and solid hurtled into her midsection, and a strong hand clamped down on her right wrist. She was literally swept off her feet, then sent tumbling across the hood of a parked car, landing hard on her back on the graveled area separating curb from sidewalk.

Dazed, she felt the fingers of her right hand being pried off the grip of her revolver.

"I believe that's two you owe me, *migra*," she heard Raul Devlin say.

Chapter Six

Nate Abrahamson had just climbed out of the car in front of the federal building when Simon Ybarra stepped from the shadows to confront him. Ybarra's constant companion, Hans Uhlmann—a short, burly man whom Abrahamson had once heard called the Butcher of Buenos Aires—hung back, hands in his pockets, hat brim pulled low on his forehead, watching them closely through heavily lidded eyes.

"Where have you been?" Ybarra demanded. "I have hunted all over Albuquerque for you."

Abrahamson glanced over his shoulder at the FBI agent who'd escorted him on his evening prowl. With a curt hook of one thumb, he signaled the agent to go on into the building without him. Only then did he turn his full, scowling attention on Ybarra. "I told you to stay away from me. Ever since El Paso, people are asking questions."

"People? What people, my dear Abrahamson? Surely you are not worried about that young woman who seems to have been pressed into service as your aide-de-camp? I hardly consider her a threat to, ah, our arrangement."

Abrahamson grunted. "Don't underestimate Tally Gordon. I suspect she's sharp enough to have you pegged—you and your trained gorilla." He looked at Uhlmann, who listened impassively but said nothing. "Tell me, is it true that your friend there used to be Argentina's number one hit man?"

Ybarra seemed amused. "Hans's reputation follows him everywhere. Actually, though, this is a labor of love on his part. He volunteered to help us when he heard, via the grapevine, that we were looking for Raul Devlin. Hans once served in the Argentine Army under Devlin, and Devlin had him court-martialed for some petty infraction—rape and murder, as I recall. He would like very much to settle the score."

Abrahamson stared coldly at Ybarra. "Let's get one thing straight. There's to be no more killing, you understand? If you or Uhlmann or any of your other people get trigger-happy again like you did down there on the border the other night, our deal's off."

Ybarra was no longer amused. Squaring his shoulders, he stepped back, and Uhlmann moved in closer like a trained attack dog ready to spring into action. "I assure you, the men in the van did not shoot to kill. Their orders were to seize Devlin, and to accomplish that they had to prevent that woman from snatching him out from under their noses." He paused, lowering his voice. "Besides, my dear Abrahamson, you do not give orders—you take them. The ruling council of the Protectors expects full value for its investment."

"No more killing," the man from Washington said firmly.

Ybarra shrugged. "I do not intend to argue the point. Now tell me, what have you found out this evening?"

"Nothing."

"Nothing? What do you mean, nothing? You've been gone for hours...."

"I've been following up some leads. Every one of them turned into a dead end."

Ybarra exchanged glances with his silent companion. He then studied Abrahamson, as if trying to determine if Abrahamson was lying.

"What you are saying is that you have found no one who has seen Raul Devlin. Is that correct?"

"No one who admits to it."

"I understand there is a faculty member at the university who has maintained close ties with the Movement. Have you interviewed him?"

"Anastacio Olivera? I haven't been able to reach him, but I left word for him to call me. Gordon was supposed to take the message. I'll check in with her and see if she's heard anything."

"Please do."

Ybarra turned to leave, but Abrahamson reached out and caught his sleeve. "There's the matter of the money," he said.

"Ah, yes." Ybarra reached into an inner pocket and brought out a fat envelope. He handed it to Abrahamson and smiled. "This brings the total to fifty thousand. I must say, your services do not come cheaply."

Abrahamson stuffed the envelope into his own pocket. "You get what you pay for, and what you're paying for is the head of Raul Devlin. Consider it money well spent."

"THOSE PEOPLE IN THE CAR, who were they?" Tally demanded, glancing nervously at her gun, which lay in Raul Devlin's lap.

He laughed dryly. "I have no idea. I was too busy trying to save your neck to get the license number."

Tally's apprehensiveness gave way to irritation. "That's not funny, Devlin! I want to know who they were!"

"I wouldn't worry about it, *migra*. I doubt they were interested in running you down. They must have been following you and you got in their way. But you'll have to take that up with the man you work for. He seems to think he and his allies are above the law."

"The man I work for is Uncle Sam," Tally said stiffly. She thought of Abrahamson and all that he hadn't told her about the case. "And no one's above the law in this country."

Devlin's cheeks crinkled in a cynical grin. "You're not just attractive, *migra*, you're also too quixotic for your own good. Like Cervantes's lovable hero, you see things not as they are but as you wish they might be." The cynicism faded, as if he was suddenly afraid she'd think he was making fun of her. "I'm familiar with the symptoms. I have a recurring case of the same disease."

They were in Tally's car, parked in the lot of a restaurant half a mile from Olivera's apartment. Devlin was at the wheel, Tally seated on the passenger side. The Border Patrol radio was crackling just loud enough to be heard above the rock-and-roll music throbbing from the café next door.

What now? Tally asked herself. Should she make a break for it? He wouldn't shoot her, even if he did have her gun. If he wanted her dead, he could have let her be hit by that car a few minutes ago. He could have killed her himself as she lay dazed on the sidewalk. For that matter, he could have killed her in El Paso. He didn't—and that told her something: Raul Devlin might be a dangerous man, but he was not a cold-blooded murderer.

"I don't consider myself quixotic," she said aloud, adopting a defensive tone. "I consider myself quite practical." What right did he have to analyze her?

"Forgive me, *migra*. When I used the term quixotic, I was thinking not of naivete, but of idealism. A naive person couldn't achieve straight A's in law school while working full time at a demanding job such as yours."

Tally cocked her head and looked at him. "How'd you know I...?" Why ask? After handcuffing her the night before in El Paso, he must have examined every scrap of paper on her desk, even her grade reports, looking for the photographs. What's more, he must have done it quickly, knowing she'd phoned for assistance and that at any minute armed officers could come charging into the apartment.

Devlin reached across and patted her hand. "That's the cardinal rule for a good soldier," he said with a smile. "Know your enemy."

Tally edged away from him, withdrawing her hand from under his. "You've certainly got that right, Devlin. We *are* enemies. I represent the law, and you're a criminal who's evading arrest—it's as simple as that. If you stop running and give yourself up, maybe I'd be willing to listen to what you have to say." She'd listen, she thought, but would Abrahamson and those sinister friends of his? They'd just as soon put a bullet in Devlin's brain.

His lighthearted manner disappeared. "If I give myself up, I'm a dead man—you know it, and I know it. I have no wish to die, certainly not until I've done what I set out to do."

"And what's that?"

He shrugged off the question. "Why talk about it, *migra*? We're enemies. Remember?"

Tally glanced again at the gun, sensing that it was time to back off. From what she'd seen of Devlin, from what Olivera had told her about him, she didn't think he'd deliberately harm her, but she couldn't be sure. What was it Olivera had said? If she kept poking, she might find out things she really didn't want to know. The thought disturbed her. She'd become fascinated by Devlin. He was unlike any man she'd ever known. But she was afraid of him, afraid of unlocking those dark mysteries Olivera had hinted at. Still, not knowing if and when he might explode, she decided it might be better to tread carefully. "We don't have to go on being enemies," she ventured.

"Don't we? I told you—I have no intention of surrendering to you or anyone else."

"You don't have to be afraid of me," she said, trying to put him at ease.

"Afraid of you?" Again he smiled. "Hardly. I have a great deal of respect for you. In fact, the more I think about it the more sure I am that I'd like to have you in my corner."

That was the opening she needed. "Then give me back my gun."

He studied her for a moment, then made his decision. He picked up the revolver and handed it to her gingerly, butt first. "Careful, *migra*. We both know it's fully loaded. Before you do anything foolish, hear me out, will you?"

Tally's hand tightened on the grip of the gun, and instinctively she thumbed off the safety. Wild thoughts tumbled through her mind. Finally she had him. All she had to do was get on the radio and . . .

Not a chance, she thought. He had to be lying to her again. He had to have slipped out the cartridges while she was still dazed, and now he was testing her. Well, it wouldn't work.

Turning to one side, she held the revolver up to the light and flipped out the cylinder magazine.

She could see that there were five shells in the magazine, with the sixth chamber empty—the way she always left it for safety's sake. For all practical purposes, the weapon was fully loaded.

Was he out of his mind?

She pointed the muzzle at the floor, made sure the safety was reset and then dropped the gun into her purse. "All right, Devlin, you have the podium. Talk."

"I need a favor, *migra*."

Tally made a face. "Stop calling me *migra*. What sort of favor?"

"I need—what's the expression?—space. I need room to operate, without having to look back over my shoulder every step of the way to see who's closing in on me. I need to know what the other side is doing. As I said before, I'd like to have you in my corner."

She shook her head. "Sorry, Devlin. I might be willing to look the other way if you agreed to go back where you came from, but I won't turn informer for you. I take my job too seriously."

"I'm sure you do. You have a well-defined sense of justice. But, then, so do I." He paused, choosing his words carefully. "You heard what the professor told you about the Movement...."

She looked at him sharply. "You were listening in?"

"I was outside, at the window, Tally. You don't mind if I call you Tally, do you?"

"Tally's fine. As for the professor, he told me enough. He said you're mixed up with some group that's trying to set up a confederation of Central American states."

Devlin nodded. "The Movement. And didn't I hear him tell you that there's another group that's every bit as determined to see that the confederation never gets off the ground?"

Tally nodded. "The Protectors."

"And he told you what kind of people they are..."

"Yes. He said Simon Ybarra personally had killed some of his closest friends."

Devlin stared straight ahead for a moment, as if reliving a secret memory. Finally he said, "Ybarra and Uhlmann will stop at nothing to get their hands on me. I can't prove it, but I've got a pretty good idea that it was Uhlmann who murdered the doctors and nurses who treated me in Mexico. The killings had his sadistic touch."

Tally tightened her grip on the strap of her purse. It would take only a second to grab the gun from the purse if she needed it. "Some people seem to think *you* killed them."

"Did Abrahamson tell you that?"

"He suggested as much." She hesitated. "Did you?"

Devlin shook his head slowly. "I did not. I did steal the medical files, but that was all. The files contained photos of my reconstructed face, and I wanted to go deep underground for a while."

"I see. You wanted to avoid being recognized by the Protectors." She hesitated. "There's something you should know, Devlin. I think Uhlmann and Ybarra followed me to Albuquerque."

He reached down and switched on the ignition. "Then I've got to get back and check on the professor. If Ybarra and Uhlmann are in Albuquerque, it was probably the two of them who followed you to his place."

"No one followed me. I made sure of it."

He shook his head. "I don't believe in coincidence. It may have been them in the car that took a run at you."

Tally thought about it. "Possibly, but that's a big building. They couldn't know what apartment I was watching."

"I wonder . . ." He backed out of the lot and pulled into the street. "How about it, Tally? Will you grant me the favor I ask? Will you give me breathing room?"

She thought it over. "I'd like to, Raul, but I can't. I've got a job to do." Raul. How easily the name came to her lips.

He didn't press the point. Not then.

Five minutes later, they were knocking on the professor's door.

From behind them they heard a man say, "If you're looking for Dr. Olivera, you're wasting your time. He's gone."

They turned and saw a man in shirtsleeves standing in an open doorway across the hall. The sign on the door said Manager.

"You saw him leave?"

"A while ago," the man said. "A cab came for him."

Tally and Devlin exchanged glances. Devlin thanked the man, and they left.

"I was worried," Devlin said as they returned to the car. "I was afraid Ybarra and Uhlmann had gotten to him, but he seems to be safely on his way to California. It's just as well."

Tally took the keys from him and slid behind the wheel. As she buckled her seat belt, Devlin put his left arm up over the back of the seat, the tips of his fingers brushing the silken hairs on her neck just above the upturned collar of her trench coat. "It's your move now, Tally," he said softly. "Where do we go from here?"

"We?"

"We—the two of us."

"I'm still thinking about it."

"You've got to decide. We're running out of time."

She glanced at him. "Will you reconsider and give yourself up—at least get out of the country?"

"Not until I do what I have to do."

"Then you leave me no choice, Raul. You entered this country illegally, and I've got to take you in."

"You know what will happen if you do, don't you?"

Tally didn't want to think about it. She'd already thought about it and knew there was only one answer. "You'll be deported," she said, knowing she was lying.

Devlin shook his head slowly. "It will never come to that. I will be 'interviewed' by certain people, and when I refuse to lead them to Dr. Fuentes, I shall be summarily executed."

Tally closed her eyes, trying to shut out the idea. "My government won't allow that to happen," she murmured, wishing she could be sure.

"Your government has delegated its authority in the matter to Abrahamson, and Abrahamson has obviously sold out to the Protectors."

"You have no proof!"

"I have all the proof I need. So do you, if only you'd stop and think about it."

Steeling herself to the inevitable, Tally leaned forward and reach for the microphone mounted under the dashboard. As she did so a chill ran down her spine. Was it coincidence that when she moved, he was no longer touching her? His nearness gave her a reassurance, a warmth she couldn't quite explain. "I've got to take you in, Raul." She picked up the microphone, and he made no effort to take it from her. "If you want me to help you . . ."

"You *will* help me?"

"I didn't say that. I said—I started to say—that if you want me to help you, you've got to tell me just what it is you intend to do when you find Fuentes." She'd already picked up enough bits and pieces to construct her own scenario, but now she wanted to hear the story firsthand.

He shook his head. "It's better that you don't know."

Tally pressed down the microphone transmit button. "This is Agent Gordon of Border Patrol. I need..." She hesitated.

Devlin looked at her. He said nothing.

Tally lowered the microphone. "I don't understand you, Raul. You could be miles away from here by now and—"

"—and you could be lying dead in that street. Is that what you were going to say, Tally?"

The radio broke in: "Repeat, Gordon. Your last transmission incomplete."

Tally glanced down at the microphone. "Something like that, I suppose."

"I need you, Tally. It's as simple as that."

"For what?"

"I told you. You're the one who can give me some breathing room. It's not much to ask, is it?"

The radio sputtered, and Tally recognized Abrahamson's voice. "Gordon, what's your location?"

Tally looked at Devlin out of the corner of her eye. "How much breathing room, Raul?"

"Two days—three at the most."

Abrahamson's tone sounded even more curt than usual. "Gordon, where are you?"

Watching Devlin, Tally began to wonder who was captor and who was captive. She wasn't sure why, but she wanted to trust him. "You'll be out of the country within three days?"

"You have my word."

Tally took a deep breath. "On one condition. You've got to take me with you."

"I what?"

"I go along. I want to keep an eye on you. I want to make sure you don't get into any more trouble."

He laughed dryly. "Sorry, but the answer is no." Was there a note of regret in his tone? "It's too dangerous."

"Then no deal." Tally raised the microphone.

Devlin smiled and reached out and took the hand that held the microphone. He kissed her fingertips. "You drive a hard bargain, Tally."

"Then you agree to take me along?" Oh, boy, how would she ever explain this to Abrahamson? she wondered.

"Under protest."

"I have your word you won't try to slip away and do anything else illegal?"

"You have my word." Again, that disarming chuckle. "We might make a good team after all. You know how the Border Patrol operates, and I know the people we're dealing with. Together, we can..." He let the sentence dangle. Giving her a quick kiss on the cheek, he twisted around and opened the door. "I'll phone you later."

Tally grabbed at his sleeve. "Hey, where do you think you're going?"

"I've got to find a phone and call some people who've offered to help me. It may take a while. Where can I reach you?"

"At the Howard Johnson's on the interstate. But—"

Devlin was half out of the car. Suddenly he turned and leaned back across the seat, his hands reaching out for her shoulders, drawing her toward him. His lips grazed the tip of her nose, then closed upon her mouth, tentatively at first, as if resigned to yield to the slightest resistance on her part. But she didn't resist. Closing her eyes, she lost herself in the promise of his kiss, shutting out all else, the glare of the restaurant neon, the sounds of the night, the inner voice of reason that told her there was no way she could have any sort of romantic relationship with this man. It was all so utterly hopeless. And yet...

Her arms circled his neck, pulling him tighter as her lips parted, melding with his, coolness giving way to moist warmth and warmth to fire, a muffled murmur rising from her throat. "Raul . . ."

He pulled back and gave her a last hug. "Till later, partner," he said softly. "I shall call you no later than midnight. You have my word on it."

And then he was gone.

The radio crackled. "Gordon! Come in, Gordon!"

"Oh, shut up!" Tally muttered, turning down the volume.

"I TOLD YOU to stay put at the motel and take messages," Abrahamson grumbled. "I tried half a dozen times to reach you. What do you mean chasing off that way?"

Tally struggled to hold her temper. "Professor Olivera was leaving town and there wasn't much time. I couldn't reach you, so I went out there myself and interviewed him."

Abrahamson turned to the FBI agent who had brought him to the motel and instructed him to have someone intercept Olivera at the airport. "Tell him we'll send him on his way by military jet later on. If he objects, tell him he's a guest in this country, and if he wants to keep his green card he'd better cooperate."

"That's not fair," Tally protested as the FBI agent left the room. "The professor hasn't done anything wrong. You have no right to threaten him."

"Don't tell me what I can and can't do! Olivera's probably working hand in glove with Devlin." Abrahamson sat down on the edge of the bed and looked up at Tally. "So what did he have to say?"

Tally gave a detailed report of the conversation, but omitted mentioning her encounter with Devlin. She fully intended to keep her part of the bargain, but she hadn't yet decided how to handle the man from Washington.

When she was finished, Abrahamson shook his head as if to say he didn't believe a word of it. "Olivera was the only solid lead we've developed, and you blew it."

"He promised to call me later and tell me where we could find Fuentes."

"That isn't what he said and you know it, Gordon! He said he'd *think* about it and then call you. The only way we're going to get the information from Olivera is to sweat it out of him, face-to-face. If we—"

The phone rang and Abrahamson grabbed the receiver, grunted acknowledgment, and then hung up. He looked grimly at Tally. "The FBI just got word from the local police. Olivera's body has been found in a cab on a side street a few blocks from his apartment. He and the cabdriver both had their throats cut. Nice work, Gordon..."

TALLY KNEW she had to talk to someone she could trust, someone who could help her, and Blaine Murchison was the only person who came to mind. He might not be the man she wanted to marry, but she respected him professionally. Blaine had earned several commendations for his investigative work, and although he'd certainly never admit it, she suspected he admired her for keeping faith with Pop by following in his footsteps. If only he wasn't such a damn chauvinist...

As soon as Abrahamson left the motel, she put in a call to El Paso and told Blaine what had happened. She'd half expected he'd blow sky high and read her the riot act, let her know in no uncertain terms what an idiot she'd been to trust Devlin. And he would have been right, of course. Whatever his shortcomings, he was almost always right when it came to police work. He was as sharp an investigator as Pop had been. Damn! She should have listened to her head, not her heart.

But Blaine didn't explode. Like an understanding priest hearing a penitent's confession, he simply listened to what she had to say, asked a few straightforward questions, then told her not to worry.

The knuckles of Tally's hand went white as she clutched the receiver. "Blaine! I've put my whole future on the line, and you tell me not to worry! If Abrahamson finds out, I've had it!"

"Calm down, girl. I'm not going to say anything to Abrahamson, so why should you?"

Not good enough, she thought, ignoring his use of the word girl. "He's bound to find out when he finally catches up with Devlin."

"You're wrong there." Blaine lowered his voice. "The word's out on the street in Juarez. In case you haven't heard, Abrahamson isn't really interested in talking to Devlin. Fact is, he doesn't want Devlin talking—to anybody."

Blaine was only reinforcing the theory Tally herself had all but accepted, but she still found it troubling. "He intends to kill him, doesn't he?" she asked softly.

Blaine ignored the question. "Look, Tally, you're in way over your head on this one. You're being used, and I don't like it—I don't like it one bit. All I can tell you to do is go with the flow and let things take their course. Abrahamson gets his marching orders from way up high. Nobody in Washington is going to question him as long as he gets results."

Tally was suddenly angry and frustrated. "I'm not going to stand by and let an...let a man be murdered!" she protested. She'd started to say "innocent man," but even if he wasn't a murderer she was convinced Raul Devlin was anything but innocent.

"You don't have any choice."

"I may not have a choice, but I do have a conscience. Maybe if I talked to the chief, he could get in touch with someone at the justice department."

"The chief's hands are tied. Besides, the department would come on him like a ton of bricks if they even suspected one of his agents was playing patty-cake with a fellow like Devlin.''

Tally bristled. ''We are not playing patty-cake, Blaine,'' she said sharply. ''I'm just trying to do what's right.''

''Sure, Tally.'' His tone suggested he didn't believe it.

''Really, Blaine! I've got nowhere to turn. I can't trust Abrahamson, I can't go to the chief, I can't—'' Blaine was right. She *was* in over her head. ''Tell me, what do I do now?''

''You asking me as a friend, or as one cop to another?''

''As a friend.''

''All right, then, I'll tell you. Play along with Abrahamson, but don't stick your neck out any farther. He's bound to show his hand sooner or later, and when he does, let me know and I'll take it from there.''

Tally shook her head slowly. ''He's awfully shrewd. He may never show his hand.''

Blaine wouldn't accept that. ''I don't know a hell of a lot about Abrahamson, but I've got a hunch he's met his match. Devlin is one smart hombre. He'll manage to do whatever it is he figures on doing, then slip out of the country. Any man who can survive the kind of wounds he suffered in Central America has something extra going for him. It'll take a lot more than an overage, Ivy League hotshot like Abrahamson to stop him.''

''How'd you know about Devlin being wounded?''

''Abrahamson told me, of course. Didn't he fill you in, too?''

Tally frowned. ''Every time I ask a question, he practically accuses me of snooping into matters of national security.''

Blaine laughed. ''So maybe the man's a... What's the word for a guy who hates women?''

''A misogynist,'' Tally supplied. ''I think it's more than that. He's been letting a couple of creepy types follow us around. I have to wonder where they fit into the picture.''

"Hans Uhlmann and Simon Ybarra," Blaine mused. "I've wondered about them myself. I don't—" He broke off, then came back on the line a few seconds later. "Got to run, girl. I have a minor crisis at this end. Keep in touch, hear?"

"Wait, Blaine! How should I handle it when Devlin calls me later to make arrangements to meet me?"

"I wouldn't count on him doing that, Tally. He's probably well on his way by now."

"But if he does phone, what do I do?"

Blaine was silent for several seconds. Then he said, "Play along with him, then call and let me know where we can find him. I'll pass along the word to Abrahamson, but I'll manufacture a story that'll keep you out of it."

Tally hesitated. "How do we know Abrahamson won't start shooting the minute he sees Devlin?"

"You have a crush on that son of a gun, haven't you?" There was a faintly mocking tone in his voice.

"Of course not! I just don't want to see anybody get hurt, that's all."

"Okay, girl. I'll try to set it up so there are some of our own people on the scene. They'll see that your boy doesn't get hurt. Fair enough?"

"Fair enough, Blaine. Thanks."

TRUE TO HIS WORD, Raul phoned just before midnight to say he'd taken care of his other business and was ready to meet her. "I understand there's a snowstorm moving down through southern Colorado," he added. "If it slows us up, I may need more than those three days you promised me, *migra*."

Migra. Tally chewed at her lower lip. So, he was back to that name. Why did he have to remind her of who she was? It just made things all that much more difficult. "I'm sure that can be arranged," she lied. "Where do you want to meet?"

Raul gave no indication that he noticed the coolness in her tone. "Are you familiar with Old Town?"

"I've been there a few times."

"There's an arts-and-crafts shop just off the plaza—a place called La Tienda Zacatecas. Do you know it?"

"No, but I'm sure I can find the place."

"All right, be there at twelve-thirty."

Tally checked her watch. That would be cutting it close, she knew. She needed time to call Blaine and have him make arrangements. "Can we make it one o'clock?"

"Is anything wrong, *migra*?"

"No, nothing's wrong," she said quickly. "It's just that I . . . I want to make sure I'm not followed."

"I see. All right, then one o'clock it is. I suggest you park a few blocks away and come in on foot."

"You'll be inside the shop?"

"No, La Tienda Zacatecas will be closed. I'll station myself nearby so I can see you arrive, just in case."

Did he suspect she might betray him, or was he merely being extra cautious? It was hard to tell. "I'll be there."

"I'm looking forward to it. Do you know something? We're going to make a great team . . . Tally."

Don't count on it, she thought.

As soon as he hung up, she put in a call to Blaine. She had mixed feelings about what she was doing, and she tried to tell herself it was for Raul's own good. If Abrahamson managed to track down Raul on his own, there was no telling what would happen.

Blaine was still at the office. That didn't surprise her. Most of Blaine's underworld contacts were night people.

"You were wrong," she began. "Raul Devlin did call. And he wants me to meet him."

"What did you tell him?"

"I told him yes, of course, just as we'd agreed."

"Where and when?"

Tally told him.

"Any idea where Abrahamson is now?"

"He's still out with the FBI, as far as I know. He ordered me to stay here in my room and take messages."

"And that's just what I want you to do, girl. I'll handle it from here on out."

"You won't let anything happen to Devlin?"

"Not a chance. Look, I've got to get cracking. You owe me one."

That was what she was afraid of, Tally thought as she hung up. She didn't want to be in Blaine's debt, but it looked as though she didn't have much choice.

Leaving her door ajar so that she could hear the phone if it rang, she walked across the hall to see if Abrahamson had returned while she was on the phone. He hadn't said when he was coming back, just that he wanted to look through Olivera's personal papers. As usual he'd been purposely vague.

Tally knocked on his door several times, wondering what Blaine would tell Abrahamson. Some fanciful tale of an anonymous tip from sources in Juarez? It would have to be something like that. How else could Blaine keep her out of the picture?

Suddenly Tally started to have second thoughts about the whole thing. If Blaine couldn't pull it off, she'd be the one responsible for leading Raul to his death. Whatever else he'd done, Raul trusted her, and now she'd betrayed him.

She knew she had to be there when they arrested him. Surely Abrahamson wouldn't kill Raul in front of witnesses—but there might not be time for Blaine to get his own people in place. That, or Abrahamson might send them away on some pretext, then claim later he'd shot Raul when the fugitive tried to escape.

No, Raul wouldn't be safe until he was behind bars. With an attorney to represent him, no one in the government would dare make an attempt on his life.

Perhaps she should hand in her badge now and take Raul on as her first client, Tally thought as she returned to her own room and gathered up her coat and shoulder bag. After all, she'd certainly researched the case.

She went outside to her car, unlocked the front door and then, as an afterthought, opened the trunk and unclipped her handcuffs and chemical-mace canister from the gunbelt she'd packed away in the bag with her Border Patrol uniform. She dropped the cuffs and canister into her purse, which was already heavy from the weight of her service revolver. She didn't know if she'd need the extra equipment, but better to be prepared.

Five minutes later, she was parked on a side street just outside Old Town, one ear cocked to the car's police-radio scanner as she planned her next move.

The radio calls she'd heard on the way over from the motel were routine, nothing to indicate Abrahamson was deploying his men. That didn't prove a thing, she knew. Abrahamson played everything close to the vest, and it was likely he'd ordered his people to use a tactical channel that couldn't be heard on Border Patrol scanners.

She wished she knew if Blaine had gotten through to him, wished she knew what Abrahamson intended to do.

It was almost twelve-thirty, still half an hour to go before the scheduled rendezvous.

Maybe Raul would arrive early.

And if he did...what? Would he see the others closing in and know he had been betrayed?

Oh, hell! It was her doing, and she had to face up to it. Let Raul think what he liked, just as long as he came out of it alive.

She turned off the ignition, got out of the car and headed into Old Town, hugging the inside of the sidewalk, trying to be inconspicuous.

A few restaurants were still open, their late-hour diners spilling out onto the covered walkways of Old Town as the witching hour drew near. Brushing past them and waving aside invitations to join the merriment, Tally strode briskly into the heart of the renovated district.

At the main plaza, she stopped to get her bearings. She'd only been here a few times, passing through on vacation, and she had no idea where to find La Tienda Zacatecas.

She decided to start walking in ever-widening circles around the plaza, peering up darkened alleyways, hoping to spot a sign.

Again, she checked her watch. Twelve forty-five. She had to hurry.

Chapter Seven

From the shadows of a doorway half a block off the plaza, Raul watched as Tally came into view. He'd chosen their meeting place carefully. The shop was bounded on one side by a narrow alley that wound through canyons of low-rise adobe buildings, and on the other side was the shell of a business block that had recently been gutted by fire and was now being rebuilt; all that remained of the latter was a high, stuccoed wall and an interior courtyard stacked with piles of lumber and other construction materials. He'd checked out the courtyard earlier in the day after calling on Gabriel Zuniga, the proprietor of La Tienda Zacatecas, who'd arranged the rendezvous with Anastacio Olivera. He'd decided it offered a number of possibilities in case he had to leave in a hurry.

But you wouldn't try to trick me, would you, Tally? he wondered, smiling. *After all, what have I ever done to you? Perhaps I've told you a few lies, but we can't let that stand in the way of our relationship, can we?*

Raul felt a twinge of remorse that he'd had to shame Tally by trussing her up and leaving her a prisoner in her own apartment for her colleagues to find. Still, it couldn't have been helped.

He watched her disappear down one of the streets leading off the plaza, and he remained where he was, motionless in the shadows, waiting to see if she was being followed.

He had a feeling something was wrong. Tally had seemed very much on guard when he'd talked to her on the phone an hour earlier. Not exactly nervous but hesitant, as if fearful of spooking him.

You know, migra, I really couldn't blame you if you did try to turn me in. You have a sense of duty, just as I do, and when the final hand is dealt we shall have to see whose values prevail. I hope it doesn't come to that, because I need you. I really do.

He waited.

A few minutes later, he saw her reappear from a different side street. She stopped, looked across the plaza, peering into doorways and up at the tiled rooftops, and then started down another side street.

Raul still didn't move.

You're doing one of three things, Tally, he told himself. *You're trying to find La Tienda Zacatecas. Or you're on a scouting expedition to familiarize yourself with the territory. Or, possibly, you're trying to draw me out. Which is it?*

The minutes ticked by.

Tally entered the plaza the third time, looked around, then started down the street leading to La Tienda Zacatecas.

Raul stepped out of the doorway and headed after her.

Then he saw them: Two men and a woman, arms linked, sauntering across the plaza, laughing, as if they'd just left a restaurant where they'd had an exceptionally good time.

Raul ducked into the next doorway, wondering if the trio had spotted him. Probably not, he thought, but he couldn't take any chances.

The two men and the woman disappeared into the next side street, and still Raul waited.

He checked the time. Exactly one o'clock.

He struck out again for La Tienda Zacatecas, hugging the inside walls of the buildings flanking the plaza, keeping to the shadows.

At the mouth of the side street leading to the meeting place, he stopped and looked around.

No one was in sight.

He turned the corner and was halfway down the block, just a few doors from La Tienda Zacatecas, when he saw two dark figures spring out of the alleyway bordering the shop.

"Hold it right there, Devlin!" one of them shouted, raising his arm.

Raul wheeled and sprinted back the way he'd come, in the direction of the plaza.

Three more figures were blocking the route. He had only the briefest glimpse, but he was sure they were the two men and woman he'd seen a few minutes earlier.

Raul edged toward the inside of the sidewalk.

"He's making a break for it!" one of the men yelled.

The other man raised his hands, and Raul saw the muzzle flash as two quick shots were fired in his direction.

I seem to have misjudged you, Tally, Raul thought grimly as he darted into the courtyard of the building adjacent La Tienda Zacatecas.

Pausing long enough to flip over a steel drum that was sitting alongside the entrance to the courtyard, he gave it a kick that sent it rolling noisily out onto the stone pavement of the sidewalk. Then he turned and sprinted toward the darkness at the rear of the courtyard, where during his earlier reconnaissance he'd noted a suite of rooms stripped down to bare studs. Just beyond the suite was a boarded-up window that, he knew, overlooked yet another alley.

He entered the first of the rooms, a long, empty foyer where the air was stale and dusty and the floor gritty with builder's sand.

He'd scarcely cleared the doorway when someone pounced upon him, sending him sprawling. He felt a ring of cold metal clamp down on his right wrist, and he heard Tally say, "I've thought it over and I'm dissolving the partnership, Raul."

"Pity," he muttered, rolling over and reaching out for her, and finding that she had fastened the other half of the handcuffs to her left wrist. He struggled to his feet, pulling her with him.

"Are you all right?" she asked worriedly.

"No, *migra*," he replied, "I'm not. I feel terrible."

He raised his left hand and touched her cheek. "In fact, I hate myself for having to do this."

The hand that was upon her cheek drew back, became a fist, and the fist slammed into her jaw.

Tally gave a little cry, then slumped.

Slinging her over one shoulder in a fireman's carry, Raul headed for the boarded-up window and freedom....

"INCREDIBLE!" ABRAHAMSON BELLOWED as he prowled the courtyard, the beam of his flashlight stabbing into every nook and cranny. "We had him completely boxed in, and you people let him get away! I want to know how he did it!"

One of the FBI agents stepped forward. "He had help. We know that much. Just before we took up our positions, we saw someone—a woman, I think—standing in the doorway of that shop next door. She must have managed to get into the courtyard just ahead of Devlin, because she's nowhere around now."

Abrahamson glared at him. "Whoever fired those shots can't hit the broad side of a barn!"

"We weren't trying to hit Devlin, sir, just let him know we mean business."

Abrahamson turned on his heel and headed for the foyer where other agents were prowling about, looking for clues.

"Look here," someone said, shining his flashlight at the sand on the floor. "He must have stumbled over something because he went down hard. And over here—" the flashlight beam shifted a few feet to one side "—this is where the woman was waiting for him. You can see the smaller footprints. It looks as if she bent down to help him up after he stumbled."

Abrahamson studied the floor. "I don't know," he said. "It looks like more like they engaged in a wrestling match. What's that over there?"

One of the agents bent down and picked up a thin canister that was lying on the floor. He examined it. "It's one of those CN gas devices—you know, chemical mace, like the various police agencies use."

"I see," Abrahamson said, nodding knowingly. He was beginning to see a great deal. And he wasn't at all surprised. "Any indication it's been used?"

"No, sir."

The agent who'd been talking to Abrahamson in the courtyard came inside. "You want to put out an APB on them?"

Abrahamson threw up his hands in exasperation. "I do not!" he snapped. "We've got too many people involved in this already!"

TALLY GROANED AND SAT UP, blinking as she peered into the cold, hollow darkness that was all around her. Her jaw ached and her left wrist was sore where the steel of the handcuffs pressed into the flesh. She couldn't see Raul, but she knew he was there, still chained to her. She could hear him breathing.

"You hit me," she murmured, moving her lips as little as possible.

"You left me no alternative, *migra*," he said softly. "If we'd waited to discuss things like intelligent human beings, your friends would have been all over us. Given their superior firepower, I suspect they meant business."

"I didn't—" Why try to deny it? She'd arranged the trap. She hadn't known the details, but she was the one who'd made it happen. He had a right to be annoyed.

Jerking up their linked forearms, Tally massaged her manacled wrist with the fingertips of her right hand. "You're my prisoner. You know that, don't you?"

He laughed. "That's a moot point, *migra*. Neither of us is going anywhere until you unlock these bracelets."

"Not a chance. And I'll ask you again to quit calling me *migra*, Raul Devlin." She removed her right hand from her left wrist and felt around. They were sitting on a thin rubber mat that covered a metal floor of some sort. A very cold metal floor. "Where are we?"

"In the back of a delivery van that, fortunately, has no windows."

"Another of your getaway cars?"

"I'm afraid not. The van's parked in a lot a few blocks from where we ran into one another, and it was a case of any port in a storm."

"I see." She patted softly at the floor by her side and found her purse. Slowly, carefully, she moved her right hand to reach into the purse.

"If you're looking for your revolver, save yourself the effort," Raul said. "I removed it when I went through your purse looking for the key to the handcuffs. What did you do with the key, anyway?"

"Forget it!"

"I could take it from you."

"You could if you knew where to look."

Again he laughed. "That invites a very thorough search."

She edged away from him, as far as the handcuff chain would allow. "Don't try it," she warned him, patting about with her free hand in search of something to use as a weapon.

"I wouldn't dream of it. I might punch you in the jaw in a moment of extreme urgency, but undress you against your will? Never. That would be loutish and uncouth."

Her fears began to subside, and she smiled in spite of herself. "And you're nothing if not couth—a real officer and a gentleman."

"My military career may be over, but old habits die hard, you know."

"I'll bet." Quietly, she unsnapped the closure on her purse and felt around inside for her canister of chemical mace. If she could disable him for a few seconds, maybe she'd have time to unlock the cuff from her left wrist and use it to truss him up the way he'd done her in El Paso.

But the canister wasn't there. She must have dropped it in the scuffle.

She sighed. "So what do we do now?"

"We?" He sounded amused.

"We seem to have become inseparable, for the moment at least."

"That depends, Tally."

"Depends on what?"

"On whether you intend to keep your part of the bargain and give me a few days to do what I have to do."

"You don't stand a chance, Raul. By now, Abrahamson has probably put out an all-points bulletin on you."

"I doubt it. If Abrahamson is in the Protectors' pocket, he has to be discreet. How could he ever explain ordering a full-scale manhunt for someone who'd done nothing more than sneak across the border? I'm guilty of a few misdemeanors, if that."

Tally turned her head to look at him. Her eyes were gradually becoming accustomed to the darkness inside the van, but she still couldn't see his face. His head and shoulders were a form without shape, blending into the blackness. "Murder is hardly a misdemeanor," she said.

"Murder? What do you mean, murder?"

"Olivera's dead, and so is the cabdriver who was taking him to the airport. Somebody cut their throats."

She felt him stiffen. "This had to have happened while we were together earlier. You don't think I had anything to with it, do you?"

"If I did, I wouldn't have come tonight. I'd have sent Abrahamson's people in and let them do whatever they liked. I came on my own because I wanted to see that you got a fair chance." She paused. "Where'd you go after you left me?"

"I told you. I had some business to take care of."

"What sort of business?"

"I had to arrange to get another car. Also, Olivera had given me the name of another man he thought might have a lead to Dr. Fuentes's whereabouts."

"What's this other man's name?"

"Cordova. He lives in—" He stopped short. "Since the partnership has been dissolved, you wouldn't be interested."

"Why should I? You've done nothing but lie to me from the moment we met."

Shifting his weight and leaning forward across her outstretched legs, he pushed aside the dark curtain that separated the cargo compartment from the driver's seat. He peeked out. Tally blinked as the glow of a nearby streetlight spilled into the cargo area.

"We've lied to each other," he corrected her, drawing shut the curtain and settling back against the van's side wall. "Now it's time to stop lying and start leveling. Why did you tell Abrahamson about our meeting?"

"I didn't—not directly. I went through a third party, someone I trust. This third party set it up so that there'd be other people to keep an eye on Abrahamson after he tagged you."

Raul thought it over. "You know, *migra*, I've had my doubts about you, too. Wherever I find you, I find trouble. Tonight, for example, someone obviously followed you to the professor's."

Ignoring his continued use of *migra*, Tally shook her head vigorously. "I told you before—no way. I used all sorts of evasive tactics."

"There's another possibility."

"Abrahamson?"

He nodded. "He could have planted some sort of tracking device in your car. He had every opportunity to do so.

The Protectors would have known your every move, and when they killed Olivera your Mr. Abrahamson would be miles away, with the perfect alibi."

Tally thought about it. It made sense. Blaine was right: she *was* in over her head. "I'll ask you again, Raul. What do we do now?"

He held up their linked wrists. "Unlock the handcuffs and let me go."

Simple question, simple solution. All she had to do was release him and walk away. She could drive back to the motel, and when Abrahamson returned she could tell him that she'd tried to help set up Raul Devlin but that again he'd been too crafty. After all, she had Blaine as a witness to the fact she'd wanted to do what was right.

She couldn't do it. She just couldn't let Abrahamson execute a man who was only trying to do his duty.

"It looks like you're stuck with me," she said. "I seem to have lost the key."

"Then we'll have to find a hacksaw, won't we?"

"Those handcuffs are government property. You mess around with them, you're in real trouble."

Raul reached around with his left hand and gingerly touched her jaw with his fingertips. "I'm sorry I had to knock you out," he said softly.

"You pack a mean right."

"It was a left," he said. Leaning over, he kissed her lightly on the lips, then pressed his cheek to hers. "Time to be on our way, Tally. We have a lot of ground to cover."

"Where are we going?" She didn't want to leave the van—not just yet. She had an idea, and she needed time to carry it out.

"Denver. Come on." He eased forward and again reached out for the curtain that screened the front seats.

Her left hand closed over his right while her right hand fished silently through the purse on the floor beside her, searching for pen and paper. She found her notepad, but not her pen. Her fingertips touched the cold metal of her lipstick, and she decided it would have to do. "Wait," she said. "I'm still woozy."

"Take a few breaths. That should perk you up."

"All right." She hoped he couldn't see that she was using her right hand to scrawl a message in lipstick on the notepad.

"Any better?"

"A little. Just give me a minute more." She kept writing, hoping that whoever found the note would be able to read it. "Do you have contacts in Denver—people like Professor Olivera, I mean?" The more information she could pack into the message, the better.

"Not really. We'll be pretty much on our own."

"It won't be easy. They've got a description of the car you took from the lot in Socorro."

"That thought has occurred to me."

"You've lined up another car?" The tip of the lipstick poised over the notepad.

"We're wasting time." He moved forward on his hands and knees, dragging her left wrist with him, and almost touching the unseen notepad.

"All right," Tally said, scraping her heels along the matting on the floor to cover the sound as she ripped off the piece of notepaper she'd been writing on. She wadded up the paper, then dropped the lipstick and notepad back into her purse. "I'm ready."

Raul pushed aside the curtain and slid into the driver's seat, pulling her with him. Looking around carefully for any sign of movement outside, he opened the door of the van and stepped down. "My car is close by."

Tally glanced about to get her bearings. The Sheraton Hotel was a block away, and Old Town just ahead. "We could take mine," she suggested. "It's parked just down the street, and it has a police radio."

"Too easy to spot," Raul said. "Besides, it might be bugged. We'll take mine."

Tally drew back. She had to swing by her car to leave the note she'd scribbled. It wouldn't do any good to drop the note in the van. Even if the driver came back and found it, it wouldn't mean anything to him. "At least let me stop and get my gear out of the trunk."

"You won't need it."

"My uniform is in the trunk. If I lose it, they'll take it out of my pay."

"Buy another. I'll give you the money. Come on."

Tally stood her ground. "But I may have another set of keys packed away. I mean, we can't walk around like this forever!"

Raul shrugged. "More's the pity. All right, we'll stop and pick up your things..."

NATE ABRAHAMSON STARED at the smudged, hot-pink scrawl on the crumpled paper. One of the FBI agents had found it in the spare-tire well in the trunk of Tally's abandoned Border Patrol car. The note consisted of one word: Denver.

Denver.

Abrahamson smoothed out the note and folded it carefully. He slipped it into a pocket of his jacket. "I want them—both of them," he said gruffly. "Set up surveillance on all roads leading out of the city."

"They've got at least a two-hour head start," the FBI agent pointed out. "And we don't have any idea what kind of car Devlin's driving. I think we'd be better off with some plain, old-fashioned roadblocks."

"I don't want to stop them," Abrahamson growled, "but I do want to know where they are every step of the way." He looked around, shaking his head. At least half a dozen other FBI agents had converged on the scene, along with the Border Patrol officers who'd shown up unexpectedly to assist in the stakeout. Nincompoops! It had taken them ninety minutes to turn up Tally Gordon's car, another fifteen minutes to discover the wadded-up note in the trunk. Even that cowboy Blaine Murchison had a better handle on things than the vaunted FBI. He'd call Murchison, tell him to scoot on up here to Albuquerque. If nothing else, Murchison knew the Gordon woman and might be able to anticipate her actions. It was worth a try.

The FBI agent Abrahamson had been speaking to hadn't given up. "The woman is his prisoner," he said. "Who knows what Devlin will do to her?"

Abrahamson eyed him coldly. "The woman is also a trained law-enforcement officer. She should have realized what she was getting into when she pinned on that badge."

He turned on his heel and stomped off, back to the car where Simon Ybarra and Hans Uhlmann were waiting, puffing on cigars.

"What did you find out?" Ybarra inquired.

Abrahamson told them that Tally had apparently been taken prisoner, and that she and Devlin were probably on their way north to Denver.

"My," Ybarra observed, fanning away a thick, blue cloud of smoke, "she's a troublesome little witch. I'm afraid we shall have to deal with her forcefully when next we meet."

"You keep your hands off the woman," Abrahamson growled. "I couldn't stop you from getting to Olivera and that cabdriver, but if you try taking out a law officer you're going to have every cop in the country climbing your frames. I mean it. I won't lift another finger to help you."

Ybarra smiled cruelly. "Spare me your pious preachings, Abrahamson. You shall do exactly what I say. I have detailed records of all our transactions, and they are more than enough to send you to prison for the rest of your life. *¿Entiende?*"

Abrahamson glanced over his shoulder to assure himself no one else was standing near. "My deal was to help you find Devlin, and through him, Fuentes. Murder wasn't part of it. Leave the woman alone."

"I assure you, I shall not touch the woman," Ybarra said solemnly. He turned to Uhlmann. "I shall let my friend here handle it."

"Gladly," said the Butcher of Buenos Aires. "She is as good as dead...."

THE JOKER GOES WILD!

Play
this
card
right!

See
inside!

HARLEQUIN
WANTS TO <u>GIVE</u> YOU
- 4 free books
- A free digital clock/calendar
- A free mystery gift

IT'S A WILD, WILD, WONDERFUL
FREE OFFER!

HERE'S WHAT YOU GET:

1. *Four New Harlequin Intrigue® Novels—FREE!* Everything comes up hearts and diamonds with four exciting romances—yours FREE from Harlequin Reader Service. Each of these brand-new novels brings you the passion and tenderness of today's greatest love stories.

2. *A Useful, Practical Digital Clock/Calendar—FREE!* As a free gift simply to thank you for accepting four free books we'll send you a stylish digital quartz clock/calendar—a handsome addition to any decor! The changeable, month-at-a-glance calendar pops out, and may be replaced with a favorite photograph.

3. *An Exciting Mystery Bonus—FREE!* You'll go wild over this surprise gift. It will win you compliments and score as a splendid addition to your home.

4. *Money-Saving Home Delivery!* Join Harlequin Reader Service and enjoy the convenience of previewing four new books every other month, delivered to your home. Each book is yours for $1.99—26 cents less per book than what you pay in stores. And there is no extra charge for postage and handling. Great savings and total convenience are the name of the game at Harlequin!

5. *Free Newsletter!* It makes you feel like a partner to the world's most popular authors…tells about their upcoming books…even gives you their recipes!

6. *More Mystery Gifts Throughout the Year!* No joke! Because home subscribers are our most valued readers, we'll be sending you additional free gifts from time to time—as a token of our appreciation!

GO WILD
WITH HARLEQUIN TODAY—
JUST COMPLETE, DETACH AND
MAIL YOUR FREE-OFFER CARD!

GET YOUR GIFTS FROM HARLEQUIN
ABSOLUTELY FREE!

Mail this card today!

Printed in the U.S.A.

PLACE
JOKER
STICKER
HERE

PLAY THIS CARD RIGHT!

YES! Please send me my four Harlequin Intrigue novels FREE along with my free Digital Clock/Calendar and free mystery gift as explained on the opposite page.

180 CIH RDAY

NAME _____
(PLEASE PRINT)

ADDRESS _____ APT. _____

CITY _____

STATE _____ ZIP CODE _____

Prices subject to change. Offer limited to one per household and not valid to current Intrigue subscribers.

HARLEQUIN READER SERVICE® "NO RISK" GUARANTEE

- There's no obligation to buy — and the free books remain yours to keep.
- You pay the lowest price possible and receive books before they appear in stores.
- You may end your subscription anytime — just write and let us know.

IT'S NO JOKE!

MAIL THE POSTPAID CARD AND
GET FREE GIFTS AND $9.00 WORTH OF
HARLEQUIN NOVELS — *FREE!*

BUSINESS REPLY MAIL

FIRST CLASS   PERMIT NO. 717   BUFFALO, NY

POSTAGE WILL BE PAID BY ADDRESSEE

HARLEQUIN
READER SERVICE

901 Fuhrmann Blvd.
P.O. Box 1867
Buffalo, NY 14240-9952

NO POSTAGE
NECESSARY
IF MAILED
IN THE
UNITED STATES

Chapter Eight

They'd traveled all night on winding back roads that took them through a succession of sleeping villages Tally never had heard of. Now and then she could pick out signs pointing the way to the major highway, and she hoped that Raul would turn and follow the signs. Surely by now Abrahamson would have had time to order roadblocks set up—if he'd found the note she'd left.

She peeked at the fuel gauge. It indicated they had just over a quarter tank of gas left. Maybe if they stopped somewhere, she could...

Raul geared down for a steep hill. The handcuff chain tugged at Tally's left wrist as he moved his right hand to work the stick shift.

"This is uncomfortable," she complained, jerking back her wrist and massaging it with her free hand.

He laughed. "It was your idea, not mine, *migra*. As far as I'm concerned, you can unlock the bracelets at any time."

"The handcuffs stay."

"Suit yourself."

She settled back in her seat and closed her eyes. What a night it had been! Not only had a key witness been murdered, but she'd been punched out and abducted by the man she was trying to help. On top of everything else, she'd been a party to car theft.

"You know, of course, they'll be looking for this car," she said, determined to keep Raul off guard.

"I don't really think so."

"It's a stolen car."

"What gave you that idea?"

Tally opened her eyes and glanced across at him. In the dull glow of the dashboard lights, she could see he was amused. She didn't have to inquire further. It was clear to her that the switch had been prearranged. After leaving Old Town, they'd driven to the airport and waited until a man drove up in a Dodge and parked nearby. The driver had scurried into the terminal, carrying a suitcase. Raul had gotten out of his car, pulling her with him, and got behind the wheel of the Dodge. The keys were under the floor mat.

"You have quite a network of little helpers, don't you?" she'd remarked as she transferred her carryall to the new car and made a show of searching for handcuff keys, which she knew weren't in the bag.

He'd shrugged. "The Movement has a great many friends in this country, if that's what you mean."

She remembered Olivera telling her that not everyone trusted Raul, that some of Federico Fuentes's followers were unsure as to just where his loyalties lay. "How do you know you can count on these people? How do you know they won't turn you in?"

"I just have to take my chances. Now try to get some sleep."

They drove for another hour, in a silence so complete that Tally found herself dozing off. Finally the blackness of the night began to give way to the soft light of dawn. It was getting colder by the minute, and the skies were spitting snow.

Tally looked again at the fuel gauge. The needle was almost down into the red zone.

"You're going to need gas pretty soon," she said.

"There's a town a few miles up ahead—Chama. Should be something open there."

She squirmed, seeking a more comfortable position. "I hope so. I want to rinse out my mouth. I'm still tasting blood from where you slugged me."

Raul held up their chained wrists. "If you're going off in search of the ladies' room, this may present a bit of a problem."

Yes, she had to agree it might indeed. "If I unlock the cuffs, will you give me your word you won't try to escape?"

"Scout's honor," he said solemnly, raising his right hand, and her left, and holding up three fingers.

Tally folded her arms across her chest, jerking his right wrist with her. "You're no Boy Scout, Raul Devlin."

He laughed. "How about my word as an officer and a gentleman?"

She glanced at him out of the corners of her eyes. "You're not an officer anymore, either."

"Ah, but I am a gentleman. Unlock the handcuffs and I'll prove it."

"You're out of your mind! You'll take off the minute I get out of the car!"

The lights of a Texaco station came into view, and he started to slow down. "Try me," he said.

"No."

He shrugged. "All right. We'll just sit here and have somebody fill the tank and we'll be on our way. We won't have to stop again for hours—long, cold hours."

Tally knew she couldn't let the opportunity pass. She had to get another message to the people who by now were scouring the countryside for them, and she couldn't do it if she was sitting here in the car. "If you double-cross me, Devlin, so help me, I'll..."

He pulled up in front of the station's only pump, then leaned over and gave her a quick kiss on the cheek. "Unlock the handcuffs, Tally."

"Turn your head."

"Anything to oblige."

She reached inside the shaft of her right boot and brought up the key she'd pinned to the lining. She unlocked her half of the handcuffs, and just as quickly refastened that half to the steering wheel. "Don't go away," she said, snatching the key from the ignition. "I'll be right back."

He just smiled.

Tally made a beeline for the rest room at the rear of the station.

Now all she had to do was get on the phone, and . . .

The phone wasn't in the rest room. It was in the office, in clear view of the gas pump. Should she chance it? Raul was securely cuffed to the steering wheel, and she had the ignition key. It would take only a minute to call for help, and Raul couldn't lift a finger to stop her. All he could do was sit there, watching helplessly, as she sealed his fate . . .

. . . and then what?

She hesitated, then made her decision.

Oh, rats! I'll just play this one out!

When she came back out of the rest room, he was sitting in the car, studying a road map. "Your turn," she said, getting into the car and leaning over to unlock the cuff she'd left fastened to the steering wheel.

And then she realized that the engine was running.

"How'd you do that?" she demanded.

"The same way I did this." He held up his right hand, and she saw the handcuff dangling from his wrist. Somehow he'd managed to free himself from the steering wheel.

She shook her head. "My, aren't we tricky!"

"I prefer devious," he said.

"You were testing me, weren't you?"

"Yes."

"I assume I passed?"

He nodded. "With flying colors. Here's your graduation present." He reached into his jacket pocket for her gun and handed it over.

Tally hefted the revolver appraisingly. Then, making sure the safety was set, she dropped it into her purse, along with the keys she was holding. "Your turn. The men's room is right around the corner."

"I know."

She stared at him. "You know?"

"Of course. I paid it a visit when I went to see if there was a phone back that way. There wasn't, of course. The only phone is in the office."

She pouted. "How'd you know I wouldn't scrawl a message on the mirror in lipstick? I've seen that done before—in the movies."

Raul reached into his coat pocket and brought out her lipstick, pen and notepad. "This is how I knew," he said. "I removed them from your purse while you were sleeping."

Tally found herself smiling. "That's what I like about you, Raul. You're such a trusting sort."

HIS GARMENT BAG slung over his shoulder, Blaine Murchison stepped up to a pay phone in the airport terminal and made his call. Despite the chill in the air, his husky frame was slick with sweat. Blaine wasn't a coward, not by any means, but there was one thing in life he dreaded—flying. Flying had terrified him ever since that night he'd been scheduled to ride as observer in the chopper that carried Zach Gordon, Tally's father, to his death. Blaine had tickets to a rodeo that night, and Zach had volunteered to fill in for him. The memory still gave him nightmares.

Blaine glanced back at the commuter plane that had brought him up from El Paso. It just sat there on the tarmac, sleek and silvery, oblivious to Blaine's nervous glare.

You're not getting another chance at this ol' boy, Blaine said silently to the plane. *I'm taking the bus home when all this is over.*

But would it ever be over?

His number answered, and for the next few minutes he talked and listened, mostly listened, nodding now and then in agreement.

Right, he was beginning to have doubts about Abraham-son himself.

Right, something would have to be done.

Right, he'd handle it.

But what about Tally Gordon? he asked. Whatever he did, however he handled Abrahamson, Tally's life was in danger.

Have no fear, the voice on the other end of the line said. Raul Devlin needs her. Devlin is not likely to do away with the one person he thinks can help him.

"What do you mean 'not likely'?" Blaine demanded. "You've got to do better than that!"

"We'll make every effort to guarantee her safety," the voice said calmly. "If Agent Gordon gets hurt, it will be Abrahamson's fault, not ours."

"In that case, I'll take him out right now!"

"You will do nothing of the sort, inspector. You will sit back and wait until he finds Devlin. Only then will you be permitted to deal with the traitor. Is that clear?"

"But—"

"Is that clear, inspector?"

"Right," said Blaine. It was just as clear as could be.

Damn, why had he taken on this job, anyway?

RAUL HAD NOTICED the two-tone blue Chevrolet station wagon on their tail ever since he and Tally had crossed the Colorado state line north of Chama. Several times he'd slowed to give it a chance to overtake him. It hadn't. It had hung back, most of the time out of sight, but on long, open stretches he caught frequent glimpses of the heavy-duty Chevrolet, relentless in its pursuit, but its driver seemingly unwilling to close the gap.

He didn't mention it to Tally because he didn't want to worry her. She had enough on her mind.

But then so did he. Not only did he have a mission to ac-complish, but now he had other factors to consider.

Other factors? *What a graceless, unpoetic way to describe it!* he thought, glancing at her. *I think I'm actually falling in love with this woman.*

He'd known it ever since Alamosa...

He hadn't needed gas, when they'd reached Alamosa, but he'd pulled into a Texaco station anyway, ostensibly to study his road map. A sheriff's car was stopped at a pump in the next aisle.

Tally, who'd dozed off after leaving Chama, woke up when he came to a stop. She looked around bleary-eyed, and ran her fingers through her sleep-mussed hair. "Where are we?"

"Alamosa. Time for another pit stop."

"Oh." She'd buttoned her coat and grabbed her purse. "I'm going to run over to that restaurant next door and get us some coffee. Do you want me to pick up something to eat?"

Raul had shaken his head. "Just coffee. I'm afraid food might make me sleepy."

She opened her door and got out of the car, then leaned back inside. "You *will* be here when I get back, won't you?"

"You have my word on it."

"For whatever it's worth," she'd said, smiling. What a pretty smile, he'd thought. She straightened up and walked away from the car, with a toss of her head to free her long, tawny hair from the collar of her trench coat.

Raul had watched her disappear into the restaurant. He'd thought, *I don't know what it is about you,* migra, *but you bring out dangerous thoughts and you generate desperate dreams. You are the woman I've never known, the woman I'll probably never get to know. You are fire and ice, steel and satin, a woman determined to prove herself and yet troubled by her own uncertainties. I don't understand you at all, and perhaps that's what makes you fascinating.*

An attendant had come out to the car, and Raul had him check the oil, water and battery, then tipped him a dollar.

"You can't be too careful," he'd told the attendant. "I'd hate to have a breakdown out in the middle of nowhere."

"Where you bound?" the attendant inquired affably, pocketing the money.

"West," Raul lied. "Toward Silverton and then on into Durango. My wife and I are on holiday."

"You shouldn't have any problem then. I heard on the radio that the worst of the storm is passing to the east."

Raul had glanced at the restaurant, thinking how easy it would be to take off and leave Tally there. It might have even been the kindest thing he could do for her. There was sure to be trouble ahead, possibly even gunplay, and he didn't want her mixed up in it.

But he hadn't left her behind. He'd waited, and when she'd come out of the restaurant, carrying two steaming plastic cups of coffee, he was glad he'd waited.

FIFTY MILES beyond the starboard wing tip of the Air Force executive jet, the Spanish Peaks towered in haughty grandeur against the icy blue of the midmorning sky. The twin-engine plane was cruising at an altitude only a few hundred feet greater than the twin summits, and the snow that swirled around the rocks and ridges of the peaks conjured up an ethereality bordering on the supernatural.

But of the four passengers in the cabin, only the normally dour, sharp-tongued Nate Abrahamson was impressed. His companions clearly had other things on their minds.

"Spectacular," Abrahamson said, cupping his hands to his eyes as he looked out, grunting his approval. "Really spectacular."

Blaine Murchison glanced across at him. Blaine had been sitting there with his eyes half-closed, his cowboy hat pushed low over his brow, worrying about flying and doing some serious thinking about Tally. The interruption was an unwelcome one. He said nothing.

Ybarra and Uhlmann were seated in the pair of seats just behind Blaine, their heads close together, talking. Blaine couldn't hear what they were saying over the high-pitched hum of the jets, but he suspected it had to do with Devlin.

"You like the mountains, Murchison?" Abrahamson asked.

Blaine shrugged.

"I've lived in Virginia the past five years," Abrahamson said, "and we have mountains there. Nothing like this, though. Hills, really—rolling hills with trees and valleys, quite picturesque, but they can't compete with the brutal rawness of the Rockies." He settled back into his seat. "Climbers speak of conquering this mountain or that, but they never really do. Whether they reach the top or not, the mountain conquers them, becomes part of them, part of their souls. The climbers may think they've won, but they haven't. The mountains will be there long after the men and women who conquered them are dead and buried."

You and Devlin—you're both poets as well as double-crossing bastards, Blaine reflected. *No wonder the world's going to hell in a handcart.*

"You ski, Murchison?"

"Don't have time for it. Me, I get a few hours off, I like to saddle up and go out riding."

"I used to ski when I was younger. My hometown in Massachusetts is just a few hours from Stowe, Vermont. We'd drive up to the Green Mountains on weekends, six or seven of us crammed into a little Volkswagen, sharing expenses, living for those few minutes of thrills and exhilaration that come when you push off with your poles and maneuver your way down a difficult run, the wind in your face, knowing that the slightest mistake can cost you a broken leg or worse."

Big deal, thought Blaine. *I'm risking more than that in this little pile of tin. One of our agents is down there somewhere, held prisoner by a wild-eyed revolutionary, and all you can do is yammer on about skiing. You want to talk*

*about how we're going to nail Devlin, fine. But if you just
want to make idle conversation, I couldn't care less.*

"You don't like me, do you, Murchison?"

Blaine pushed up the brim of his hat and stared at the
man from Washington, still trying to size him up. Abrahamson was thin and sharp featured, almost frail looking,
but Blaine knew he was tough as nails. "You've got a job to
do. I know how it is. It's just that I'm worried about Tally."

Abrahamson frowned. "She's just going to have to look
out for herself. If she'd done as she was told and stayed there
at the motel, she wouldn't have been taken hostage."

"She's a good cop," Blaine said grudgingly. "I don't
really take to the idea of women doing men's work, but
Tally's a lot like her daddy—determined as anything."

"The two of you used to have something going, I understand."

Blaine nodded.

"That's one reason I wanted you along on this," Abrahamson went on. "You know how she thinks, how she's apt
to react in a given situation."

"I suppose so."

Abrahamson leaned forward in his seat, studying Blaine.
"You think she'll turn him in if she gets the chance?"

"She'll do what she thinks is right. That's the way she is."
He gave a little flick of his head to indicate Ybarra and
Uhlmann. "I know she's uptight about those two gents. She
figures they're bad news. She told me so."

A thin smile played at the corners of Abrahamson's
mouth. "What about you? Haven't you yourself wondered
where they fit in?"

Blaine shrugged. "They're with you. That's all I need to
know."

Abrahamson lowered his voice. "It seems to me that your
heart really isn't in this pursuit. Since you have no reason to
take Devlin's side—every reason not to, in fact, considering that he's abducted Tally Gordon—I can only assume
you're motivated by your resentment of me."

Why should I resent you? Blaine thought bitterly. *All you did was breeze into El Paso and take over my operation, cutting your own deal with Guerrero, making me look foolish.* He said nothing.

"How old are you, Murchison?"

"Thirty-five. Why?"

Abrahamson frowned. "I've been working for the government since before you were in grade school. I've done a lot of things for my superiors, and I don't mind saying I've done them well. I haven't always been happy with the methods I've had to use nor the objectives I've been directed to seek. But that's neither here nor there. Whenever I've been ordered to—"

"You happy with your present objective?"

"I can't discuss certain aspects of the Devlin case. You know that."

"I know," Blaine said. "National security, right?"

Abrahamson's eyes narrowed behind his thick-rimmed glasses. "Inspector, you've picked up bits and pieces of the story. I'll let you believe what you want to believe." He removed his glasses and began polishing them with the wide end of his maroon-and-blue striped tie. "You like jigsaw puzzles?"

Blaine stared at him.

"Jigsaw puzzles are made up of a lot of little pieces, and until the last piece falls into place the picture is incomplete. I'd advise you to keep that in mind."

More double-talk, Blaine thought. "When you buy a jigsaw puzzle, there's always a picture on the box showing you what you'll eventually come up with if—"

"If you're patient," Abrahamson cut in. "But some people lose patience and give up. Some get sloppy and lose pieces, and when they do they never see the big picture."

"You're telling me to be patient?"

"I am."

"It's not easy for a man to be patient when he knows damn well somebody he likes is being used."

Abrahamson snorted. "We're all being used, one way or another. You, me, Devlin, them—" he glanced past Blaine, in the direction of Ybarra and Uhlmann "—everybody. It's a simple fact of life." He stared at his glasses, decided they weren't yet clean enough and started polishing them again. "Personally I don't much care for some of the people I'm forced to work with. Nor do I care for their methods. But then—" he made a feeble attempt at a smile "—you may remember that famous quote attributed to Leo Durocher of the Dodgers—'Nice guys finish last.'" The man from Washington unbuckled his seat belt and stood up. "Keep that in mind." He turned and made his way forward to the cockpit.

Blaine watched as Abrahamson leaned through the open door and spoke to the pilot, an Air Force colonel who'd been pressed into service after a hurried call to Washington. The pilot nodded, adjusted a dial on the instrument panel and handed a microphone and headset to Abrahamson.

Blaine sensed a stirring in the seats behind him, and he knew that Ybarra and Uhlmann also were wondering what Abrahamson was up to.

A few minutes later, Abrahamson came back to his seat and buckled up. "A change in plans," he announced. "We're going to set down at Alamosa. A Colorado state patrolman thinks he spotted them in a Dodge."

"Did he try to stop the car?"

Abrahamson shook his head. "The patrolman was ordered to call in the location and then back off. We can't afford to bring in state or local law enforcement on this."

"What about them?" Blaine cocked his thumb toward Ybarra and Uhlmann, who were staring at them questioningly.

"I'm going to send them on to Denver on this plane. They won't like it, but they'll have to live with it. Our people in Denver are trying to track down Fuentes, and I'll tell them that Ybarra and Uhlmann might be of some use in that phase of the operation.''

"Then why don't we go on to Denver, too?" He didn't really want to. He was more than happy to be getting off this plane.

"Because I still think that Devlin is the key to finding Fuentes.''

"I DON'T KNOW about this," Tally muttered as she fought to regain control of the Dodge after it fishtailed dangerously on a patch of snow-dusted ice on a curve west of Fort Garland. She wasn't used to winter driving, and her stomach muscles were knotted with tension.

Raul, on the other hand, seemed very much at ease as he sat in the passenger seat, watching the miles go by, and it occurred to Tally that he actually enjoyed the chase. "Look at it this way," he said. "If our friends are following us, they have to drive through the same storm. It's no easier on them than it is on us.''

"That's a comforting thought," Tally said. Her knuckles were white as she tightened her grip on the steering wheel and gently pumped the brakes. "I don't know why I'm doing this anyway. It's one thing to let you talk me into not turning you in, but it's something else to actually drive the getaway car.''

He grinned. "You make it sound like we're Bonnie and Clyde.''

"That's what it feels like." She stole a quick glance at him and noticed that he'd slipped off the handcuff that had been fastened to his right wrist. "You mind telling me how you unlocked the cuffs?''

"Why?''

"Professional curiosity.''

He shook his head. "It's a trade secret.''

"I thought we didn't have any more secrets. I thought we trusted each other.''

"Oh, we do. We most certainly do. I gave you back your gun, didn't I?"

"You probably took all the bullets out of it."

"No, it's loaded with five rounds. Check. You'll see."

Tally shook her head. "You certainly like to live dangerously, don't you?"

He laughed. "Is there any other way?"

THE COLORADO STATE TROOPER was waiting for Nate Abrahamson and Blaine Murchison. He was parked on the side of the U.S. 160 at the intersection of Colorado 159, which leads south to the Costilla County seat of San Luis before cutting across into New Mexico. They pulled up in front of him, and he waved them back to his car.

"They've got maybe an hour's head start on you," the trooper said. "They stopped for gas back down the line a ways, and the woman went next door and got coffee and sandwiches. I cruised by and made sure it was the same car I saw earlier."

"Did you radio ahead to have your people watch for them on the other side of La Veta Pass?" Abrahamson asked.

"Yes, sir. I told them not to get too close, though—just keep an eye on the car from a distance." He paused to listen to his radio. "It's going to be touch and go, I'll tell you that. The way this storm's kicking up, there are all sorts of accidents for us to cover and we can't be everywhere at once."

"Just do what you can. That's all we ask."

"Sure. But all of us in the state patrol would feel a lot better if we knew what this was all about. What're these people supposed to have done?"

"Sorry," Abrahamson said. "I can't tell you."

"It's classified," Blaine said gruffly, turning up his coat collar as protection against the cold wind. "You know—a matter of national security."

TALLY COULD BARELY MAKE OUT the sign jutting above the snowbank at the side of the road, next to the turnout where, on better days, one could pause and gaze at the scenery. La Veta Pass Summit, the sign read. Elevation 9,416 Feet. But today the view ended abruptly in a white, windy nothingness, which hooted and howled and whistled, as if to remind them that they were unwelcome visitors in a savage land. Any second, she knew, the rear wheels could lock on the ice and the Dodge could go hurtling off the highway and down the mountainside, rolling end over end and exploding in a ball of fire as it slammed into rocks buried just below the mantle of snow.

"Do you want to pull over and let me take it again?" Raul asked. His tone was cool and casual, but she knew he was worried, too.

"I'll manage," Tally replied, gritting her teeth. "It should be easier going when we get down off this pass. If we— Hang on!"

A hundred feet ahead, an orange-and-black box-shaped thing was lumbering out onto the roadway, and Tally tapped on the brakes to slow the Dodge. The car skidded, then slid sideways straight downhill.

Tally wrestled with the wheel in a futile attempt to bring the car under control. "He's not even looking!"

The box shape was a battered, two-and-one-half ton truck, its sides painted with the logo of a rental agency. The truck's dual rear wheels were churning up a thick spray of snow as its driver gunned the engine to give the heavy vehicle enough power to pull away from the turnout where it had been parked.

The Dodge picked up speed as it slid downhill toward the truck, and Tally and Raul braced themselves for the inevitable collision.

Seeing them, the driver of the truck spun his steering wheel frantically, aiming at the inside lanes, and the truck joined the Dodge in a sickening downhill skid.

Then the Dodge sideswiped the truck, crumpling the car's right front fender and causing the driver of the truck to lose what little control he still had over his vehicle. The truck made two complete spins and careened toward the outside lanes, where the turnout ended in an abrupt drop.

Suddenly the truck jolted to a stop as its front wheels rode up and over a tightly compacted snowbank, leaving the vehicle teetering on its undercarriage, its front end jutting out over the chasm.

Its forward movement slowed by the collision, the Dodge skidded to the inside lane and came to a halt. Tally and Raul jumped out, just as the driver of the truck threw open his door and hopped down into the snow, losing his balance on the hard-crusted mound and sliding to a bruised and breathless halt, on his bottom, at Tally's feet.

Raul stepped forward to help the driver to his feet. "Are you hurt?"

The driver, a dark, heavyset man wearing a thick parka and jeans, glanced around, dazed, blinking. He seemed more than unduly worried about something.

"That snowbank was the only thing that saved you," Tally said, stepping forward to examine the truck teetering on the brink of the chasm. As she moved past the driver, she was sure she smelled liquor on his breath. "You were lucky."

The driver rubbed his neck, as if to indicate the seriousness of his injuries. "It was your fault," he grumbled. "You were driving too fast."

"You should have looked before you pulled out."

"My foot slipped on the pedal," the truck driver said. "Even so, you shouldn't have hit me."

"Is there anyone with you?" Raul asked.

"No, no one," the truck driver said quickly, glancing up at the aluminum walls of the cargo compartment.

"Okay," Raul said. "We'll go on down the mountain and send up a wrecker to help you back onto the highway."

"No...wait!" the truck driver called out, grabbing Raul's arm as Raul turned. "My insurance people, they'll want to talk to you."

"We're in a hurry."

The truck driver's eyes narrowed. "Who pays for the damage she caused? Just look. It'll cost me a thousand dollars or more to have my truck repaired."

Raul stepped back and examined the shallow scrape along the side of the truck. "It will cost you fifty dollars, if that." He reached for his billfold. "I am prepared to offer you a hundred."

"A hundred dollars! I am a poor man, a victim of circumstances. I cannot—"

Raul cut him short. "A hundred dollars. Take it or leave it."

The truck driver thought about it for all of three seconds, then held out his hand and grudgingly accepted the settlement.

As Raul counted out the bills, Tally cocked her head and listened. "What's that I hear?"

The truck driver stared at her in perfect innocence. "I don't know, lady. What's it sound like?"

"Screams. I hear people screaming."

"I got my radio on," he said quickly.

Raul checked his watch, then glanced at Tally. "We've got to get going." He started for the car.

Tally frowned. "I'll be right there," she said. She turned and walked around to the other side of the truck, picking her way carefully through snow that in places came almost to the top of her boots. She paused to inspect the padlock on the rear doors.

"What are you hauling?" she called out to the driver.

"Some stuff of my brother's. He's moving."

Tally's right hand dipped into her purse and brought out a small, black leather case. "Is there anyone in the back of the truck?"

The driver looked back over his shoulder, as if to assure himself that Raul had returned to the car. "Nah, just furniture. Mattresses, dressers, a stove and refrigerator—stuff like that."

Without taking her eyes off the driver, Tally stepped to the rear of the vehicle. "Would you mind undoing the padlock?"

"Hey, lady, you got no right to—"

Tally flipped open the case to display her badge and identification card. "Border Patrol. Now open that door."

The truck driver took a step toward her, thrusting his hands into his pockets. "I don't have the key," he said morosely.

"Who does have a key?"

The driver took another step. "My brother. Like I told you, it's his stuff, not mine."

Tally put away her ID case. She reached up and pounded on the side of the cargo compartment.

The voices Tally had heard grew stronger. The voices were speaking in Spanish.

"Unlock that door!" Tally insisted.

The driver took another step toward her. "Sure, lady. Anything you say." His hands came out of his pockets, and he was holding a vicious-looking blackjack.

Pivoting on the balls of her feet, Tally spun sideways and seized his right wrist, twisting it sharply and causing him to drop the weapon and squeal with pain. In the same fluid motion, she brought his extended arm, palm up, over her right shoulder, and thrust her hip into his midsection, sending him tumbling to land in a heap in the snow several feet away.

When he looked up, dazed, he saw her pointing a gun at him. Tally was holding the weapon with both hands, and the driver seemed to know she meant business.

"Unlock the door," Tally said calmly.

Raul, whose only glimpse of the action came when the driver tumbled forward from behind the truck, leaped out of the car and ran to Tally. "What's going on?"

"I believe we have a smuggler," Tally replied. She motioned to the driver with the barrel of her gun. "On your feet and up against the side of the truck. Move!"

Eyeing the gun, the driver did as he was told.

Tally kicked his feet wide apart and frisked him. She removed his keys and billfold, checked his driver's license, then stepped back. "Is this your name? Eddie Valdez?"

The driver just grunted.

"Mr. Valdez, you're under arrest. You have the right to remain silent. Whatever you say can and will be used against you in a court of law. You have the right to an attorney. Should you..."

Tally finished intoning the required warning, then glanced at Raul. There was a twinkle of accomplishment in her eyes. "If you're through playing with those handcuffs, how about putting them on him?"

Raul grinned. "But of course, *migra*. It's always a pleasure to see a professional at work."

Tally put away her gun and pulled herself up onto the tow bar at the rear of the truck. Using Valdez's keys, she unfastened the padlock and rolled up the door.

"Oh, my God!" she gasped. The cargo compartment was jam-packed with thinly clad men, one woman and a couple of children, pressed together for warmth, clutching bundles that held everything they owned.

As Tally tried to do a head count, they instinctively edged back, toward the deepest and darkest recesses of the cargo compartment. The shift in weight caused the truck to rock.

"*¡Esta bien!*" Tally shouted. "*¡Quiero ayudarles!*" It's all right! I want to help you!

She motioned to them to move toward her, but they only edged farther back, wide-eyed and afraid, causing the truck to seesaw even more, crunching against the frozen snowbank.

And then the front of the truck took a sickening dip.

Tally clawed at the metal floor of the truck, trying desperately to keep the vehicle from sliding over the side. "Raul!" she screamed. "Get up on the tailgate! We've got to counterbalance it somehow!"

As Raul vaulted nimbly up onto the bed of the truck, Valdez saw his chance. Still handcuffed, he darted for the Dodge parked nearby, its motor running.

"Valdez!" Tally yelled, looking back over her shoulder at the escaping smuggler.

"Hold it!" Raul yelled from his perch on the tailgate. A small, black pistol had appeared in his right hand. "One more step and you're dead!"

Valdez stopped.

"That's better. Now get over here and get up on this tailgate! Tell these people to bail out or they're going to go over the cliff."

Valdez reluctantly climbed onto the tailgate and spoke to the Mexicans in a burst of Spanish. One by one, the human cargo moved toward the rear, clutching their meager belongings. They looked worriedly at the newcomers, then at Valdez, and jumped down into the snow.

Tally counted twenty-seven in all. She glanced at Raul. "We'll take as many as we can carry down the hill, then send back a truck for the others. Some of them have white patches on their faces. That means frostbite. They need medical attention."

"Of course," Raul said.

When the last of the human cargo had jumped clear, Tally and Raul slid off the tailgate and onto the ground. Valdez started to follow them, but Raul raised his pistol and pointed it at him. "If it were up to me, I'd leave you on there and give the truck a push."

"No, please!" Valdez shouted.

"But it isn't up to me," Raul said, stepping back from the tailgate. "The lady is in charge." He glanced at Tally. "What do you want to do with him?"

"He's a prisoner," she said. "He has to go to jail."

"Let me off here!" Valdez screamed.

Before any of them could move the truck lurched and swayed, its metal undercarriage squeaking as it continued to press against the icy mound that supported it. The forward section reached the high point of its seesaw ride and started down again. Any second it would plummet to destruction.

Chapter Nine

The truck tumbled end over end in a shower of snow, gathering momentum as it bounced off the rocks. Then, as they watched, the recently filled gasoline tank ruptured, the truck burst into flames and exploded with a mighty roar.

Valdez, who'd jumped clear at the last second, sank to his haunches in the snow and held his head in his hands, moaning as he realized how close he'd come to dying.

Putting away her gun, Tally grabbed the smuggler by the collar of his parka and hauled him to his feet. "You're still under arrest," she reminded him crisply. "Into the car—the front seat—and no tricks." She nodded to Raul. "You drive, huh? We'll put the woman and her kids in the back and take them down the mountain."

Raul turned to the oldest of the men and in Spanish instructed him to get the woman and her two children into the back seat of the Dodge. He said he and Tally would arrange to send vehicles for the others.

"What will happen to us?" the man asked.

Raul glanced questioningly at Tally. *"Migra?"*

Tally avoided his eyes. This was the part of her job she hated, but someone had to do it. "You'll be sent back across the border," she replied in Spanish, directing her remarks to the man. "You have to have papers."

"But there is no work in my village," the man said, his eyes pleading.

"I'm sorry," Tally said softly. "It's the law."

"What about him?" Raul asked, gesturing at Valdez sitting in the front passenger seat of the Dodge.

Tally said, "He's going to jail, and I hope they throw away the key. Come on."

She climbed in back with the illegal aliens, keeping her eye on Valdez, while Raul drove. They headed down the highway to a truck stop at the foot of the pass. Tally sent a wrecker up to the summit to pick up the other aliens, and then arranged by phone for a bus to come in from nearby Walsenburg to collect all twenty-seven members of the group and turn them over to immigration authorities.

Twenty minutes later, after buying hot chocolate and candy bars for the people they'd hauled down from the pass, she, Raul and a sullen Valdez were on their way again. Tally had put Valdez in the back seat and herself up front, and now, loosening her seat belt, she twisted sideways so that she could see both Raul and Valdez, who was dismally contemplating his handcuffs and his future. "You didn't tell me you had that gun," Tally said to Raul, lowering her voice and hoping Valdez was too busy feeling sorry for himself to listen to what she was saying. She was annoyed with Raul, but also inexplicably amused.

Raul checked the rearview mirror to make sure the highway was clear on the uphill side, beyond the truck stop. Only then did he ease the car out onto the road, keeping a sharp eye out for icy patches, and smiling an innocent, blue-eyed smile. "Wasn't it Cervantes who wrote, 'Never look a gift Beretta in the mouth'?"

"It wasn't Cervantes, it was Shakespeare. And he was referring to horses, not automatic pistols."

"Same difference."

"Anyway, we're not talking about gift horses—we're talking about you holding out on me. You're just full of surprises."

He laughed. "Would you have it any other way, *migra*?"

Valdez muttered something under his breath, and Tally gave him a dirty look.

"What do you want to do with him?" Raul asked, cocking his thumb at their prisoner.

Tally had already decided. "There should be a federal magistrate in Pueblo. We'll drop Mr. Valdez at the police station there and I'll call immigration to take over."

Raul frowned. "I don't know that I care to go parading into a police station. The local gendarmerie might not be as understanding as you."

Understanding or just plain stupid? Tally wondered. "You can wait in the car. I'll book Valdez and come right back out. Fifteen minutes tops—that's all it will take."

Raul glanced again at the rearview mirror. "Whatever you say. But we've got to get cracking. We're already behind schedule, what with this snowstorm and the accident up there on the pass."

"It couldn't be helped."

"My, what an eloquently simple definition of fate—a sequence of things that can't be helped. Sheer poetry, my dear. I salute you."

"Sheer pragmatism," Tally corrected him. "Tell me, have you had it all this time?"

"Had what?"

"That pistol you pulled to persuade our friend here to pitch in and lend a hand when we were getting those people off the truck."

Raul patted the inside breast pocket of his jacket. "Of course. This little Beretta has served me well over the years."

"Has it?" Tally wondered if she was about to get a glimpse of the dark side of Raul Devlin. "Have you ever had to shoot anyone with it?"

"Never."

"Then how has it served you?"

"You might call it negative insurance."

She cocked her head and puzzled over the term. "What's negative insurance?"

"It's knowing you have a hidden resource to call upon if your back is to the wall. It's a disagreeable resource, true, but it's there nonetheless. I consider it something of a test of character to find ways to avoid having to use it."

"But now your back really is against the wall, isn't it?"

He glanced at her, and his lightheartedness was gone. "It really is, Tally. . . ."

"Have you thought of what you'll do if you don't find Fuentes?"

He shook his head. "I don't intend to fail—again."

"What do you mean, again?"

"You know the story. Olivera told you—I heard him. I took it upon myself to protect Dr. Fuentes, and I didn't do my job properly. The Protectors ambushed us on a back road in the mountains of northern Guatemala, which nearly dealt the Movement a fatal blow. Now it's up to me to make up for my mistake. I intend to find Dr. Fuentes and bring him home. And if anybody tries to stop me . . ."

He didn't finish. There was no need to finish. The harshness of his tone said it all.

They drove on in silence for a while, approaching Walsenburg from the west, and Tally noticed that Raul was paying ever-closer attention to the rearview mirror. She turned and looked out the rear window and could see nothing behind them but a billowing wake of blowing snow.

"Is something wrong?" she asked.

"No, nothing," he said quickly.

"You're lying."

He reached into his pocket, pulled out his Beretta and dropped it into his lap. "That's right, my dear. I'm lying."

Tally again looked back. She could still see nothing. "What did you see?"

"A two-tone Chevrolet wagon—a Suburban, I think it's called. It's been on our tail all the way from the New Mexico line."

Instinctively Tally unsnapped her purse so that she could get her own revolver out quickly. "The Protectors?"

Raul nodded. "I'd bet on it. I don't know how, but they seem to know our every move. My hunch is that they planned to make their move up on the pass, but after that accident there were too many witnesses on hand and they didn't want to chance it."

Tally looked at him worriedly. "Any ideas?"

"Not a one. If it hadn't been for this storm I would have taken a chance on chartering a plane at some small airstrip along the way, but it's just as well we didn't. Your Mr. Abrahamson probably would have called in the Air Force to shoot us down."

"He's not *my* Mr. Abrahamson," Tally corrected him. "I just wish I knew for sure whose Mr. Abrahamson he was— Uncle Sam's or the Protectors'."

She looked back again. No sign of the Suburban.

It was noon when they entered Walsenburg. They'd made good time the first part of the trip, from Albuquerque to Alamosa, even after the Protectors had picked up their tail. But now it was slow going with the blizzard that was whipping down along the front range, buffeting the few cars and trucks that dared venture into its fury.

Tally took a map from the glove box and folded it out on her lap. "We can pick up Interstate 25 here. It's another two hundred miles to Denver."

"Two hundred *long* miles," Raul noted. "This storm's getting worse by the minute."

She looked at him. He was wearing the same dark blue blazer, gray wool slacks and white shirt he'd had on when they met in Juarez. "Let's hope we don't get stranded. You're hardly dressed for a hike through the snow."

"You may have a point."

Several stores were open in downtown Walsenburg. Leaving Tally in the car to guard Valdez, Raul went into one of the stores and bought a heavy parka, sweater, gloves and insulated hiking boots. He'd left his luggage in his hotel room in Juarez. He made a mental note to call his contact there and tell him to pick up the things and distribute them to a needy family. There was so much need in Juarez, he thought.

It was twelve-fifteen when he came out of the store, wearing the parka and gloves and carrying his other purchases.

The Suburban was parked a block away, on the other side of the street, a few doors removed from the entrance to a small bank. He could barely see the outline of the vehicle through the falling snow.

He adjusted the fur-lined hood of his parka to mask his face and walked right on by the Dodge, pointedly refraining from looking at it. He then crossed the street at the intersection light. Hugging the inside of the sidewalk, as if to escape the worst of the blowing snow, he sauntered past the Suburban.

The Suburban had New Mexico license plates and there were two men in the front seat. They were wearing dark coats and snap-brim hats, and they had what the *coyote* Guerrero had so appropriately described as the look of undertakers.

Raul passed within three feet of the vehicle. Glancing at it casually, as any local might, he nodded pleasantly and walked on, past the bank and around the corner.

The Protectors. No mistaking them.

He and Tally had best be on their way, get at least as far as Pueblo that night. Pueblo, he'd noticed on the map, was a city of about one hundred thousand, far larger than Walsenburg. They'd have a better chance of going to ground there while they made travel arrangements. The first thing they'd have to do would be to get rid of the car they were driving. That scrape on the right side made it stand out like a sore thumb, and he didn't want to attract attention.

He stepped into a shabby café, forced down half a cup of bitter black coffee, and then went to the pay phone on the back wall and looked up the number of the Huerfano County sheriff's department.

After completing his call, he left, walked around two blocks and entered the side door of the store where he'd bought his new clothes. He watched from the window.

A few minutes later, he could see a sheriff's car pull alongside the Chevrolet Suburban. Two uniformed deputies got out and approached the car from either side, right hands brushing the leather holsters on their hips.

Raul didn't wait to watch the rest. He left the store, walked directly to the Dodge, got in and drove north to pick up the interstate.

They'd have a ten or fifteen-minute head start, he guessed. Maybe twenty or thirty minutes if they were lucky. It all depended on how long it would take the Protectors to convince the local law that they had no intention of robbing the bank they appeared to be casing.

He and Tally, with their prisoner, would have to move fast.

BLAINE HAD SEEN the school bus loading its passengers at the truck stop, and he knew immediately that they were illegal aliens. His years on the Border Patrol had given him almost a sixth sense about such things.

He swung the rental car in front of the parked bus and got out, ignoring Abrahamson's protests that they were wasting valuable time. Flashing his badge at the bus driver, he asked what had happened, and when he was told, he stepped back and cocked his thumb toward the office. "Everybody inside!" he bellowed. *"¡Pronto!"*

As Abrahamson looked on impatiently, Blaine interviewed the aliens one by one, firing questions at them in gruff, Tex-Mex Spanish. He began each interrogation with a single, broad question: "The man and woman who stopped and helped you—what can you tell us about them?"

"They were very nice," a small, worried-looking woman from Morelia said, nervously fingering the bundle on her lap. "They brought us here, and the man bought us hot chocolate and candy bars. The woman, called Tally, told us not to worry, that we would not have to go to jail but would be sent back to Mexico." She gazed up at Blaine, and there was a flicker of hope in her dark brown eyes. "Can we not stay in this country? We have families—"

Blaine wasn't interested in sad stories. "Did this Tally seem to be afraid?"

"Afraid?"

"Of the man, afraid that he was going to hurt her, I mean."

The woman from Morelia smiled knowingly. "No, *señor*. She was not in the least afraid. In fact, I even saw her put her arms around him and kiss him on the cheek as they went back outside to their car."

Blaine gritted his teeth. "Did you see him point a gun at her?"

"No, *señor*."

Blaine frowned. "You're not telling me the truth. I know he had a gun. Others have already told us so."

The woman from Morelia shook her head vigorously. "He did, *señor*, but he only used it to keep our driver from escaping. The woman had a gun, too."

Blaine turned to Abrahamson to translate. When he was finished, he added his own interpretation: "I don't care what she says. Tally's still being held against her will. Damn! If I ever get my hands on Devlin, I'll—"

Abrahamson eyed him coldly. "You'll follow orders, that's what you'll do. I'm not going to let your personal feelings screw up this case, Murchison." He glanced at the woman from Morelia. "Ask her if she heard them say anything to one another that might indicate their plans."

Blaine put the question into Spanish.

The woman from Morelia shook her head.

"What about the prisoner?" Blaine prodded her. "What were they going to do with him?"

The woman shrugged.

"Answer me!"

She just stared at him.

"You want to go to jail?"

"No, *señor*," the woman said quickly.

"Then tell me what they said about the prisoner."

There was anguish in the woman's eyes. Did she suspect Tally and Devlin were on the run? Probably. Tally, true to form, had befriended the lot of them, Blaine knew, and the woman didn't want to say anything that might be harmful to her. "They speak always in English. I do not understand English very well."

Blaine stared at her. "You won't like it in jail very well, either. They'll lock you up in a cell and you may never see your family again. Do you want that?"

"No, *señor*."

"Then tell me what they said."

The woman bowed her head. "They talked about taking the driver to a city called Pueblo."

"Where in Pueblo?"

"The police station, I think."

Blaine looked at Abrahamson. He told him what the woman had said.

"Let's get moving," Abrahamson said. "We're not all that far behind them." He headed for the door.

"Señor?" The woman was standing, tugging at Blaine's sleeve as he started to follow Abrahamson.

Blaine brushed away her hand. "Go back out and wait with the others," he said brusquely.

"*Señor*, we won't have to go to jail, will we?"

"That's not my concern, woman."

"IT'S MY FAULT," Raul said glumly, using his coat sleeve to wipe away the fog that had formed on the inside of the windshield. "One of the first lessons they taught us at the Point was to always expect the unexpected."

"You can't plan for every eventuality," Tally said sympathetically. "Neither of us had any way of predicting this."

A hundred yards ahead, two giant tractor-trailer rigs straddled the interstate at crazy angles. One of the rigs was canted precariously, its rear wheels lodged in a ditch. The other's cab was twisted back, its bumper jammed squarely against the tangle of hoses and chains connecting the two sections of its massive companion.

They'd been stopped for almost half an hour, theirs the fifth vehicle in line. A Trailways bus headed the motion-frozen procession, followed by two passenger cars and a small truck.

Somewhere behind them, its presence cloaked by the blowing snow, was the Chevrolet Suburban. Both Raul and Tally knew it. Only Valdez, who had dozed off in the back seat, was unaware of their danger.

Raul casually unzipped his parka and slipped the Beretta out of his waistband. Palming it in an attempt to keep it concealed, he transferred the pistol to the right-hand side pocket of his parka.

Tally glanced back out the ice-glazed rear window, then at Raul. "It might not be the Protectors. What if it's Abrahamson, or the Border Patrol, or any other law-enforcement agency, for that matter? What will you do when they make their move? Come up shooting?"

"I haven't thought about it," Raul replied. In fact, he had, but he'd failed to come up with an acceptable answer.

"Much as I dislike Abrahamson, I'd have to side with them, Raul. You know that, don't you?"

He nodded. He knew all too well. Tally Gordon had her duty, just as he had his, and if it came to a showdown...

Ahead, he saw a state trooper walking down the line, holding a red-lensed flashlight, pausing at each vehicle to inform motorists it wouldn't be long now. They were waiting for a wrecker from Walsenburg, and as soon as the tangle was cleared they'd all be on their way.

When the trooper had finished talking to them and had gone on, Raul brought out his Beretta and handed it to

Tally. "Hold on to this for me, if you would," he said, starting to get out of the car. "I want to have a look."

"You get back here!" she said sharply. "They may remember you from Walsenburg."

"I've got to take that chance, Tally. We've got to know what's happening back there."

"Then *I'll* go," she said, putting the Beretta in her purse and opening her door. "You stay here and keep an eye on the prisoner."

Valdez roused and glanced from one to the other, wondering what was going on.

Tally got out of the car and squinted north into the raging blizzard. She could barely make out the rear end of the bus that was stopped at the head of the line, its caution lights blinking.

Her coat collar turned up, her hands thrust into her pockets, she walked back down along the column of vehicles, scuffing through snow that was beginning to drift across the highway. There'd be time to get back to the car when she saw the wrecker coming, she knew. More than enough time, judging from what she'd seen of the snarl that was causing the delay.

Always expect the unexpected, Raul had said.

Yes, and whatever can go wrong will go wrong. Words to live by.

She counted off the vehicles stopped behind the Dodge.

Ten, eleven, twelve . . .

She stopped.

The Suburban that Raul had pointed out to her in Walsenburg was the thirteenth.

She kept walking, slowly, not wanting to appear nervous or attract attention. She didn't think they'd recognize her but she didn't want to take a chance. She came abreast of the Suburban and glanced inside, but didn't recognize the men within. She walked a few car lengths farther, then turned slowly and started back toward the Dodge.

Had the men in the wagon noticed her? She had no way of telling. The way the snow was swirling about, visibility was no more than two or three car lengths.

Walking faster now, she reviewed the possibilities.

They'd gotten only a glimpse of Raul on the street in Walsenburg—hardly enough to recognize him in, say, a police lineup. But they might have talked to those Mexicans she and Raul had helped, and they could have fleshed out the description.

Tally heard a noise from behind her, and she glanced back over her shoulder and saw a huge truck rumbling along on the inside shoulder of the highway. The truck had a crane mounted on its bed.

All right, what now? she asked himself.

Take the worst-case scenario. Assume they'd recognized Raul, knew he was traveling in the Dodge. They'd either try to grab him here and now, or they'd wait and attempt to take him before he got to Pueblo. The Chevrolet Suburban was far more powerful than the Dodge and would be less bothered by road conditions.

Which would it be? Stay and fight, or run and take their chances?

She walked back to the Dodge and got in. She took Raul's Beretta out of her purse and handed it to him. "Good news and bad news," she announced.

"What's the good news?"

"It's not Abrahamson nor any of his people."

"And the bad news?"

"That Suburban is only a few car lengths behind us."

Raul unzipped his new parka and tucked the Beretta into his waistband. "Any bright ideas? I seem to be fresh out of inspiration."

She thought about it. What if they pulled out suddenly and headed back to Walsenburg? There hadn't been much clearance between the Suburban and the car directly in front of it, a foot or so at the most. It would take the driver of the

Suburban a few minutes to maneuver around and follow them.

No, she decided. That wouldn't work. They might have a momentary advantage, but there was no place to hide in Walsenburg. The Protectors were bound to find them.

They'd have to make a run for it—north.

The rear window of the Dodge had iced over. Raul found a plastic scraper in the glove box, got out and rubbed the window clean. As he scraped, Tally looked back out through the newly cleared glass and saw two figures approaching from the rear of the line. They were walking on either side of the stalled vehicles, hands in their pockets, heads down against the snow.

She and Raul had no choice. They had to go back to Walsenburg.

Raul started to get back into the car, but Tally motioned him to the passenger side. "Let me drive," she said. "You ride shotgun and tell me if they get close."

She shifted into low and prepared to swing out of line and make a fast U-turn. It would take even more time for the two men to get back to the Suburban, and the added seconds would work in their favor—unless the men started blasting away at Raul then and there. They wanted Raul alive, she knew, because he was the only one who could lead them to Federico Fuentes. But if they saw their quarry getting away, they might get desperate.

The men were only a car length behind the Dodge now.

Neither Tally nor Raul saw the third figure loom out of the blowing snow until that figure was almost alongside the Dodge.

It was the state trooper who'd talked to them earlier, who'd told them of the delay. The trooper tapped on the side window, and Tally rolled it down a few inches, shifting the car back to neutral as she did so.

"Traffic's going to be moving any minute, ma'am," the trooper said, his breath a frozen cloud. "Keep your lights on and try to stay in sight of the vehicle in front of you."

Then he was gone.

Tally watched the mirror. The trooper said something to one of the men approaching from the left side of the column of cars. The man appeared to argue with him, but the trooper was adamant. The man turned and walked back toward the Suburban. The trooper signaled to the second man, and the latter retreated, too.

Another idea suddenly occurred to Tally.

Slamming the gear shift into low again, she jockeyed the Dodge around, slipping and sliding every inch of the way, until it sat squarely across the road, blocking both northbound lanes. Then, turning off the ignition and pocketing the key, she pointed to the bus at the head of the line.

"What do you think?"

"I think you're a genius, *migra*—that's what I think!" he exclaimed. "Let's go for it."

Grabbing the sack containing his shoes and sweater, he climbed out of the Dodge and motioned Valdez to follow him. Valdez didn't seem at all interested in accompanying them, so Raul reached in, grabbed him by the collar and hauled him out.

Pausing long enough to collect her carryall from the trunk, Tally joined them on the steps of the waiting bus.

Raul was smiling at the driver. "I need three tickets to Pueblo," he said. "Our car seems to have broken down and we're in a hurry...."

ON A GOOD DAY it takes a leisurely forty-five minutes to drive from Walsenburg to Pueblo on Interstate 25, which runs north and south, parallel to the front range of the Rockies. On a good day, the four lanes of concrete ribbon extend as far as the eye can see across the undulating, brown land of the foothills, beyond which the peaks of the high mountains jab proudly into the crisp, blue sky. On a good day, it's a pleasant trip, even a relaxing one.

But this wasn't a good day. It was a terrible day. Ground blizzards swirled angrily across the pavement and visibility was a car length or less. The few vehicles that had ventured out into the storm stayed close together, each driver keeping a careful eye on the slow-moving taillights ahead, trusting blindly that whoever was leading the procession knew what he was doing, always hoping he didn't jam on the brakes and cause a chain-reaction pileup.

It was after five o'clock and nearly dark when the Buick that Nate Abrahamson had rented in Alamosa entered Pueblo from the south. Blaine Murchison was at the wheel, fighting not just the weather but his own emotions. The thought of Tally—*his* Tally—casting her lot in with a man like Devlin made him furious. Damn fool woman!

"You've got to hand it to him," the man from Washington said, a touch of admiration in his voice. "That was some maneuver back there by Walsenburg, blocking the highway and then hopping aboard the bus."

"I'll hand it to him all right," Blaine said fiercely, tapping the brake pedal with his toe as he slowed to watch for the downtown exit. "You can have what's left of him when I get finished."

Abrahamson gave a dry little laugh. "You think so? I've got news for you. Devlin could eat your lunch any day of the week. He's tough."

"We'll see about that."

"You're not going to get the chance. As soon as we nail him, you're on the next plane back to El Paso. I don't need any hotheads on my team, Murchison."

Blaine glanced sharply at him. "You were the one who sent for me."

"That's right, I did. And I think maybe I made a mistake. You're supposed to be a first-rate investigator, but I'm beginning to have my doubts."

"Oh?"

"See that wagon up ahead, the big one?"

Blaine squinted at the two-tone blue Chevrolet Suburban that was swinging out to pass another car directly ahead of them. "What about it?"

"Has it occurred to you that we've seen it half a dozen times since we left Alamosa?"

"Nothing unusual about that. U.S. 160 feeds into Interstate 25, and the two of us just happen to be going in the same direction. Strictly coincidence."

"I don't believe in coincidence," Abrahamson said. "Stay on his tail, Murchison. I want to see where he's headed."

Again Blaine turned to look at his companion. "We don't have time. We've got to get to the police station and see if Tally's checked in yet with the smuggler."

"No hurry. She and Devlin aren't going anywhere. We've got them boxed. I've been listening to the weather reports on the radio. The highway is closed by drifts north of here, and it has been for the past hour."

"But—"

"I said to follow that wagon."

Blaine realized it was pointless to argue. He pulled out to pass the car directly ahead of him, and the Buick skidded and spun around, facing oncoming traffic. Angrily, Blaine twisted the wheel and tried again, the car fishtailing as he struggled to keep it under control.

"Try to keep us in one piece," Abrahamson muttered.

"This damn road's like a skating rink," Blaine said. "That wagon you want me to tail must have four-wheel drive."

By the time the Buick picked up speed and passed the car ahead of it, the Suburban was nowhere in sight.

NOBODY IN HIS RIGHT MIND would venture out on a night like this, the ticket clerk at the bus terminal told them, glancing out morosely at the snow swirling around the streetlights when Tally asked directions to the police station. He was so right, Tally thought. Nobody but the fools, the hunters and the hunted.

"I'm freezing my butt off," Eddie Valdez grumbled, trying to thrust his hands into the slit pockets of his parka but only half succeeding. His right wrist was shackled to

Tally's left, and to further discourage him from attempting to escape, Raul was walking on his other side.

"It's only a few blocks more," Tally informed the smuggler, adjusting the strap of her carryall so that it would ride more comfortably over her right shoulder. "When we get there, you'll be a lot warmer than those people you let suffer in the back of your truck."

"Look," Valdez said, in wounded innocence. "I just picked up some hitchhikers back in New Mexico—that's all I can tell you, lady. Geez, you try to be a nice guy, and look what it gets you."

"It gets you two to five in the federal slammer," Tally fired back. "If you've got a record, and I suspect you do, it'll probably be more like five to ten. Consider yourself lucky. If we hadn't looked inside that truck, you could be facing twenty-seven counts of manslaughter."

Valdez made another unsuccessful attempt to put his right hand into his pocket. "I want a lawyer."

"Be my guest," Tally said, yanking his hand down. "Just as soon as we get you booked."

Raul spoke up. "I'm not all that familiar with the law, but doesn't the arresting officer have to appear in court for the hearing?"

"Ordinarily yes," Tally replied. "But they'll probably let me just give an affidavit."

"Affidavits take time. And time is something we don't have."

"I know." How well she knew. "But I'm not going to let our friend here waltz."

The police building, which was only a few blocks south of the bus terminal, was nearly invisible in the storm, and they were in front of it almost before they realized it.

Raul stopped and looked around cautiously. "This is as far as I go. I'll wait for you outside."

Tally stepped in front of Valdez, blocking his way. She reached out with her right hand and rested it on Raul's shoulder. "Promise?"

"You have my word on it."

The smuggler leaned in to hear what they were saying. "Look," he grumbled, "it's cold out here. You two want to snuggle, do it on your own time, huh?" He again tried to shove his right hand into his pocket.

"Oh, shut up!" Tally exclaimed, jerking on the handcuffs. She looked at Raul, then impulsively raised up on her toes and kissed him on the cheek. "Be right back."

Leading the reluctant Valdez, she headed for the entrance of the building. By the time she'd gone a dozen paces, Raul was out of sight, lost in the savagery of the storm.

Suddenly Tally was aware that she was not alone on the snowswept walkway. Two dark figures, one tall, one short, were standing just outside the doorway, and when they saw her they began moving toward her. Both were bundled up in heavy overcoats, and both had hats pulled down low over their eyes.

"You will give us your prisoner," the taller of the two men said in a heavily accented voice.

He was carrying a gun, and the gun was pointed directly at Tally.

Chapter Ten

This wasn't happening, Tally told herself. Not on the walk-way leading up to a police station, in the middle of an average American city. This was something out of a Grade B fifties movie.

"Who are you?" she demanded, lowering her right hand from the shoulder strap of her carryall. The bag thudded to the concrete by her right foot. Her fingers moved toward her purse and toward the service revolver that was in it.

The tall man, the one holding the gun, ignored her question. Stepping in close, he grabbed the terrified Eddie Valdez by the front of his parka. As he did so, he saw the short length of case-hardened steel chain that joined Valdez and Tally. His face screwed up in a thin, evil smile. "It's nice to know that you've finally come to your senses and decided to turn him in, Agent Gordon. Now if you'd be kind enough to unlock the handcuffs..."

Tally stood her ground, wondering how he knew her name. "I'll unlock the cuffs when I get my prisoner inside the police station—not before."

"You'll do it now!" the second man snapped. Tally looked at him and saw that he also had drawn a gun.

She couldn't fight them, she knew—not two men who clearly had the drop on her, with her left wrist locked to Valdez's right wrist. "All right," she said. "Let me find the key."

Both men watched her closely as she unsnapped the flap on her purse and reached inside.

The gloved fingers of her right hand grazed the grip of her revolver, and she hesitated. Perhaps if she could throw herself to one side, using Valdez as a shield, she could...

No, she told herself. You don't use prisoners as shields.

She groped for the keys.

"Slowly," the first man instructed her.

"And carefully," the second man said. "Very, very carefully, Agent Gordon."

"I'm not an idiot," Tally said, still wondering how they knew her name. She tried to sound flustered and frightened, and it wasn't at all difficult.

She found the key and handed it over, and the shorter man stepped in and unlocked Valdez's side of the cuffs. As he did so, the shorter man sneered at the smuggler. "I hope that plastic surgeon in Mexico City didn't charge you too much, Devlin. He really botched the job."

Valdez gulped. "Huh?"

The taller man laughed. "The operation not only made the poor fellow ugly, it addled his brain. Whoever would have thought the great Devlin would meet his Waterloo at the hands of a woman?"

Oh, my God! Tally thought. *They think Eddie Valdez is Raul!*

The second man tossed the key back to Tally, and it slipped through her fingers and fell to the snow. "We were advised that you might be difficult, Agent Gordon," he said, pocketing his gun as Tally bent down to recover the key. "We obviously were misinformed."

"I told you, I'm not an idiot, and I'm not very heroic, either." She wasn't, she knew. But she was determined.

The taller man put away his gun. "There are more than enough heroes in the world, Agent Gordon. Heroes have an unpleasant way of upsetting the natural balance of things." He thumped at Valdez's chest with the heel of one hand. "Am I not right, Devlin?"

The smuggler gave him a pleading, wide-eyed look. "Hey, man, you got it all wrong. The name's Valdez—Eddie Valdez. I don't know nobody named Devlin. Honest."

Tally glanced coldly at the cowering Valdez. There was a chance yet, if only Valdez would play along. He had to for his own good. The two Protectors would probably kill him—both of them, for that matter—if they realized they'd made a mistake. "Sorry, Raul, but I guess it's all over between us. It was nice meeting you. Write to me when you get back to Argentina."

Valdez clawed at his captor's coat sleeves. "Wait a minute! Don't listen to this crazy broad! The clown you want, is his first name Raul? There was a guy with us she kept calling Raul—never did hear the last name, but it must have been him."

The taller man looked questioningly at his companion, then at Tally. "There is a second man?"

Tally raised the forefinger of her left hand to her temple and made a little, circular motion. She had to keep them off balance, just for a minute longer. "Probably brain damage from that plastic surgery in Mexico City," she said. "The poor man has been insanely jealous ever since we met. He even thought the bus driver was coming on to me."

"Bus driver?" said the shorter man. "What's this about a bus driver?"

Tally wondered if she'd gone too far. Maybe the two Protectors didn't know how she and Raul had slipped aboard the bus at the roadblock north of Walsenburg. "You don't think we walked here in this snowstorm, do you?"

"Let's be on our way," the taller man said, grasping Valdez by the upper arm.

"Hey!" the smuggler yelped. "You gotta believe me! I'm not Devlin!"

The Protectors grabbed Valdez, one on each arm, and started to lead him away. It was the opportunity Tally had been waiting for. Her right hand dipped into her purse and brought out her service revolver. "Freeze!" she shouted, leveling the gun at the trio.

The sequence of events that followed would forever remain a blur in her mind. The wind had picked up and the blowing snow had even further reduced visibility. Tally was vaguely aware of shapes moving on either side of her, and for a few seconds she thought they might be innocent passersby. But what passersby? As the ticket clerk at the bus station had said, only a fool would venture out on a night like this.

The fools, the hunters or the hunted.

"Abrahamson?" she called out, not taking her eyes off the two men who'd just snatched Eddie Valdez. She didn't trust Abrahamson, but she felt more comfortable with him than with these two strangers.

"Gordon? Is that you?"

"Over here. I'm—"

Dimly, she could see Valdez break free from his captors and start to run. Then the shooting started.

Bullets whizzing around her, Tally dropped to the icy walkway and rolled over, clutching her revolver with both hands, keeping it pointed in the general direction of the two Protectors.

She saw someone trot up the walk, slipping and sliding on the ice. Was it Abrahamson? She couldn't be sure.

Scrambling to her feet, she moved forward, and as she moved she caught a glimpse of Valdez running back toward her, holding his head with both hands, screaming.

Tally lunged at the smuggler, knocking him off balance and sending him sprawling into a snowbank at the side of the walkway. She dove on top of him to shield him, again rolling over and coming up on her hands and knees with her revolver at the ready.

"Abrahamson!" she shouted at the top of her lungs, firing a shot into the air to attract his attention.

There was a second of ominous silence.

Then the shorter of the two Protectors appeared out of nowhere and grabbed her right wrist, twisting it to deflect the muzzle of the gun. His companion came up from behind her and reached down and seized the collar of the cowering smuggler.

"Abrahamson!" Tally screamed again. "I need help!"

The shorter man slammed her back down into the snow and continued to wrestle for possession of her gun, one knee jammed against the side of her head, dazing her.

Tally heard another shot, from a distance, and the man who was struggling with her jumped up, one foot securely planted on Tally's right wrist. She could see him reach into his coat pocket and bring out a gun. He raised it and took aim at the figure obscured by snow.

Tally squirmed about and, with her left hand, the cuffs still jangling from her wrist, punched as hard as she could at the back of his knee, knocking him off balance as he squeezed off several quick shots.

She could see him standing over her, his dark eyes blazing coals of anger. He drew back the foot he'd pinned her wrist with and started to kick her, and she rolled free, out of reach.

She remembered thinking, *The third time's the charm, Raul. You've helped me out twice. One more time? Please?*

She heard another shot and the man who'd tried to kick her fell on top of her, screaming. He was holding his chest with both hands, and blood was spurting out from between his fingers.

RAUL HAD BEEN STANDING in a doorway across the street from the police station when he saw the Suburban pull over to the curb and park only a few yards away. He'd pressed back into the doorway, his right hand reaching for the Beretta, wondering if he'd been spotted.

Two men had climbed out of the Suburban—the same two Raul had seen in Walsenburg—and walked quickly toward the entrance of the police station.

Tally would already be in the station, booking her prisoner, Raul had known, so she was safe for the moment. But she'd be coming back outside in a few minutes, and he didn't want her running into a reception committee of Protector musclemen.

He'd moved out of the doorway and started to cross the street, directly in front of the parked Suburban. He glanced at the wagon that had dogged them every mile of the way from New Mexico. How was it possible that the Protectors had been able to follow his every move? They had to have some sort of tracking device.

Peering into the blowing snow to make sure he wasn't being watched, he went up to the driver's side door of the Suburban and tried the handle.

The door was unlocked.

He opened it and stepped into the driver's seat, his nose wrinkling at the heavy stench of stale cigar smoke that greeted him, then quickly shut the door. He made a cursory examination of the interior, saw nothing that seemed out of order, and then decided to risk switching on the ceiling light for a closer examination.

The first thing he noticed was what appeared to be a radar detector clamped to the dashboard, its sighting barrel pointed straight forward. A partially open map lay between the front bucket seats, and it was weighted down by a thermos that was leaking coffee. The ashtray was full of cigar butts, and crumpled sandwich wrappings littered the floor.

Messy, messy, he thought.

He bent down and patted his hands around the space under each of the seats.

He found nothing under the driver's seat, but his search under the other seat turned up a short-barreled submachine gun with a silencer. He examined it and saw that it was an Ingram Model 11, a weapon he'd been familiar with since his army days. The Ingram was a favorite of Central American paramilitary groups because it was simple to operate—and deadly.

With a few practiced twists, Raul removed the bolt, rendering the submachine gun useless. He stuffed the bolt into his pocket.

He put the weapon back where he'd found it and looked around.

There were two canvas satchels in the back seat. He'd have to check them out, but later.

He leaned over and opened the glove box and looked inside. The compartment contained some papers indicating that the wagon had been rented in Albuquerque less than an hour before he and Tally had picked up their Dodge at the airport there. It also contained two boxes of nine-millimeter ammunition.

The plot thickens, he thought. *They knew exactly what we'd be doing, which way we were headed. It's as if they were reading our minds.*

As he closed up the glove box, his gaze fell on the object clamped to the dashboard. Strange. He'd never heard of any rental companies equipping their cars with radar detectors. On the contrary, rental companies would encourage their customers to comply with speed laws, not try to outsmart them.

He examined the device, then smiled grimly as he unfastened it and smashed it against the steering wheel. So the two Protectors did have a homing device! Very clever. Next question: what were they homing in on? Electronic tracking devices such as this one needed specially designed targets to get a fix on. Nothing elaborate: Raul recalled seeing targets as small as matchbooks. Was it something that had been planted on him—not likely, he thought—or on Tally? He'd have to find out. He ripped out the wires dangling from the broken scope and turned to reach for the two satchels in back.

It was then that he heard the shooting, and he knew that Tally was in trouble.

He threw open the door, jumped out of the Suburban and ran toward the police station, drawing his pistol as he ran.

He heard Tally shout, "Abrahamson! I need help!" He knew she was somewhere close by, but she was nowhere to be seen in the raging swirl of the blizzard.

Wait! He saw something moving off to his right, and he moved in on it.

The something was a man. He was short, and bundled in an overcoat, with a hat pulled low over his eyes, and he was standing over someone who was sprawled on the ground. The short man saw Raul and started blazing away.

Raul dropped to the pavement and fired, and his target pitched forward atop his intended victim.

Someone yelled, "There they go! Get them!"

There were half a dozen more shots.

Raul rose to a crouch and inched forward, trying to make out what was happening.

He heard a man call out, "Tally! Where are you, girl?"

Raul cupped his hands to his eyes, squinting into the wind-driven snow.

And then he caught a glimpse of her. She was getting shakily to her feet. She was splattered with blood, and a man wearing a cowboy hat was reaching out for her.

Raul pocketed his Beretta and walked away.

When he got back across the street, the Suburban was gone.

BLAINE PLACED Tally's carryall bag on the floor by her feet and looked down at her long and hard, shaking his head. "You better ask the desk sergeant if he's got someplace you can go and change your clothes. You've still got clumps of snow and ice all over you. And you're splattered with blood."

"I'm all right," Tally said. "Just shaken up a little. Let me get my breath."

"You're lucky Abrahamson and I came along when we did. Those turkeys meant business."

She looked at Blaine. "How'd you know where to find me?"

"Those wetbacks you helped out—they told us where you were headed. It took a little persuasion, but they talked."

Tally didn't ask what sort of persuasion. She knew from experience that Blaine wasn't the gentlest of interrogators. "How is Abrahamson?"

"Don't know yet. He took a slug in the shoulder, and they hauled him off in an ambulance. I figured as soon as you feel up to it, we can go to the hospital and look in on him."

"What about Valdez?"

"Who?"

"Eddie Valdez, my prisoner. I was bringing him in to book him for transporting the illegals." She glanced down at the handcuff chain dangling from her left wrist. "Those men we ran into outside made me release him. They thought Valdez was..." She didn't finish the sentence. She didn't want to talk to Blaine about Raul. He'd never understand.

But Blaine already knew. "They figured Valdez was Devlin." He grinned. "They're in for a big surprise when they start interrogating him."

"Maybe he managed to get away from them."

"Maybe. There was some blood in the snow, over near where Abrahamson was shooting it out with them, but no way of telling who else was hit besides that guy you snuffed."

Tally looked at him. "I didn't shoot anybody."

"You sure?"

"Positive."

Blaine shrugged. "Maybe it was Devlin." He sat down on the bench next to her. "You want to tell me about him now?"

Tally avoided looking at him. "No," she said softly.

"What do you mean, no?" Blaine bristled. "That son of a gun kidnapped you back there in Albuquerque and made you go with him!"

"He didn't make me do anything. I went along because I wanted to."

"You wanted to?"

Tally nodded. "That's right. I wanted to make sure he got out of the country—alive. Abrahamson wants to kill him. I'm sure of it."

Blaine jumped to his feet. "You realize what you're saying, girl? You were under orders to help Abrahamson collar him, and you decided on your own to—"

"I'll do my job, but I won't be a party to murder," Tally cut in.

"Whatever gave you the idea Abrahamson wants to ice him?"

"You said so yourself—when I talked to you on the phone last night."

Blaine shook his head. "I said that was the word on the street. You can't believe everything you hear."

"It's true, Blaine. I know it's true. Abrahamson has been working with the Protectors all along, feeding them information."

"You've flipped your lid, girl. I've been with Abrahamson every step of the way since Albuquerque. Hell, if he'd been in touch with them I would have known it."

Tally stood up and picked up her carryall. "I don't know how he's doing it, but he's managing somehow to keep in touch with them. They know every move we make." She slung the strap of the bag over her right shoulder, then looked down at the handcuff dangling from her left wrist, as if noticing it for the first time. She unlocked the steel bracelet and dropped the handcuffs and keys into her purse. "Let's go on up to the hospital."

She started for the door, but Blaine grabbed her arm. "I want to know about Devlin. Where is he now?"

"I have no idea. Please let go of me."

"You can't protect him, girl."

Tally glared at him. "Don't call me 'girl,' *Inspector* Murchison!"

"I want to know where you left him when you came waltzing up to the station house with Valdez."

Tally tried to shake free of his grip, but he wouldn't let go. "I'll ask the desk sergeant if someone can give me a ride to the hospital."

"You know, of course, that if any of this gets out, you're in big trouble. You can kiss your job goodbye."

"I plan to, anyway."

Blaine frowned. "It's a good thing for you that your daddy isn't alive. He'd take you across his knee and whip some sense into you."

Tally batted away his hand. "Drop dead, huh?"

She walked away to search out the desk sergeant.

Ten minutes later, a Pueblo police cruiser dropped her off at the front door of the hospital, just as an ambulance pulled up to the emergency entrance, its siren wailing. Tally wondered if it was the same ambulance that had brought Abrahamson from the police station earlier.

"You've have a busy night," she told the patrolman who'd given her a lift from the police station.

"If it's not one thing, it's another," he agreed. "That call you just heard—somebody took a header off the bridge into the Arkansas River. Went right through the ice, he did. They just got the call a few minutes before we left the station."

"I hope the victim's not hurt too badly," Tally said, reaching around to get her carryall from the back seat. "Thanks for the ride."

"Anytime."

At the front desk, Tally showed her credentials and was told that Abrahamson had been taken up to surgery, but that one of the residents who'd treated him when he was brought in was still in the emergency room.

"Better not bother him just now," the duty nurse informed her. "I was just back there and they're really busy."

Tally nodded. "I heard that somebody fell off a bridge."

"He fell all right, but he was shot first. At least, they were setting up for a gunshot wound. That's all I know."

Tally's heart skipped a beat. Her first thought was of Raul. *They chased him down and tried to kill him!*

"How do I get to the emergency room?"

"If you'll wait a little while—"

Tally spun around and raced out the front door, then down the driveway to where she'd seen the ambulance pull in. The ambulance crew was just leaving, wheeling out an empty gurney, when she ran up to them.

"How is he? The man you just brought in?"

The driver shook his head sorrowfully. "There was nothing the paramedics could do for him. He was dead when they pulled him out of the water."

Oh, no! she thought, starting to tremble. "I've got to see him." She started for the door of the emergency room.

"Hey, you can't go in there!" the driver called after her.

But Tally was already inside, her badge case in her hand. She flashed the badge at the first nurse she saw. "I want to see the shooting victim who just came in."

The nurse nodded to a cubicle partitioned off by white sheeting. There, in the middle of the cubicle, was a table, and on the table was a body.

Tally walked over and stared down at it.

Eddie Valdez had retired from the smuggling business. Permanently.

THE SURGEON SMILED reassuringly as he talked to Tally and Blaine in the hallway outside Abrahamson's room. "There's nothing to worry about," he said. "He's got a nasty wound in his left shoulder that will slow him up for a while, but judging from those other scars he's a tough old bird. He'll be fine."

"How long do you figure he'll be here?"

The question came from Blaine, and Tally knew exactly what he was thinking. With Abrahamson out of action, he'd be in line to take over the case—that and whatever glory accrued to the person who brought in Raul Devlin.

The surgeon shrugged. "Three or four days. Gunshot wounds can be tricky. I don't want to take a chance on infection."

"Can we talk to him?" Tally asked.

"I'd rather you didn't. I gave him a pretty stiff jolt of Demerol after I stitched him up, and now I want him to get some sleep."

"It's important."

"Very important," Blaine spoke up. "A matter of national security, in fact."

Tally winced.

The surgeon threw up his hands. "All right, but don't be surprised if he drifts off on you before you're finished." He looked at his watch. "I'm going down the hall to look in on another patient. I'll be back in five minutes. See that you're out of there when I return."

They slipped into the room and found Abrahamson turned on his right side, staring at the door.

"I heard you talking out there, and I wondered how long it would take you to talk your way past that quack," he grumbled in a thick voice. "It's about time you showed up to fill me in." He looked at Tally, then at Blaine. "She okay?"

"I'm fine, Mr. Abrahamson." As if it made any difference to him! she thought.

Abrahamson scowled at her. "I didn't ask you, Gordon. I asked Murchison."

"Yeah, she's fine," Blaine said. "Look, I wanted to ask you if you—"

"Anybody else get hurt down there in front of the cop shop?"

"Two men were killed," Tally said.

"Oh? Who?"

"One of the attackers and a fellow named Valdez," Blaine said. "The attacker was carrying a Costa Rica passport issued under the name Ignacio Lazaro, but it could be a phony. We won't know until we check it out."

"Who's this Valdez?"

"He's the smuggler I was bringing in," Tally replied. "They thought he was Raul Devlin."

Abrahamson shifted about, seeking a more comfortable position. "Doesn't make sense killing Devlin. They wanted him alive."

Blaine moved in closer to the bed and lowered his voice. "The way I figure it, this Valdez got caught in the cross fire and took a slug in the back. He ran south, and was halfway across the bridge when he saw a car coming and figured it was them—them or us, I don't know. He climbed over the railing, figuring to hide, but lost his footing and fell into the river."

Abrahamson looked at Tally. "You buy that, Gordon?"

She shrugged. "I don't know. I was there, but the storm was so bad I couldn't tell what was happening."

Abrahamson studied her, then turned his attention to Blaine. Tally came closer to the bed and stood next to Blaine. She wanted to hear everything that was said between the two men.

"The locals turn up anything, inspector?" Abrahamson asked.

"Nothing."

"Where do you suppose Devlin got to?"

"Hard to say..."

Abrahamson glanced at Tally. "Where'd you leave him?"

It was the question Tally had dreaded. Did she follow her head or her heart? Her every instinct told her that Raul was a decent, honorable man—just as Olivera had said—and that he was only trying to fulfill what he considered an obligation. And yet she had a sworn duty to bring him in, despite her suspicions of Abrahamson. She'd ignored that duty, and now she had to face up to it. They'd been seen together on the bus, and at the bus terminal. She couldn't lie about that. It would be too easy for Blaine to learn the truth. All she could do was hope that Raul's talent for staying two steps ahead of his pursuers would continue to serve him. "Across the street from the police station," she said.

Abrahamson settled back, his head on the pillow. "Not even going to ask what you and Devlin had in mind, Gordon." He yawned. "Talk about it tomorrow."

Blaine bent down over the bed. "Mr. Abrahamson?"

Abrahamson gave him a confused look, then closed his eyes.

"Mr. Abrahamson?"

"He's asleep," Tally said, stepping back from the bed. "Remember what the doctor said."

"Yeah," Blaine said. "It looks like I'm going to have to take over for him." Taking Tally's arm, he led her out of the room. "What I want you to do, girl, is find a motel room somewhere and get some rest yourself. As soon as this storm lifts, I'm sending you back to El Paso."

That's what you think, inspector, Tally wanted to say.

THE CAB FARE came to eighteen dollars and fifty cents, and Tally paid it with a twenty-dollar bill and started to pocket the change. Then she read the disappointment in the cabbie's face, remembering how he'd had to fight ice and snow every foot of the way as he hauled her to one motel district after another. She remembered what the clerk at the bus terminal had said about how nobody in his right mind would even venture out on a night like this. "Keep it," she said, handing back the dollar bill and two quarters he'd given her. It wasn't much of a tip, but it was all she could afford. She was down to her last few dollars, and unless she could cash a check somewhere she'd have to use her credit cards to buy meals after her money was gone. She hoped her purchases in Albuquerque hadn't brought her balance over her credit limit, because she was counting on a cash advance from MasterCard to help pay her first month's rent on her new law office. Tally Gordon, big-time detective, she thought ruefully.

She got out of the cab, slung the strap of her carryall over her shoulder and looked west on Highway 50, where surrealistic splashes of neon glared through the whiteness of the storm.

Find a motel somewhere, Blaine had told her. And that was exactly what she intended to do: find a motel, one certain motel.

Raul had to be holed up somewhere close by, she knew. The highways leading in and out of the city were closed, and Pueblo wasn't all that large. It was a working-man's town, with a bare minimum of hotel and motel rooms.

This was her last chance. She'd checked out all the other places in town. If she didn't find him in one of the motels on Highway 50, she might as well give up and carry out the second part of Blaine's instructions by getting some much-needed rest.

But she wasn't going back to El Paso. Not until she found Raul again.

Slogging on through the drifting snow alongside the highway, she started checking out the half dozen motels, one by one.

At the last motel, the woman in the office seemed nervous. She shook her head, almost before Tally came out with the name Devlin.

"There's no one registered here by that name," the woman said quickly.

"Do you mind if I look for myself?"

"I certainly do mind. You can't—"

Tally showed her badge and ID card. "Official business," she said.

Room 24 was rented to a Kevin Shannon—the name Raul had used in Juarez.

Tally asked for a key to Room 24, and the woman handed it over. "Won't do you any good," she said with a smug little smile. "As far as I know, Mr. Shannon never even went back to the room. He just paid cash, took his key and walked off."

"Walked off where?" Tally demanded.

"I have no idea."

"Thank you."

"Anytime. Have a nice evening."

Tally walked back outside and stood in front of the motel, wondering what to do next. She'd exhausted just about every possibility.

Kevin Shannon.

Of course! He'd used that name because he knew she'd recognize it!

But why had he left right after checking in?

She started backtracking, rechecking each of the other five motels, using her Border Patrol credentials when necessary to persuade the clerks to let her see their registration cards.

Raul had taken a room in the third one she tried. This time he'd registered as Tally—Gordon Tally.

"Why didn't you tell me before that he's here?" Tally asked the young woman behind the counter.

"Your description didn't sound a thing like him," the young woman replied innocently. "I mean, he's a real dreamboat, and you made him sound rather ordinary."

Tally had to laugh in spite of her aggravation. "There's nothing at all ordinary about the man," she said. "Do you know if he's in now?"

The clerk reached for the phone. "Let me ring back there and find out for you."

"No," Tally said, "that won't be necessary. I want to surprise him."

Walking to his room, she paused long enough to fish her handcuffs out of her purse and slip them into the pocket of her trench coat.

A minute later, she was standing face-to-face with Raul in the doorway of his room.

He grinned at her. "I was wondering how long it would take you to show up, *migra*."

"Ah, but you knew you could count on that distant early-warning system of yours," she said accusingly.

"Distant early-warning system?"

"The desk clerk called you from that first place you checked in, didn't she? You had it all worked out."

"A very sweet lady," Raul said with a wistful sigh. "I told her I had a mean-spirited ex-wife who'd vowed to follow me to the ends of the Earth to make trouble. I told her my ex-wife was a bit unbalanced and took childish delight in impersonating police officers. What's more, she'd even hired some private detectives who were every bit as corrupt as she. The clerk was more than happy to oblige me."

Tally managed to suppress a smile. It wasn't easy. "The woman looked like she'd be a sucker for a fast line of patter. All you had to do was bat those dark lashes of yours, and you had her eating right out of your hand. You're a wolf in sheep's clothing if I've ever seen one." Then she laughed and leaned in and kissed him on the mouth. Her eyes locked on his, holding his attention as his warm and willing lips pressed against hers. She took the handcuffs from her pocket and clamped one end of them around his right wrist.

Chapter Eleven

Raul didn't even try to resist. They stood in the open doorway, ignoring the freezing cold and the blowing snow, their bodies pressing together, each of them drawing inner fire from the other. And for a moment, the harsh realities of the here and now were forgotten in the desperate hunger of a kiss that said everything that could possibly be said.

After a while—a minute or an hour, Tally wasn't sure which—Raul scooped Tally into his arms, their mouths still joined in gnawing passion. Raul carried her to the bed and lowered her onto it, then eased himself to his knees at the side of the bed, running his fingers through her wind-tangled hair.

"Raul..." she murmured as his lips left hers and floated across her chin and down her neck, coming to rest in the soft hollow of her throat. "Thank God you're all right. I don't know what I would have done if I'd lost you."

"You haven't lost me, Tally. I've been here, waiting for you. I knew you'd come."

"Raul..." She hesitated, not wanting to talk about what had happened at the police station. She tried to shut it out of her mind, if only for the moment. But she couldn't. The memory was too vivid, too terrifying. "Raul, they killed my prisoner, Valdez. I let them think he was you."

"The Protectors?"

Tally nodded. "They were waiting for us there at the police station—two of them. I don't know how they managed to track us, but they did."

Raul said nothing, and she sensed he was holding out on her again. This time she didn't press him, but went on with her story, telling him how Valdez had fled the scene and had later plunged to his death from the bridge. As the words poured out, her eyes misted with tears and she clutched at him, reassuring herself with his warmth and nearness. She had indeed come very close to losing him, she knew, and if she had, her life never again would be the same.

She could feel his muscles tighten as she described how, in all the confusion and clamor, someone—she didn't know who—had shot the man who was attacking her when she was down in the snow, and she knew he was reliving the same memory that was torturing her.

He didn't want her to dwell on that part of it. Or was it that *he* didn't want to dwell on it? "Was anyone else hurt?" he asked, his words muffled against her throat.

Tally brushed at her eyes with the backs of her hands, wiping away the tears. She felt ashamed breaking down this way. She hadn't cried since the night Pop died. "Abrahamson was wounded in the shoulder, but the doctor says he'll be all right."

Raul raised his head and looked at her. "That was very convenient, I'd say."

"What do you mean?"

"I mean that Abrahamson must know how obvious it is he's made a deal with the Protectors. He's pushed his luck too far. What better way to divert suspicion? That wound is a perfect badge of innocence."

Tally perked up. Suddenly she was a cop again, sorting out facts, trying to get at the elusive truth. "You know, I never thought of that, but it's possible."

He rested his cheek upon her chest and closed his eyes. "The man who was killed there at the station—what was his name?"

"He had a passport identifying him as Ignacio Lazaro but Blaine isn't sure that's his real name."

Again Tally could feel Raul's muscles tense. "The inspector has good instincts. Ignacio Lazaro has been dead for a year. I know. I shot him myself—just as I shot the man who appropriated his name tonight, there in front of the station. Lazaro, the real Lazaro, had set off a bomb that killed twenty people who'd come to hear—"

"It was you, then?" She'd had a feeling all along it had been Raul who'd come to her aid.

"Yes, it was me."

She didn't want to pursue it. Pulling his face up to hers, she kissed one corner of his mouth. "Let's not talk about it now, darling, please."

"You're trembling."

"Delayed reaction, I guess." A nervous little laugh bubbled up from her throat. "In five years with the Border Patrol, I never once had to draw my weapon. Then I met you, and it's been one gunfight after another." She tugged at his shoulders, drawing him up onto the bed with her, and kissed him again. "You're trouble, Mr. Devlin. Nothing but trouble."

Unbuttoning her trench coat and laying it aside, he slipped first one hand and then the other under her sweater, tenderly caressing her rib cage, working his way higher until his fingers were grazing the undersides of her breasts. She could feel the chill of metal against her bare flesh, and she realized he still was wearing the handcuff she'd clamped on him when he opened the door to greet her.

The joke had gone on long enough.

Fumbling for her purse beside her on the bed, she groped for the key, then unlocked the handcuff and tossed it aside. Her lips moved away from his, brushed across his cheek, then settled on one ear. "I don't think we really need the bracelets anymore," she murmured, nuzzling him.

"We never did, Tally. You captured my heart and soul the day we met."

Again she laughed, lightly this time. "The poet I can handle. It's the other side of you I have trouble with, Raul." She closed her eyes. "Do that some more. Please..."

Pushing up her sweater, he pressed his face to her breasts, and his tongue began tracing a message all its own. "I love you, Tally," he said, his breath tickling her flesh as he spoke the words. He raised his head and looked up at her. "And that's not just the poet who's saying so."

She nudged his head back down between her breasts and ran her fingers through his hair. "Don't talk, Raul. Just make love to me."

His arms circled under her, holding her tightly as he rolled over on the bed until she was on top of him. Only then did she reopen her eyes, looking down at him, wanting him more than ever.

She smiled and reached down to take off her boots. "If I were any sort of woman, I'd go into the bathroom and get out of the rest of these wet things and slip into a clinging negligee and douse myself with cologne and..."

He smiled back. "If you were any other sort of woman, you wouldn't be the woman I love."

Tally snuggled down and kissed him again on the mouth, and as their parted lips joined, their tongues probing, she could feel his hands slide up under her skirt and begin to tease down her bikini briefs. She wriggled about to help him, shuddering with anticipation at the softness of his touch.

Before she realized it, the two of them had become one, untroubled by the clothing they still wore, sharing a delicious ecstasy, whose sensual rhythms grew in intensity with every passing second. They clutched at one another, continuing to kiss as their combined passion flamed in the hungry, moaning fury of fulfillment.

Later, happy, satiated, Tally pushed herself a bit away from Raul and whispered his name.

He said something, but said it too softly for her to understand.

"Raul, you know what I'd like to do? I'd like to run off and find a desert island somewhere and pretend there's no one else in the world except you and me. I'd like to forget that any of this has happened."

"Any of this?"

"Except for these last few minutes."

He rolled onto his side, moving her with him, and cradled her head in his arms. "I'm supposed to be the poet, my dear, while you're the hardheaded pragmatist." He blew softly against the side of her neck, under her ear. "You've managed to get our roles reversed."

"I'm in love with you, Raul Devlin. I want to be with you. I want you safe."

"That's very sweet of you, but the fact is that the two of us are on a collision course—"

"We've already collided, darling. Or haven't you been paying attention?"

He chuckled. "I have indeed, and someday perhaps we can find that desert island. But at the moment..." He sat up, swung his legs off the bed, and leaned over to reach his pants on the floor. "Are you sure you weren't followed here?"

She reached out for his hand. "Isn't it a little late to worry about that?"

He raised her fingers to his lips and kissed them. "Not at all. You give me that much more reason to want to go on living. And if I'm going to go on living, I have to know what the other side is up to."

He got up and walked to the window, parting the thick draperies just enough to look outside.

"I wasn't followed," she said, smoothing out her wool skirt, then settling back on the pillow and clasping her hands behind her neck.

He turned away from the window and faced her. His handsome face was a mask of grim determination. "Tally, I want you to do something for me."

"What?"

"Undress."

She raised up and stared at him. "Just like that? I mean, we—"

"Just do it."

"Really, Raul, I—"

"Take off all your clothes."

"But—"

"Please do it. For me."

"All right." Sitting down on the edge of the bed, she tugged off her knee-length wool socks, then stood up again and unzipped her skirt, letting it fall to the floor by her feet.

"My panties are in there somewhere," she said, motioning sheepishly to the tumbled bedspread.

"The sweater, if you please."

She pulled off the bulky knit, then dropped the bra that was dangling loosely from her shoulders. With a toss of her head to shake her long, auburn hair from her face, she sat down again on the edge of the bed, demurely folding her arms across her chest. "Your turn," she said, "but if you want to know the truth, this hardly seems all that sexy."

"You're the sexiest woman I've ever met, Tally, but sex has absolutely nothing to do with this," he said, picking up her sweater and examining it carefully, his fingers tracing the hems. He dropped the sweater onto the bed, then checked her skirt, socks and boots, and finally her trench coat, giving it the closest scrutiny of all.

Tally rummaged around for her panties and bra. "You might as well be thorough," she said, handing him her wispy underthings.

Raul grinned. "I think we can safely cross those off the list."

Her eyes narrowed as she studied him. "Do you mind telling me what you're looking for?"

"A homing device of some sort."

She gasped. "You don't think that I—"

He shook his head quickly. "No, sweetheart, I don't believe you've betrayed me, not intentionally. But I *do* suspect that someone—undoubtedly Abrahamson—has planted a tiny piece of equipment somewhere among your belongings.''

''No way! He's never had the opportunity.''

''Opportunity is something one creates for oneself. It would have taken Abrahamson only a second to drop an electronic bug in your things.'' He turned, went to the window and peeked out again. ''You remember that big Chevrolet wagon that followed us up from New Mexico? I saw it pull up and park across the street from the police station when you were walking in with Valdez. I looked inside the wagon and found a tracking receiver. My guess is that the receiver has been locked in on you—on whatever device they planted on you—from the very beginning.''

Throwing her arms above her head, Tally twirled about in her nakedness. It annoyed her that he suspected she'd allowed herself to be used, however unwittingly. If he loved her, surely he had more respect for her ability than that. ''All right, take a good look,'' she said angrily. ''I'm not wired.''

He stepped up to her and put his arms around her.

''You have a magnificent body, my love.''

''I don't feel magnificent. I feel like an insect under a laboratory microscope.''

He gave her a quick kiss on the cheek. ''Better get dressed.'' He leaned over the bed and picked up her purse. ''May I?''

''Why not?'' she said, her anger subsiding as she gathered up her things. ''I think we've progressed beyond the point of having any secrets from one another.''

Raul dumped the contents of the purse onto the bed and poked through them. When he was finished, he reached into his pocket and brought out the ballpoint pen, lipstick and notepad he'd taken from her to prevent her from leaving a message in the service station rest room at Chama. He added the pen, lipstick and notepad to the pile on the bed, and then turned his attention to Tally's carryall.

He found the homing device wedged into a narrow slit in an inside seam of the first pocket he checked. The device, cased in black plastic, was about an inch square and less than a sixteenth of an inch thick.

"You know, it's truly amazing what they can do with microchips these days," he commented, holding out the device for Tally to see. "Any idea who might have planted it?"

She took it between thumb and forefinger and peered at the deceptively innocent looking thing. "It had to have been Ybarra," she said. "He came to my room in Albuquerque, looking for Abrahamson." She shuddered as she remembered the encounter. "All he had to do was home in on this and he'd know exactly where I was?"

"The device has a limited range—a few miles at best. But if he knew which way we were headed, no problem. When he got in the general vicinity, he could easily pinpoint your location."

If he knew which way we were headed . . .

Great!

Tally handed him back the homing device. "Raul, I have a confession to make," she said sheepishly.

He smiled. "You want to tell me about the message you left for him in Albuquerque—the one you wrote in lipstick and left in the trunk of your car?"

She stared at him. "You knew?"

"I guessed." He glanced at the contents of her purse on the bed. "When I looked at that lipstick, I noticed the tip was mashed. You haven't had the lipstick out since we left Albuquerque, my dear, and if you had you're hardly a sloppy person—you wouldn't have handled it that way. Conclusion—you used the lipstick, probably when we were sitting in the dark in that van, to write a note. I should have suspected something when you insisted on going back to your car to get your bag out of the trunk. That's when you left the note, isn't it?"

She nodded.

"What did it say?"

"Just one word—Denver." She looked at him. "I'm sorry, Raul. At the time, it seemed the right thing to do."

He shrugged. "What's done is done. You have your job, and I have mine."

Tally zipped up her skirt, then sat down on the bed and put on her socks and boots. "It proves one thing," she said. "Abrahamson is working hand in glove with the Protectors. I mean, the Protectors had the tracking unit in their car. And—" She looked up at him. "We've got to get out of here."

He smiled. "We've got some breathing room. I told you that I found the receiving unit in the wagon? I smashed it."

"Raul, you said that you saw the Suburban pull up while I was going into the police station with Valdez?"

He nodded.

"But there were two other men there on the steps waiting for us! They were in front of us, not behind us! Don't you see, Raul? There were two teams of Protectors looking for us!"

Before he could respond, the phone rang and he snatched up the receiver. He listened, then said, "You've been very kind and I appreciate it. Perhaps I can repay you someday."

He hung up and turned to Tally. "Is your offer still good? I mean, the two of us working together?"

"I thought we'd already sealed the partnership." She got to her feet and repacked her purse. "Who was that on the phone? Your distant early-warning system?"

"It was. A couple of unsavory-looking men came around asking questions. It took you fifteen minutes to run me down after leaving that place where I first checked in. It shouldn't take them any longer than that to show up here. I suggest we be on our way."

Tally went to the window and looked out at the blizzard. "We're not going to get very far in this."

Raul put on his parka and opened the front door. "We don't have any choice."

IT WAS ALMOST ONE in the morning when they arrived in Colorado Springs, after using Tally's Border Patrol credentials to hitch rides north from Pueblo aboard a succession of highway-department snowplows assigned to clear the interstate. Tossing down her canvas carryall containing her uniform and the change of clothing she'd bought in Albuquerque, Tally jumped from the cab of the plow and into Raul's outstretched arms. "It's taken us four hours to travel forty miles," she said. "I think we've seen the last of the Protectors. Even if they suddenly sprouted wings, they wouldn't be going anywhere in this."

Raul hugged her. "I told you we'd make a great team."

Tally smiled at the pressure of his arms around her waist. It was a comfortable sort of pressure, gentle yet solidly reassuring. But she knew the snowplow operator was watching them, and in a few hours, their pursuers would be questioning the man, trying to pick up their trail. With the highway between Colorado Springs and Pueblo closed, the Protector teams in Pueblo wouldn't be able to move in on them, but they could call Denver to have someone pick up the trail at that end. The Protectors seemed to have resources that just wouldn't quit.

She picked up her carryall. "We'd better let this fellow get back to work," she said. She looked up at the cab of the plow and waved, then turned and, taking Raul's hand, led him into a nearby coffee shop. "He said that the highway between here and Pueblo won't be open until tomorrow afternoon at the earliest. We can either stay here in Colorado Springs tonight, or we can try to rent a car and drive on up to Denver. Neither of us has had much sleep lately, so it might be a good idea to stay here."

Despite the late hour, the coffee shop was doing a brisk business with southbound motorists stranded by the blizzard that had swept down over the Rockies. They managed to find an unoccupied table in back, and Raul ordered coffee.

"The interstate is open to Denver," he said, keeping his voice low to avoid being overheard by the other diners. "It's only another sixty miles north, but the more distance we can put between ourselves and our friends, the better."

Tally studied him. There were dark rings under his eyes, and his normally healthy complexion had taken on a gray cast. He was practically out on his feet, she knew. He'd been on the run constantly since El Paso, and he hadn't slept in at least three nights. "Raul," she asked softly, "why are you doing this?"

Raul smiled patiently. "Because I have to. It's as simple as that."

"Why do you have to?" Tally persisted. "You left that hospital in Mexico City with a new face and a whole new identity. You have connections, money, imagination, talent. You could have gone anywhere in the world, and no one would have been able to find you. But as soon as you set out to find Fuentes, you became a marked man."

A sadness crept into his eyes, which were reddened by sleeplessness. "I would have been a marked man if I'd done what you suggest," he corrected her. "I would have marked myself as a coward and a deserter, and I couldn't bring myself to do that."

"What will you do when you find Fuentes?"

"Take him home, of course. There are important elections coming up in February, and the crusade that Fuentes led for so long is foundering. The Movement no longer has a focal point. Without Dr. Fuentes at the helm, it's fast becoming a lost cause."

Tally looked across the room, avoiding his eyes, fearful of what they might yet reveal. She wanted to believe him, but she also wanted to know the truth. "You were listening. You heard what Olivera said. Some people think you double-crossed the Movement—that you set up Fuentes for assassination, but it backfired."

Raul shrugged off the accusation. "Perhaps they'll think otherwise if I return with him. Have you considered that possibility?"

"Do you know where to find him?"

"Not exactly. Dr. Fuentes has gone into hiding, cutting off contact with almost all of his former associates, not knowing who to trust. Olivera told me that he'd spent a month or so in a hospital in Denver, under an assumed name, but that he was discharged a few weeks go. Olivera said he understood Dr. Fuentes is now recuperating at a friend's ranch somewhere in the mountains of northern Colorado or southern Wyoming. Olivera was going to try to get the exact location from a contact in California and pass on the information to me when I called him tonight. Now, though . . ." He let his words trail off.

"In Albuquerque, you told me you needed two days' breathing room," Tally recalled. "You've—"

"I said three days at the most," Raul cut in.

"All right, three days. You've already used one day. It seems to me you've got an awful lot of territory to cover in the next forty-eight hours."

Raul cocked his head questioningly. "I don't suppose you'd care to give me an extension?"

"I can't, Raul! I'm already sticking my neck out for you, and who knows what Abrahamson's going to do when he catches up with us. Besides, we've got Blaine Murchison after us now. Blaine might not be the most sensitive man in the world, but he *is* an experienced investigator."

"Is he the one who came running up to you outside the police station in Pueblo?"

Tally nodded.

"Do you like him?"

"We've been friends for years."

"Were you ever more than that?"

"Why do you ask?"

"I saw him try to kiss you."

"We used to date."

"Have you slept with him?"

Tally glanced at him. "Would it make any difference—between us, I mean—if I said that I had?"

He smiled. "None whatsoever. But it would tell me something about the man. Remember what I said about knowing your enemy?"

"I don't understand."

"Simply this. If Blaine Murchison figures he owns you, he's going to act accordingly—not with cool, objective detachment. Knowing that, I'm better able to predict how he might react in a given situation."

Again Tally looked at him. *Yes, we have slept together, but no, Blaine Murchison doesn't own me. He never has, and he never will.* "It's been over for a long time," she said.

"That answers my question." He finished his coffee and signaled the waitress to bring the check. "We'd best be on our way, Tally. We've got a lot to do in the next two days." He put a five-dollar bill on the table, pushed back his chair and stood up. "Wait here. I'll find a phone and see what I can do about renting a car."

"I'll go with you," Tally said, picking up her purse and carryall.

He laughed. "You don't trust me, *migra*?"

"Whatever gave you that idea? And stop calling me *migra*..."

TALLY YAWNED and rolled down the driver's side window a few inches, letting the cold night air splash across her face. It was all she could do to stay awake, but stay awake she must. What little time they had left was fast running out, and there was so much to do.

She'd insisted on taking over the driving so that Raul could get some sleep, but he'd hardly closed his eyes.

She kept a close watch on the rearview mirror, but there were no lights in sight. They had the highway to themselves.

For the moment.

"You know," Raul said, sitting up straight and stretching, "you and I are hopeless romantics."

"Speak for yourself."

"We are," he insisted. "We've convinced ourselves we can do the impossible when reason tells us otherwise. We gamble on faith, not on fact—you even more than I, if that's possible. I risk only my life, you your whole future. Consorting with a fugitive is hardly appropriate conduct for a prospective attorney, much less a police officer sworn to uphold the law."

She laughed. "Are you trying to get rid of me, Raul? It won't work."

"You ought to think about it carefully, you know. Your friend Abrahamson is a vengeful man. When—"

"He's not my friend. He's a government agent who's gone sour. I'm going to find a way to put him behind bars. You know what he's done."

"Certainly I know. But proving it in a court of law is something else. You don't have any hard evidence, and thus far Abrahamson seems to have covered his tracks—even having himself shot in the shoulder to throw off suspicion."

"We don't know that for sure," Tally pointed out.

"No, we don't. But it fits. The point is, when all this is over, however it comes out, Abrahamson will still be a force to reckon with. He'll still be in government, and chances are he'll do everything in his power to destroy you. And as for Blaine Murchison, his pride has been wounded because he believes I've stolen you from him, and that makes him all the more dangerous."

Suddenly Tally felt cold. She rolled up the window. "Let's cross that bridge when we come to it," she said.

There were so many bridges yet to cross.

Ahead, the lights of Colorado's sprawling capital glistened dully in the pre-dawn blackness. The moon and stars had vanished behind the clouds that were shifting northward with the advancing front, and Tally knew they'd left

Colorado Springs none too soon. Within the hour, she guessed, another blinding blizzard would have engulfed the segment of interstate they'd just traveled.

Traffic picked up as they approached the city, but there was no sign that any of the other drivers were paying special attention to them. Even so, Tally had pulled off the highway several times to satisfy herself that they weren't being followed. She probably was being overly cautious, she knew, but the Protectors were everywhere. Raul had managed to destroy one of their tracking receivers, and he'd dumped the homing device in a trash can at the motel in Pueblo. But how could they know Abrahamson and his sinister friends weren't using even more sophisticated equipment? After all, as Tally had pointed out, there'd been two teams at the police station to intercept him. It was logical to assume the second team had been staked out in Pueblo, stationed there all along to join in the pursuit.

Tally shook her head in an effort to clear away the cobwebs. She couldn't let herself yield to the lure of sleep. All they needed was another accident to slow them up. She rubbed at her eyes. "What time is it?"

Raul checked his watch. "Almost five. Want me to take over now?"

"No, I'm all right."

"We'd better stop at the first decent-looking motel we see. Neither of us is going to be much good if we don't get some sleep."

Tally glanced in the rearview mirror. "I'm not so sure that's a good idea. Once the Protectors get to Colorado Springs, it won't take them long to find out that we rented this car, and then they'll know what to look for again."

"Have you got a better idea?"

Tally thought about it. "Maybe. Find a pay phone and let me check the phone book."

Thirty minutes later, Tally was pressing a button over the speaker box in the foyer of a high-rise apartment building on Denver's Capitol Hill.

It took several minutes, but finally they heard the slurred and sleepy voice of a woman say, "Who's there?"

"Karen? It's Tally Gordon."

"Tally?" There was a long pause, then the voice brightened, became more alert. "I don't believe it! Tally—you mean you're here in Denver?"

"I'm here, Karen, courtesy of a friendly blizzard," Tally assured her. "And I brought someone with me. Would you mind if we come up?"

"By all means!" The electronically controlled lock on the glass inner door of the foyer clicked. "I'm on the tenth floor, just down the hall from the elevator—apartment ten-twenty."

"We'll be right up. Ah, Karen..."

"Yes?"

"Are we interrupting anything? You don't have someone with you, do you?"

Karen laughed merrily. "You're not interrupting a thing—dammit. Come on up."

Tally and Raul walked back to the elevator, and Raul asked, "A friend of yours, I take it?"

Tally nodded. "An old, old friend."

He smiled. "She sounds like a real femme fatale."

"Then you better watch yourself, Mr. Devlin...."

Karen Yarborough met them in the hallway just outside the elevator. She was a slim, attractive woman about Tally's age, and she wore her dark hair in a braided ponytail that reached almost to the knotted belt of her white, quilted robe. She was sitting in a wheelchair, and she was wearing dark glasses set in big, round frames.

She raised her arms to give Tally a hug and a kiss on the cheek, and then reached out to shake hands with Raul, whom Tally hadn't yet introduced. Swiveling her wheelchair around, she led them to her apartment.

"Forgive me," she apologized, "but the place is a mess." She groped for a light switch at the end of a hallway leading to a small, but comfortable-looking living room that was stacked high with books, tape cassettes and papers. "The semester's almost over, and I've been up to my kazoo with papers to grade."

"Karen teaches English Lit at Metro State College," Tally explained. "We went through UTEP together."

"UTEP?" Raul asked.

"The University of Texas in El Paso," Karen said. "Didn't Tally tell you? She and I were sorority sisters. I was the swinger, and she was the serious student who was always burying herself in her books. So who ended up the college professor, and who was it who went on to break hearts right and left? One guess—that's all you get."

"Broken hearts?" Raul said with a mischievous grin directed at Tally. "'Faith, 'tis an unseemly question to ask a man who knows of naught but broken heads.'"

Karen laughed and reached out for his hands. She patted them. "Any man who knows G. K. Chesterton can't be all bad, Tally."

"Raul's a poet," Tally said. "And you know what *they're* like."

"Don't listen to the child, Mistress Karen," Raul said in a rich brogue that rolled effortlessly from his lips. "Sure and she's convinced there's something the matter with my meter."

Karen waved them to a seat on the couch. "I got my Ph.D. with a dissertation on the modern Irish poets. Are you somebody I should remember?"

"Alas, no, but would that it were so."

"But you *are* Irish, and you *are* a poet?"

"No, and yes. The Devlin side of the family is from Ireland, but I'm a native of Argentina—and a simple scribbler of high hopes and only mediocre talent."

Karen leaned forward in her wheelchair, cocking her head, but to listen, not look. "Raul Devlin. *The* Raul Devlin?"

"I don't know about *the*, but that's my name."

"I looked up your work last summer. You were reported missing after some sort of trouble in Guatemala, and several colleagues of mine told me about your writing. It's impressive—very impressive." She turned to Tally. "Aren't you glad now you dumped that rednecked cowboy who always used to call you? I mean, this man you have in tow now is in the forefront of a new wave of epic modernism. His imagery of war and death is all the talk of the literary world." She wheeled her chair toward the kitchen. "Let me put some coffee on and you can tell me about your latest work."

Tally stood up. "Karen, we're really tired. Would it be possible to bunk with you tonight—what's left of the night, that is?"

"Why, of course! If you don't mind sharing the couch, that is—it pulls out to make a double bed." Her hand went quickly to her mouth, as if she'd caught herself saying something she shouldn't have said. "I mean, I assume that the two of you are..."

"Are what?" Raul said.

"I'm afraid we are," Tally said.

Actually, she wasn't at all afraid. Not in the least. Not anymore.

TALLY LAY SNUGGLED in Raul's arms, the blanket pulled up over their heads, her face on his bare chest, listening to his heart beat, wishing that the coming dawn would skip a day, two days even.

"How long has she been blind?" Raul whispered.

"Six years," Tally said softly. "She had a skiing accident while she was in graduate school. She's also paralyzed from the waist down."

"She's a very nice woman, and she has excellent taste in poetry."

Tally smiled. "If I weren't so sleepy, I'd be jealous. Karen has been exposed to your poems, and I haven't. I feel she knows you better than I do."

He kissed the top of her head. "Not really, my love."

"We must sit down sometime and have a serious discussion about that imagery she mentioned."

"That we will. Karen's quite a woman. She seems like a very determined lady."

Tally yawned and wriggled closer to him. "So am I, Raul. I'm determined not to let anything happen to you."

"How can it? I have the luck of the Irish on my side." He began stroking her hair thoughtfully. "Do you think it was wise coming here?"

"What do you mean?"

"The last thing in the world I want to do is visit my troubles on someone else. With that homing device gone, I don't think there's any way the Protectors can trace us to this apartment, but I hate to take a chance with your friend."

"I thought about that. But this is a high-rise building. Even if they are able to track us, there's no way they can pinpoint what apartment we're in. If we see them outside in the morning, we can phone for help."

"Oh? And just who do we phone? Chances are, Abrahamson already has the local authorities on the lookout for us. Face it. We're strictly on our own."

Raul was right, she knew, and there was no getting around it. They'd made their choice, and they had to accept the consequences.

They were outlaws.

Chapter Twelve

From the tenth-floor window, Tally and Raul looked out into the first flurries of the approaching blizzard and saw Karen roll her wheelchair to the curb in front of the apartment building, awaiting the van that would come to take her to her nine o'clock class at Metro State. Karen was bundled up in a beaver coat, a bright yellow muffler around her throat and a plaid blanket covering her legs. A heavy canvas book bag was balanced on her lap.

"Truly an amazing women," Raul said, sipping at his second cup of coffee. "She's unable to see and unable to walk, and yet life goes on."

Tally put her arm around his waist, leaning her head against his shoulder. "As you remarked last night, she's very determined."

"How on earth does she manage to grade papers?"

"I asked her about that when she was fixing breakfast. She told me she has TAs come in and read the students' papers to her while she records them on tape."

"TAs?"

"Teaching assistants. You know, graduate students who want to go on and become instructors themselves."

A red-and-white van pulled up to the curb. The driver got out and slid open a wide side door, then pressed a button that lowered an electric lift platform. As Karen maneuvered her wheelchair onto the platform, she tilted her face up toward the tenth floor and gave Tally and Raul a little wave.

Tally waved back, glancing nervously up and down the street to see if anyone might be paying special attention to her friend. Tally had been having second thoughts about coming here, knowing full well that Karen's life would be in danger if the Protectors found out she'd been helping Raul. It wouldn't matter to them that Karen was a blind paraplegic. They'd torture her until they found out what they wanted to know or were convinced she didn't know anything useful. Tally shivered at the thought, hating Abrahamson more than ever.

A minute later, the van pulled away from the curb and headed north. It turned at the intersection half a block north and disappeared into traffic.

Tally gave a sigh of relief and turned away from the window. "It's going to be a long day," she said, "so we'd better—"

She stopped, aware that something was wrong, but not knowing what.

Raul was still standing at the window, his gaze locked on the man who'd gotten out of a dark blue Mercedes parked across the street and midway down the block. The man was wearing a black overcoat and was holding a black hat in one hand. The angle and the falling snow prevented them from getting a good look at his face, but there was one thing about him that was clearly distinctive: a fringe of gray hair, devoid of sideburns, that circled his bald pate like a Roman emperor's crown.

"He reminds me of someone," Tally said, sizing him up, trying to remember where she'd seen him.

The man put on his hat and strode briskly down the sidewalk, slowing momentarily as he came abreast of the Ford they'd rented in Colorado Springs. Clearly he was more than routinely interested in the Ford.

"He should," Raul muttered. "It's Ybarra."

Tally gasped, feeling her skin crawl at the mention of the name. She hadn't liked Simon Ybarra when she'd first seen him, and she didn't like him now. Even from a distance, Ybarra had an aura of evil. "I don't think I've ever seen him without a hat and dark glasses. How did he find us?"

Raul shook his head slowly. "I have no idea. The last time our paths crossed was just outside a small village in northern Guatemala's Huehuetenango province. I was more dead than alive, and I was staring at him down the barrel of this." Raul's right hand came up holding his Beretta pistol. "Ybarra and his men were moving in for the kill, but a Guatemalan army patrol came to our rescue just in time." He paused. "The next thing I knew, I woke up in a hospital in Mexico City."

Tally stepped back from the window, pulling Raul with her. "What do we do now?"

Raul put away his Beretta. "Last night when Karen spoke of that redneck cowboy you used to date, was she referring to Blaine Murchison?"

Tally nodded.

"Does Murchison know that your friend lives here in Denver?"

"I don't think so. No, I'm sure he doesn't. The last time we talked about Karen, she was still in graduate school at the University of Iowa. She didn't even get her job offer at Metro State until last August, and I know I haven't mentioned her to Blaine since then." She looked sharply at Raul. "You don't think he had anything to do with Ybarra's being here, do you?"

Raul shrugged. "You said that Murchison took charge after Abrahamson was shot, so it's possible he's been ordered to cooperate with the Protectors. I don't know." He carried his coffee cup into the kitchen, rinsed it out and placed it on the counter. "Murchison is a straight-arrow type of fellow. It seems more likely that Ybarra himself traced the Ford through the rental agency."

Tally shook her head. "There's no way on earth he could have found us this quickly, not in a city of half a million people."

Raul glanced at her. "Unless they've got yet another bug planted on you somewhere."

Tally fingered the belt of her borrowed robe. She tried to smile, but couldn't bring it off. "I knew there was a reason I didn't get dressed after my shower this morning."

Raul smiled. "No more strip searches, Tally—as pleasant as the prospect might be under other circumstances. But I think we ought to have another look at your carryall."

Tally hauled her bag to the dinette table and unpacked it, then added her skirt, sweater, trench coat and boots to the pile. Raul checked each garment carefully, even her uniform and equipment belt. He reexamined her purse, then made another inspection of the carryall.

"I can't find anything," he said at last, glumly surveying the pile of clothing, "but that doesn't mean it's not there. It could be sewn into a lining I've overlooked." He flicked his head toward the open door leading into Karen's bedroom. "To play safe, do you suppose Karen would mind if you borrowed some of her things to tide you over? The two of you are about the same size."

"I'm sure she wouldn't. We were practically sisters at one time."

Taking her by the shoulders, Raul turned her around and pointed her into the bedroom. "Then go to it, sweetheart. While you change, I'll get on the phone and check in with some contacts here."

Ten minutes later, Tally was back in the living room. She was wearing trim, gray wool slacks and a bulky-knit wool sweater, and she had a knee-length, slate-blue parka draped over her shoulders. Raul was standing at the window, looking down at the street while talking softly on the phone.

Tally sat down at the dinette table and pulled on her wool socks and boots, then transferred the contents of her purse, including her revolver and handcuffs, to the pockets of her parka.

She got up and went to the window and looked down. The Mercedes was still there, but Ybarra was nowhere in sight.

Raul finished his call and hung up the phone. "I suggest we get out of here before Ybarra has a chance to bring in reinforcements." He shrugged into his own parka, then looked thoughtfully at the pile on the dinette table. "It might be a good idea if you packed up everything in that carryall. We'll take it with us."

Tally looked at him. "Why not just leave it here? It'll just slow us up."

Raul began folding the clothes that were spread out on the table. "If they *are* using a homing device and I missed it, I don't want them barging in here and tearing up the place."

Again Tally had visions of Karen being subjected to the Protectors' wrath. "I understand," she said. She understood all too well.

She helped him pack the carryall. "What about the car we rented?"

"My guess is that Ybarra has it staked out, so we'll leave it parked down there. One of us can give the rental agency a call and tell them where to pick it up."

He zipped up the carryall and slung it over his shoulder. "Come on."

They left the apartment, locked the door and started for the elevator. An elderly woman was standing by the elevator door, jabbing at the call button with the rubber tip of her cane. She was clearly irritated.

"Top of the morning," Raul greeted her cheerfully.

The woman glowered at him as if to say, *Who are you and what are you doing here?* She didn't speak.

Raul smiled. "Going out for a walk?"

"I'm going grocery shopping—if this stupid elevator ever comes." She poked again at the call button.

"It must be out of order," Raul observed. Tally could sense a wariness in his tone. "Tell me, have you been waiting long?"

The woman sniffed her displeasure. "A good ten minutes, young man. It's a disgrace. Nothing short of a disgrace. A person pays good money and this is the service she gets!" She lowered the cane and thumped at the call button with the heel of her left hand, looking questioningly over her shoulder at Tally and Raul. "Are you folks visiting someone on this floor?"

Tally glanced around. There were six apartments on the floor, and she suspected that the woman made it a point to know the names and life histories of each and every one of her neighbors.

"No," Raul said quickly. "As a matter of fact, we're staying with some old friends on the fourteenth floor, and we decided to walk down when the elevator wouldn't come."

The woman wasn't buying that. "I saw you come out of ten-twenty—Miss Yarborough's apartment."

Tally spoke up. "We just dropped off a package that had been delivered to our friends' place by mistake."

"Your friends?"

"On fourteen," Raul said.

The woman frowned. "For your information, young man, there are only twelve floors in this building." She took a step back and raised her walking stick and pointed it at him accusingly. "I want to know what you're doing here!"

Raul looked at Tally and slapped the heel of his right hand against his forehead. "No wonder we couldn't find it, dear! We're in the wrong building!" He grabbed Tally's hand and pulled her toward a door under a sign that said, Stairs. "Come along, we mustn't keep our friends waiting. They'll be worried about us."

Inside the stairwell, he pulled out his Beretta. The light and easy banter he'd used with the woman at the elevator was gone. He was all business—cool, calculating and brusque. "I want you to do something for me, Tally."

She stared at him skeptically. "What?"

"I want you to go back to Karen's apartment and lock the door and call the police. Tell them who you are and what's happening. Have them send several cars—fast. We've got problems. Somehow, Ybarra and his people have found a way to block the elevator. They're probably making a floor-by-floor search even now."

Tally leaned over and peered down the stairwell. There was no sign of movement on the lower floors, but that didn't mean anything. The Protectors could be pressed back against the walls, waiting for them to make their move. "What are you going to be doing?"

Raul pulled her away from the railing, then gave her a kiss on the cheek. "I've got an appointment to keep. Now get going and do as I told you."

"Correction," Tally said, drawing her revolver. "If you have an appointment, then I have an appointment, too. We're partners, remember?"

"I don't want to argue."

Tally started down the stairs, pausing on the next landing down to look back at him. "Neither do I, darling. So let's move it, huh?"

"Stubborn, stubborn," he clucked, starting after her. "If you insist on coming, please stay back against the wall. I don't want to give them a clear shot at us up the stairwell."

They moved swiftly and silently, Tally leading the way, both of them pausing briefly on each landing to listen.

On the third-floor landing, Raul caught Tally's arm and held her back. "I'll take the point from here. My guess is that they've got the ground exits covered, and somebody else is working his way down from the top."

"I don't understand," Tally said, catching her breath. "They couldn't have managed all this in the short time since Ybarra pulled up."

"I'm sure they didn't. My guess is they've had the place staked out for hours, and Ybarra deliberately showed himself to draw us out. The tracking device they must be using tells the Protectors that we're somewhere in this building, but they have no way of knowing exactly where. Ybarra probably figured if he let us get a look at him, we'd panic and run and they could grab us." Raul looked around. "I've got an idea. Come on."

Taking her by the hand, he led her into the third-floor corridor and toward the back of the building, where sliding doors opened onto a balcony overlooking the roof of a parking ramp. Raul forced open the doors, stepped out onto the balcony and looked down.

"It's about a ten-foot drop," he observed. "Think you can handle it?"

Tally shoved her revolver into a side pocket of the borrowed parka. "I used to do fourteen- and fifteen-foot long jumps when I was on the girls' track-and-field team in high school."

Raul grinned. "Not bad, my dear. Not exactly an Olympic record, but not bad at all. Do you have any other talents I haven't discovered yet?"

She tapped the tip of his nose with her finger. "I'd rather keep you guessing. I'll go first and show you how it's done."

Stepping out onto the balcony, Tally gauged the distance to the roof of the parking ramp. Then, pitching down her carryall before her, she swung her legs over the iron railing, lowered herself carefully down one of the vertical bars of the railing, and then dropped onto the snow-covered roof, landing with an easy, graceful roll that left her dusted with white.

"Now what?" she asked, after he'd followed her down onto the roof.

Raul held one finger to his lips to signal her to be quiet. Stepping carefully through the snow and keeping low, he worked his way toward the rear of the roof and peered over the wall at the edge. He quickly pulled back.

"There are two of them," he whispered. "They're staked out at both ends of the alley—their cars are blocking both ends."

Tally glanced up at the balcony. It was too high to climb. They were trapped. "Did they see you?"

Raul shook his head. "I don't know. I don't think so, but I don't want to take a chance." He stood up straight and scuffed at the snow by his feet. "There's got to be some sort of a trapdoor here—a way for a maintenance person to climb up and repair the drains when they clog. Let's look around."

The roof was less than forty feet wide and thirty feet long, and it took them only a few minutes to examine it, slapping at likely-looking mounds of snow with their hands and kicking away ice with their feet.

"Here it is!" Tally said, dropping to her hands and knees and trying to get her fingers under the lip of a hinged metal plate about two feet square.

Raul bent down and together they tugged at the door.

It wouldn't budge.

"Keep trying!" Tally urged, taking off her gloves to give her a better grip.

They both strained at the metal plate.

The hinges creaked, then the seal of ice suddenly cracked and the plate swung upward.

Propping the plate open with a steel rod that dangled from a chain connected to the framework of the opening, Raul poked his head down through the opening and looked around. He raised back up. "We must be living right. There's a pickup truck right below us. All we have to do is drop down five or six feet, hot-wire the truck and take off."

Tally stared at him. "That's against the law," she said sharply. "We're in enough trouble already."

Raul looked out at the edge of the roof, and beyond. "You want to take your chances with them?"

"Not really," she admitted. "But there has to be another way."

They lowered themselves onto a stack of canvas tarpaulins on the open bed of the pickup, and Raul reached up and pulled shut the trapdoor. He vaulted to the floor of the parking ramp, then reached up to help Tally with the car-ryall.

"I've thought it over," he said, giving her a hug as he caught her in his arms. "You're right. We won't steal the truck..."

"I'm glad you came to your senses."

"... we'll requisition that little Fiat over there, instead. It'll be much more maneuverable if they come chasing after us."

"No," Tally said adamantly. "We will not requisition anything. I mean it, Raul."

"I'll leave the owner some money, just as I did in So-corro."

Tally remembered the one-hundred-dollar bill Raul had left for her in her Volvo. Abrahamson had pocketed it, and the note Raul had left, as evidence. She wondered if she'd ever get either of them back.

"We'll find another way," she said.

Raul glanced around. "There's a fire-alarm box on the wall over there. We could always pull the handle and try to slip by in the confusion when the fire trucks pull up in front of the building."

Tally sucked in her breath. "Turn in a false alarm? That's even worse!"

"Then you—" He stopped, listened, reached for the pocket in which he placed his Beretta while they were clam-bering down from the roof. "Someone's coming."

They slipped back between two parked cars and crouched low as the door leading into the main apartment building opened. They heard the voices of a man and a woman, and they shifted position to avoid being seen.

The man and woman headed for the pickup and climbed in.

"See what would have happened?" Tally whispered. "That truck would have been on the police hotsheet in no time at all. We'd both be in jail."

Raul grunted. "Your intuition is a marvel to behold. But that still doesn't solve our problem."

Tally raised herself up a bit to get a better look at the pickup. There had to be a way short of stealing. The Texas Bar examiners would take a dim view of a lawyer with grand-theft-auto on her record.

Still, the pickup did offer an opportunity....

"Come on," she said, standing up and taking Raul by the hand. "I've got an idea."

She led him boldly out onto the ramp, waving cheerfully at the middle-aged man behind the steering wheel of the pickup. The man saw them and rolled down his window.

"Hello there," Tally said with a pleasant smile, wishing she could do a better imitation of Raul's lighthearted manner. "You must be our new neighbors."

The blond woman seated beside the driver leaned forward to get a better look at Tally and Raul.

"We're the Shannons," Tally said, giving Raul a nudge to signal him to play along.

"Pleased to meet you," the driver said. "I'm Leonard Walsh and this—" he cocked his thumb at the blond woman "—is Vera. We're just moving into five-oh-three." He smiled ruefully. "We sure picked a crummy day for it, what with this storm moving in."

Vera nodded vigorously, making it clear she couldn't agree more. "If I told him once, I told him a hundred times, we should have hired it done. But no, he had to borrow this awful truck and do it himself."

Leonard gave her a dirty look. "Only three or four more loads, Vera. The money we're saving will buy you a whole new bedroom set."

"I don't need a new bedroom set. I need a new washer and dryer."

Tally glanced at her wristwatch. "I wonder if we could ask a favor of you?"

Leonard and Vera exchanged wary glances.

"Our car won't start," Raul said, turning on the charm as he picked up on Tally's lead, "and we've got a train to meet at Union Station. I wonder if we could hitch a ride downtown to someplace we could pick up a cab?"

Leonard shrugged. "I guess so—if you don't mind riding in back. Your missus can sit up here with us, but three's all the front seat will hold."

"That's very nice of you," Tally spoke up, "but I don't want to crowd you. I'll sit in back with Kevin. We love the fresh air, don't we, darling?"

"Nothing like it for putting roses in your cheeks," Raul said, climbing onto the open bed of the truck and helping Tally up. "If it gets too chilly, we'll just pull one of these tarps over us..."

The tarp went up and over them before the pickup had even left the ramp and entered the alley.

"See," Tally whispered, "where there's a will there's a way. And it's perfectly legal, too."

"If you'll overlook a few fibs."

"Fibs I can handle. Grand-theft-auto is something else, darling."

He kissed her. "I've turned over a new leaf. You're looking at a reformed man."

"Don't change too much. I kind of like the original Devlin."

He pressed two fingers to her lips. "Quiet," he said softly. "We're not out of this yet. We still have to get out of the alley."

The pickup bounced across a pothole, then came to an abrupt halt.

"This is it," Raul murmured. He reached for his Beretta, moving carefully to avoid disturbing the stiff tarp that covered them.

Tally got her own gun out of her purse.

They could hear one of the front doors of the pickup open, could feel the truck balance shift as Leonard stepped out.

Then voices. Muted voices. They couldn't tell at first what was being said.

With his left hand, Raul eased back the tarp a few inches. The voices became clearer.

"You move that thing, or I call a cop!" they heard Leonard say.

"I am sorry, but my car will not start," another voice said. This voice had an accent.

"Then shove it out of the way," Leonard said. "You're blocking traffic."

"You are in a hurry?" The voice seemed to be getting closer.

"You're damned right I'm in a hurry!" Leonard said. "We're moving furniture today, and it's already starting to snow again."

"You are moving, eh?" The voice drew nearer the bed of the pickup. "What are you hauling under that canvas?"

Tally thumbed off the safety of her revolver.

Chapter Thirteen

"None of your business!" Leonard Walsh growled. His voice was becoming louder, more agitated, and they knew he'd stepped in closer to the bed of the pickup as he argued with the man whose car was blocking his way. "I'm going to tell you one more time, Mac. Move that vehicle or— Hey, Vera, honk the horn. I see a police car coming down Thirteenth Avenue. We'll just see what—"

The rest of what Leonard was saying was drowned out in a squawking honk as his wife hammered on the horn.

Tally felt something—a hand?—poke tentatively at the tarp. She tightened her grip on her gun and got ready to jump up.

"That is not necessary," she heard the voice with the accent say. "Let me try once again to see if I can start the car."

"Well, be quick about it," Leonard grumbled. "The little lady and me, we're in a hurry."

The voices faded. Then, in the distance, Tally heard an engine kick over and rev up.

"You had it flooded, Mac," she heard Leonard say. "Now move it, huh?"

The pickup rocked on its springs as Leonard climbed back into the cab. He said something to his wife, then put the truck into gear and drove off.

Tally slipped her revolver back into her purse. "Close," she murmured.

"Too close," Raul agreed, tucking the Beretta into his waistband.

"Do you think they know we're under here?"

"I think we're all right for the moment. I know how the Protectors work. Simon Ybarra calls the shots, and he expects his men to carry out orders without question. He probably told them to block both ends of the alley and not to let anyone out without checking them over. Chances are that goon back there will stay where he is until Ybarra and the others finish making a door-to-door search of the apartment house. By then we'll have had time to cover our tracks."

Tally thought about it. "I'm still worried about Karen. If the Protectors talk to that old woman we ran into at the elevator, she's apt to tell them she saw us leave Karen's apartment. I don't want them to get their hands on her."

Raul pushed back the tarp and raised his head. He looked back the way they'd come, then sat up straight. "All clear," he said. "As far as Karen goes, better give her a call at school and tell her to keep a low profile for the rest of the day. After that, it won't matter."

"What do you mean, it won't matter?"

He put his arm around her and held her close. "I mean after today, I'll either have done what I set out to do or I'll have failed."

His tone made it clear he had no intention of failing.

Fifteen minutes later, they were getting out of a taxi and walking into the grimy, gray railroad terminal at the foot of Seventeenth Street.

"Make your call to Karen and then we'll check your bag and see about renting another car," Raul said as he slung the carryall strap over his shoulder. "I've got a lead and I need your help in developing it."

Tally laughed. "Anytime, partner. Just as long as it doesn't involve stealing..."

FOR THE FIRST FEW MINUTES, a plump and smiling Pablo Cordova was the perfect host. He greeted Raul at the front door of his stately brick home on Montview Boulevard, throwing his arms around his visitor in the traditional Latin man-to-man hug. Gushing platitudes, Cordova escorted him into the walnut-paneled library where, without taking his eyes off Raul, he airily waved away a white-jacketed houseboy who'd come into the hall from the rear of the house. What an undreamed-of pleasure, he said, to finally meet a gentleman he'd heard so much about! The stories of Raul's talents were legend, nothing short of legend. It was a bit early, true, but could he offer Raul a drink, perhaps a bite of lunch? Anything—anything at all.

When Raul was comfortably seated in a leather lounge chair, hands folded upon his lap, Cordova walked casually to the massive carved desk at one end of the library and took out a big, black automatic gun and pointed it at his guest.

Pablo Cordova was no longer the host. He was now the captor and, Raul sensed, the self-designated executioner.

"I advise you not to try anything, Major Devlin," Cordova said in a low, nervous tone, but one that was nevertheless sharply determined. "I grant you that I am hardly an expert shot, but at this distance even I cannot miss."

Raul's expression revealed not the slightest surprise at Cordova's sudden change in attitude. Slowly and thoughtfully, he studied the man and the gun he was holding. Cordova's pudgy hands were trembling and his lips were drawn tight beneath his thick, drooping mustache. He was an obviously frightened man, and Raul knew he had to handle him carefully if his plan were to succeed.

Raul smiled reassuringly. "You have my solemn promise, *señor*. I shall not move a muscle."

"Very wise, very wise indeed. Tell me, major, are you carrying a weapon of any sort?" He wagged the barrel of his gun as if it were an admonishing finger. "No, do not reach for it. Just tell me."

"I come unarmed, *señor*."

Cordova's eyes narrowed. "Why is it that I do not believe you?"

"You're welcome to search me," Raul said, mentally congratulating himself for having had the foresight to leave his Beretta with Tally.

Cordova smiled. "*¡Dios mio!* You think I would even consider getting close to you? Do you take me for an idiot? Your reputation as an expert in unarmed combat is widely known, major!"

Raul still didn't move. "However well-intentioned, it is not necessary to address me as major. I'm a mere poet, *señor*. My days of soldiering are behind me. I'm interested in ballads, not bullets."

Cordova drew in a breath and held it, as if screwing up his courage to do something he found patently distasteful. "Ever since you phoned, I have been wondering whether I should kill you the minute you stepped inside this house or let you suffer as Federico Fuentes has suffered these many months." He eased himself into a chair behind the desk and propped his elbows upon the desk to steady his wavering aim.

"And why should you want to kill me?" Raul inquired in a silky, unruffled voice.

The ripples of fat in Cordova's jowls tightened. "You betrayed Dr. Fuentes. Do not deny it. You arranged to hand him over to the Protectors, and your treachery very nearly cost him his life."

Raul shook his head slowly. "I would remind you, *señor*, that the ambush in Huehuetenango very nearly cost both of us our lives," he said gently, feeling a twinge in the scar along his right side as he remembered how the rocket shells had left their caravan a tangle of fire-scorched wrecks. "I was sitting alongside Dr. Fuentes at the time. You have only to ask him—he'll tell you."

"I have already asked him, major, and if it is any consolation in these, your final minutes, Dr. Fuentes remains convinced of your innocence." Cordova sighed. "The man is a brilliant statesman, truly one of the world's great conciliators but, alas, he is woefully naive when it comes to perceptions of loyalty. But I, being a hardheaded businessman, know better. I have kept up my Central American contacts since moving to the United States ten years ago. And my contacts tell me you were seen in the company of known members of the Protectors on at least three separate occasions before that episode in Huehuetenango. I have proof, major—eyewitnesses to your perfidy."

Raul hunched his shoulders in a shrug that said his host was talking nonsense. "Your contacts aren't very knowledgeable, *señor*. It was more like six or seven occasions. Would you like for me to enumerate them?"

Cordova straightened in his chair, his gun hand steadier now, as if his resolve had been bolstered by Raul's words. "You admit it then, eh, major?"

"I admit that I called on certain of the Protectors in both Guatemala City and in Tegucigalpa to warn them that any further attempt on Dr. Fuentes's life would backfire on them. I told the Protectors—Simon Ybarra himself, in fact—that I'd use whatever means I could to destroy them and the people they work for."

"Oh? And just who do they work for?"

Raul frowned. "I didn't come here this morning to give you a lecture on Central American politics, *señor*. You know as well as I do that the Protectors are nothing more than a gang of sadistic hoodlums used by certain vested interests who see change of any sort as a threat."

"Did Dr. Fuentes know of these approaches to the Protectors?"

"Of course not. I didn't want to worry him."

Cordova grunted. "I still do not believe you, major. Where have you been these past six months?"

"I spent part of the time in Mexico City."

"Part of the time, eh? What about the rest of the time?"

"I have been searching for Dr. Fuentes."

"Why have you come here to Denver? To this house?"

"I have heard Dr. Fuentes is hiding out at a ranch you own in this part of the country. I want you to take me to him."

"So that you can finish the job you started in Huehuetenango?"

"So I can take him home. As you know, *señor*, there are regional elections scheduled for February, and the Movement needs him."

Cordova rolled back his chair and stood up, his gun still pointed at Raul. "You are not carrying a weapon, eh?"

"I am not," Raul said, lowering his eyes to glance surreptitiously at his wristwatch. He'd been in the Cordova house less than fifteen minutes, and it seemed like hours.

"As it happens, I have a second gun," Cordova said. As he spoke, he removed his left hand from the butt of the gun he was holding and reached into his desk and brought out an old, military-style Colt automatic. Still without taking his eyes off Raul, he slipped out the magazine, then drew back the slide, ejecting the bullet that was in the chamber. "Here," he said, tossing the Colt to Raul with an underarm motion.

The gun thunked to the thickly carpeted floor at Raul's feet.

"Pick it up, major."

Raul knew exactly what Cordova had in mind. He shook his head. "I can read you like a book, *señor*. You want my fingerprints on that weapon so that when the police come you can tell them you shot me in self-defense when I tried to kill you. Sorry, but it won't work. The police would never accept your story. They'd want to know what I was doing with an empty gun."

Cordova stood up and came around from behind the desk. The room was cool, but there was perspiration on his forehead. "You are being difficult, major. I'll reload the gun after I do what I have to do."

Raul laughed dryly. "Have you ever tried to pry something from the hand of a dying man, *señor*? No, I don't think you have. It's quite difficult—I know, I've had to do it. Besides, the police would routinely run a check on the serial number of the gun and trace it back to you."

"I'll take my chances with the police. Now pick it up."

Raul still didn't move, didn't even blink. He kept his eyes trained on the hands that held the gun. "All I ask is that you put me in touch with Dr. Fuentes."

"I shall count to three, major . . ."

"What about your houseboy, *señor*? How will you explain things to him? After all, he saw you greet me at the front door like a long-lost brother."

"The young man is loyal," Cordova sniffed. "And that is more than I can say for you." He glanced down at the Colt. "Pick up the gun."

"What about the others in the house?"

"My family is away, thanks be to God. I am going to start counting. One . . ."

SIMON YBARRA WAS FURIOUS. He was surrounded by imbeciles! Not one of them was capable of thinking for himself. It had to be the soft lives they led here in the United States. They were not only *bobos*, but lazy, as well.

Ybarra had come north with only one trusted underling, Hans Uhlmann. He'd called upon the others as needed in New Mexico and here in Colorado. The others were blood-oath members of the secret society known as the Protectors, but they now lived and worked in the United States and were mere part-timers, as it were, kept in line only by the knowledge they had friends and relatives in Central America who would suffer if they forgot where their loyalties lay.

"We have checked the apartment house from top to bottom," Hans Uhlmann reported. "An old woman saw them come out of an apartment and start down the stairs. She knew they didn't belong there."

"Did you talk to the tenant of the apartment?"

Uhlmann shook his head. "She is a college professor—the blind woman you saw leave earlier. I had someone go by the college, but they must have gotten word to her. She canceled her classes and is nowhere to be found."

Ybarra reached for the car phone mounted between the front seats of the Mercedes. "They had to have been hiding in that pickup truck," he muttered. "Find it!"

"As you wish." Uhlmann started to get out of the car, then looked back at his superior. "It would be helpful if we had some cooperation from the local authorities. This is a big city."

"I will make a call," Ybarra assured him. "In the meantime, leave some men here and start searching. Time is of the essence."

Uhlmann hesitated. "You have not forgotten, have you? Devlin is mine."

"I have not forgotten," Ybarra said. "Now get started. I will make the call..."

He picked up the receiver and tapped out a number.

RAUL LEANED FORWARD, his fingers hovering over the pistol Cordova had thrown to him. If he moved fast enough, perhaps he could snatch up the Colt and hurl it at Cordova. The man was fat and slow and, by his own admission, not a very good shot. Still, Cordova could hardly miss at this range.

He hesitated. "If I am to die, *señor*, do me the courtesy of letting me know that Dr. Fuentes is safe."

"Rest assured, major, he is beyond your reach."

"And where is that?"

"He is a guest at my ranch in Larimer County, in the high mountains."

"Will you not phone him and tell him that I'm here?"

"Impossible! The phone lines have been down for a week as a result of heavy snow. Besides, Dr. Fuentes would not understand." He squinted as he sighted down the barrel of his gun. "I am counting, major. Two. Pick up the gun, I say!"

Raul knew he had to keep Cordova talking long enough for Tally to make her move. It was too risky otherwise. Not only would he die, but he would die without having carried out his mission. "If you kill me, I won't be able to tell you about the plot I've discovered."

"What plot?" Cordova snapped.

"The Protectors are already here in Denver. I saw Ybarra this morning on the street."

Cordova took one step back and rested his bottom on the edge of the desk. He kept his gun trained on Raul. "The Protectors are here?"

Raul nodded. "Ybarra and at least half a dozen others."

"Why should I believe you?"

"It's true, *señor*."

Cordova thought it over, then made up his mind. "I will deal with Ybarra just as I am about to deal with you, major."

Raul could see Cordova's knuckles whiten as he started to squeeze the trigger. "Three—"

"Freeze!" Raul heard Tally shout.

He glanced to one side and saw her standing in the doorway leading to the hall, her revolver in one hand, the case containing her badge in the other.

"Don't touch that gun, Devlin!" Tally said grimly. "You're under arrest!"

She motioned to the startled Cordova, making sure that he could clearly see the badge she was holding in her left hand. "You, Mr. Cordova. You just settle down and put away that gun. Everything's under control."

Cordova lowered his gun. "Who are you?"

"Agent Gordon, United States Border Patrol," Tally said crisply, slipping her badge back into the purse slung over her shoulder.

Cordova was still holding the gun, weighing it thoughtfully, as if wondering what to make of this. "Did you come here alone?"

"Of course not. There are others outside. We've got the house surrounded."

Cordova looked at Raul, and his dark eyes glistened with hatred. "What are you going to do with him?"

Tally stepped forward. "He's going to get just what he deserves..."

BLAINE HAD BEEN BUSY. With help from the Denver Police Department, he'd found the rental agency where a man matching Raul's description had checked out a Jeep. The man was accompanied by a young woman, obviously Tally.

"Did they say where they were headed?" he asked the clerk.

"Up to the mountains—skiing, they said."

"Tell me about the woman."

The clerk grinned. "What can I say? Real good-looking. She was in her twenties, yellowish brown hair, nice build, kind of—"

Blaine cut him off. "Did she look like she was in trouble?"

"In trouble?"

"Like she was going along with him against her will."

The clerk shook his head. "No way, man. In fact, I heard her say she didn't intend to let him out of her sight for one minute. It was obvious she had a thing for him."

Nice work, Blaine thought. *When are you ever going to learn your lesson, girl?*

"FOR A MINUTE THERE, I was beginning to have second thoughts," Raul said as Tally took off the handcuffs and dropped them into her pocket. "You cut that one awfully close."

"You told me to come on in if you weren't back out in fifteen minutes," Tally said, sliding behind the wheel and switching on the ignition. "It's been exactly fifteen minutes." She checked the rearview mirror, then swung out onto

Montview from the side street where she'd waited in the Jeep. "Did you find out what you wanted to know?"

Raul nodded. "Fuentes is on a ranch Cordova owns in Larimer County. It's an isolated place up in the mountains. That's as far as I got. He wasn't interested in talking. He just wanted to shoot me."

Tally pulled over to the curb and stopped. She reached between the seats and got the Colorado road map they'd been given when they rented the Jeep. She opened the map, and they studied it.

"Here it is," Tally said, pointing. "Larimer County is due north of here, right on the Wyoming line."

"That's a lot of territory to cover. Any bright ideas?"

Tally folded the map and stuck it back between the front bucket seats. "The county seat is Fort Collins. I suppose we could get an exact location by checking the records at the courthouse." She took his Beretta from an inside pocket of her borrowed parka and, holding it gingerly between thumb and forefinger, handed it to him. "Do me a favor," she said softly. "No more stunts like the one back there at Cordova's house, huh?"

Raul unzipped his jacket and shoved the Beretta in under his waistband. "It worked, didn't it?"

Tally gave him a dirty look. "Sure, it worked. But you almost got your head blown off."

He patted her on the knee. "You have no faith in me, my love."

Tally sighed. "What do you think Cordova will do when he finds out we snookered him?"

"You mean when he discovers his house really isn't surrounded and that you're not waltzing me off to jail?"

"Yes."

"He'll probably try to get word to Fuentes that I'm on my way up there. He'll have to send someone, though. The phone lines are down."

Tally glanced at Raul out of the corner of her eye. "What if he calls the Border Patrol and you find a reception committee waiting for us?"

"We'll cross that bridge when we come to it."

Yes, I suppose we will, Tally thought. *And then what will I do, Raul?*

NATE ABRAHAMSON SLAMMED DOWN the phone and angrily rang for the nurse. Throwing back the sheet, he sat up, cursing his bandages, the open-backed gown he was forced to wear, and everything else about the hospital. He'd been left behind, and all the action was happening many miles away. He didn't like it one bit. He had too much of a personal investment in this case, and he didn't like turning over responsibility to Blaine Murchison.

"I want my clothes!" he barked as the nurse came running. "Where the hell are you hiding them?"

The nurse pulled up short. "You don't need your clothes, Mr. Abrahamson. You need your rest. Now get back into bed and stay there."

Abrahamson swung his legs off the bed and stood up. He took a menacing step toward the woman, and she backed off. "Dammit, woman, I came in here wearing a suit of clothes, and I intend to walk out of here wearing the same suit. Now go find it."

The nurse didn't budge. "I'm sorry, but it's out being cleaned—not that it will do any good. I expect that the jacket and shirt are ruined what with all that blood on them."

"Then find me something else to wear and be quick about it. I've got to get out of here." Abrahamson's tongue was thick, his words slurred, as a result of the medication he'd received.

He took another step toward her.

"I'm going to send for the doctor right now!" the nurse exclaimed, turning and making a dash for her duty station.

"What size is he?" Abrahamson yelled after her.

Stupid woman! He went back to the bed, sat down and made a telephone call. "Abrahamson here," he growled. "I think we've finally got him. They're in a hurry, and they're making mistakes, leaving tracks anybody could follow."

He paused, listened.

Then: "The woman? She's doing exactly what I thought she'd do. She figures I'm on the take, and she's going to do everything she can to pull the rug out from under me. I'll handle her in my own way."

He listened some more, then laughed dryly. "Tough. She's playing in the big leagues now, and she's going to have to take her lumps right along with everybody else." Pause. "You arrange a car and have a helicopter standing **by**, and I'll take over. I don't care what the doctor says, I'm out of here. You tell your man to pick me up some warm clothes—a size forty-two coat, thirty-four pants, size **ten** shoes. Got that?"

Another pause. "No way, I'm going to be there myself when you move in. I've got a score to settle. Now get cracking."

Chapter Fourteen

"Better kill the headlights," Raul suggested as Tally turned off the highway and onto the narrow road leading up to the ranch. The road was walled in on both sides by ghostly white snowdrifts, and fresh tire tracks indicated several cars had come this way quite recently.

Tally slowed the Jeep and wrestled the transfer-case lever into four-wheel drive, wishing she knew whose tracks they were following.

A few minutes later, they came to the end of the trail—a trail that had taken them from the windswept banks of the Rio Grande to the wintry bleakness of the High Rockies. The blizzard had spent its fury in the canyons of the front range, and the sky was clearing. A few hundred yards in the distance, looming stark and eerie in the frozen stillness of the night, Pablo Cordova's ranch house clung to a slope at the end of the twisting road. Wisps of smoke rose from a chimney, carrying with them the fragrant scent of burning pine, and the puckered glaze of the ground-floor windows glowed with a flickering yellow light. A half-moon was nudging its way up over the ridge just behind the ranch house and overhead, errant clouds were drifting away to make room for a skyful of stars.

They'd come such a long way in such short time, Tally thought as she stopped the Jeep and gazed out across the field of snow that lay between them and the ranch house.

They'd discovered so much about themselves, and so much about one other. They'd first met in the moonlight, but before long the sun will have come up and the moonlight will be gone, and so would Raul. Would she ever see him again after tonight?

Raul reached out for her hand and squeezed it. "Do I detect poetic musings?"

She turned to him and saw that he was smiling. "You're the poet," she replied, hiding her feelings behind a mask of crispness. He was also a man of violence, as much as Simon Ybarra or any of the Protectors, but that was the dark side of him, and she didn't want to think about the dark side.

"We're all poets," Raul said. "It's just that some of us have acquired the technical skills to lay bare our souls, whereas others keep everything locked up inside, reluctant to share for fear of being looked upon as weak." He peered up at the sky. "No two of us see things the same way, Tally, and that's what makes us so uniquely human. A poet named Bourdillon wrote, 'The night has a thousand eyes, and the day but one; yet the light of the bright world dies with the dying sun.' Someone else might gaze up and—"

Tally pulled her hand from his and brushed the back of the hand against her cheek to keep him from seeing her tears. "Don't."

"Don't what?"

"Don't talk right now." *Don't make me love you any more than I do.* "It'll make it all the harder when you go."

"What makes you think I'm going anywhere?"

"You have to go someplace when all this is over, Raul. Back to Central America or Belgium or wherever..."

He put his arm around her and drew her close, his lips brushing her forehead. "There's an old saying. Let tomorrow take care of tomorrow. Tomorrow may surprise you, Tally."

Tally tried to smile, but couldn't bring it off. "You and tomorrow—you're both full of surprises."

"Would you have it any other way, my love?"

Tally had turned off the Jeep's engine, and without the defroster, the inside of the windshield had steamed up. She wiped at the windshield with her gloved hand. "So what's the game plan?" she asked, wanting to change the subject.

Raul cleared his own patch of windshield. "I'm open to suggestions. We could drive right up to the door and play it straight—tell them who we are and what we've come to do. Cordova indicated that Dr. Fuentes still trusts me, so I imagine he'd be willing to come along without too much of an argument." He paused. "The direct approach served us well at the county courthouse."

So it had, Tally recalled. She'd simply flashed her badge and said she had a warrant to serve on Pablo Cordova. The county clerk couldn't have been more helpful, even providing them with maps showing the way to the ranch.

"Somehow," she said, "I don't think the direct approach is going to work this time." She glanced at him. "You don't think much of it, either, do you?"

Raul shrugged. "The poet in me is delighted with the way everything falls so neatly into place. But the soldier part of me spots all sorts of red flags. Cordova has been thinking about this for a long time. He probably has ordered his men to kill me on sight. He's convinced that I betrayed his idol, and he wants me to pay with my life."

"But Cordova's men don't know what you look like."

"I suspect they'd shoot first and ask questions later."

Tally thought it over. "I could go in alone, Raul. I could show my ID and tell them I was sent to pick up Fuentes. They'd have no reason to suspect me. Besides, they wouldn't want to tangle with the government."

Raul shook his head. "I have a problem with that. These people have gone to great lengths to keep Fuentes's whereabouts a secret. It should be obvious by now that they don't trust your government—and with Abrahamson working so closely with the Protectors, why should they?"

Abrahamson. It all came back to Abrahamson. Tally didn't know how she'd do it, but she was determined to make him answer for his actions. It was Abrahamson who was the danger to national security, not Raul.

Raul took his Beretta from his pocket and checked the safety. He unlatched the canvas-walled door of the Jeep and pushed it open. "The moment of truth has arrived. It's time for a reconnaissance."

Staying close to the trees at the side of the road, they worked their way toward the ranch house, pausing from time to time to study the unbroken white carpet of snow that stretched before them in the moonlight.

"You don't think they saw the Jeep, do you?" Tally asked as they struggled through a waist-deep drift.

"I doubt it. The trees give us some cover, and shadows are deceptive in the moonlight."

Stepping out of the drift, Tally brushed the snow off her legs. "Something else occurs to me. The phone lines are down, but what if the people in the ranch have a two-way radio? What if Cordova realizes what we're up to and somehow gets through to them or to a neighbor? He could have sent somebody with a message. Those tracks we saw indicate someone came this way not too long ago."

Raul glanced at her. "It's not too late for you to turn back, my dear. You can go wait in the Jeep."

That's what you think, Tally said to herself. *The minute I saw you, it was too late to turn back. When was it? Five days ago. No, five nights ago. In the moonlight, on the banks of the Rio Grande....*

"Let's keep moving," she said.

When they were fifty yards from the house, Raul ducked into the trees at the side of the road and signaled Tally to stay close behind him.

"There's someone out back," he whispered over his shoulder. "I saw movement beyond the trees."

Moving in tandem through the trees, they circled around the side of the ranch house until they came to a level clearing in front of a small barn. A man stood in the clearing heaping pieces of firewood into a cart. He was huge—at least six and a half feet tall and built like a wrestler.

Raul leaned in close, his mouth against Tally's ear. "We really need a small army to handle a character like that. How's your throwing arm?"

"My what?"

He bent down and scooped up some snow, packing it into a tight ball, and handed it to her. "As soon as you see him start to head back to the house, I want you to heave this at him, then duck. I'll jump him."

Tally didn't care for the idea, but she could come up with nothing better. She took the snowball. "Be careful," she whispered.

Raul moved away and Tally lost sight of him among the trees.

Tally waited, watching the giant in the clearing. She could hear him grumbling as he worked, occasionally stopping to slap his hands together and stamp his feet.

He was wearing a heavy, knee-length coat, but she couldn't tell if he was armed.

When the man had loaded the cart with all the firewood it could hold, he grabbed the handle and jockeyed the cart around, pointing it in the direction of the ranch house.

Now.

Tally let fly with the snowball, and it glanced off a low-hanging branch, sending down a shower of white, then dropped to the ground at the guard's feet.

Tally dove for the protective cover of a tree trunk.

The man let go of the cart, and it toppled over on its side, spilling the firewood. Quick as a flash, he had his coat unsnapped and, from her hiding place, Tally could see him bring up a submachine gun he wore slung around his neck.

Raul was even quicker. Springing from the shadows at the side of the barn, he clamped one hand over the man's mouth and the other over the trigger guard of the submachine gun, dragging him back into the deep shadows at the side of the barn, kicking and squirming.

And then the man slumped.

Her revolver drawn, Tally ran to them. By the time she got to the side of the barn, the man lay in a motionless heap at Raul's feet.

"You didn't kill him, did you?" she asked worriedly.

Raul seemed hurt that she should even ask. "No, I didn't kill him. All I did was apply a bit of pressure on the carotid artery and he dozed off. Now let's get him into the barn and tie him up, and we'll have one less enemy to worry about."

He reached down to pick up the fallen hulk, and his victim suddenly came to life, snarling and grabbing out with massive hands for Raul's throat. He yanked Raul to the ground, then rolled over on top of him and began pounding his head against the packed snow.

Raul slammed the heels of his hands up under the man's chin, and the giant twisted to one side, deflecting the blow.

Tally shoved her revolver into her pocket and threw herself on the guard's broad back, locking her arms around his neck and trying to pull him away.

The giant growled. Grabbing her hair, he effortlessly plucked her off his back and sent her sprawling in the snow.

Then he went back to work on Raul, smashing his forearm against Raul's head.

Tally picked herself up and drew her revolver. She stepped in close and slammed the butt smartly against the back of the guard's neck.

He swiveled about and glared at her.

And then he slumped. For real this time.

Raul squirmed out from under the unconscious guard. "That's one I owe *you*," he muttered, rubbing his neck.

She smiled grimly. "Sorry, I couldn't find the carotid artery."

Keeping a close watch on the back door of the ranch house, they dragged their prisoner inside the barn. The near side of the building served as a workshop. In the dim light of the reflected snow, they could see two sedans and a station wagon parked side by side in the center of the building.

Relieving the unconscious man of his submachine gun, Raul searched the shelves flanking the workbench and found rope and a strip of cloth. He used the rope to tie the man securely to a post, then twirled the strip of cloth into a gag. He started to apply the gag, then waited as he saw the man stir and try to wriggle free of his bonds.

"How many others are there inside the ranch house?" Raul asked quietly.

The giant started to yell, and Raul clamped one hand over his mouth and held it there. He leaned in close, jabbing a rigid forefinger against the prisoner's ribs.

"I'm going to ask you again, and I'd be obliged if you'd give me a civil answer," he hissed into the man's ear. "You feel this?" He pressed harder with his forefinger. "You know what your gun can do. Don't make me use it on you, eh?"

He removed his hand from the prisoner's mouth, but held it poised to press down again. "How many others are there?" he repeated, this time in Spanish.

"Cuatro," the prisoner muttered.

"Four including Dr. Fuentes?"

"No, five counting him."

"Where are they?"

"They'll kill you. You know that, don't you?"

"It has been tried before, my friend. No one has managed to do it yet." Another prod with the forefinger. "Where are they?"

"Two of them are in the living room with Fuentes. Two of them are upstairs in the loft, sleeping."

"What are their orders?"

The giant stared at him, trying to pick out Raul's features in the darkness. "I don't understand."

"What have they been instructed to do in the event someone comes for Dr. Fuentes?"

"Defend him, of course—to the death."

Raul adjusted the gag over the prisoner's mouth and returned to the door, where Tally was standing guard. He'd
put away his Beretta and was holding the submachine gun
at his side. "All clear?"

Tally nodded. "As far as I can tell. But if anyone looks
out and sees that firewood scattered all over, they'll know
something's wrong."

Raul studied the open expanse between the barn and the
back porch of the house. It was twenty yards of trampled
snow, and the only place to take cover was the woodpile
midway between the two structures. "You've just given me
an idea," he said with a smile.

He ducked back inside the barn and, by feel, made a
quick search of the prisoner's pockets. It took only a few
seconds to find what he was seeking: a book of matches. He
turned his attention to the shelves.

"Mind telling me what we're looking for?" Tally asked.

"A can of gasoline, paint thinner, alcohol—anything
flammable."

"What are you going to do? Burn the place down?"

"Of course not. I just want to get their attention. But
first..." He went over to the three parked vehicles and, one
by one, lifted the hoods and yanked out wiring, tossing the
strands helter-skelter over his shoulder.

A minute later, they were back outside, dumping the
contents of a container of paint thinner onto the wood pile.
Raul struck a match and tossed it onto the pile, and then, as
the flames began spreading, ran toward the porch, with
Tally following. Motioning her to take up a position at one
side of the back door, he pressed tight against the outer wall
on the opposite side.

Reaching around, he threw open the back door and
yelled, *"¡Fuego!"* Fire! From inside the ranch house they
could hear voices, then heavy, fast-moving footsteps.
Someone shouted, then came racing through the open door.

Raul yanked him aside and chopped the side of his hand against the man's neck. The man crumpled.

A second man came out of the house, moving cautiously, holding a shotgun.

Raul snatched the weapon from him and threw it out into the snow, then stepped back, bringing his submachine gun to bear.

"Don't shoot!" Tally said sharply. "It's Blaine!"

By the light of the dancing flames, Blaine Murchison glared at Tally, then at Raul. His square jaw was set, the muscles stretched tight across his cheeks. "I was wondering when you two would show up," he said. "As long as you're here—"

He didn't finish what he'd started to say. Instead, his right forearm smashed against Raul's chest, knocking him off balance, and he lunged forward, grappling for possession of the submachine gun.

Spinning to one side, Raul ducked under Blaine's outstretched arms, then used Blaine's arms for leverage to dump him over his shoulder and down the porch steps. Raul then stepped back, waiting, his finger tightening on the trigger of the submachine gun.

Tally looked at him pleadingly.

With a shrug, Raul slipped the magazine from the submachine gun and cleared the chamber of its remaining cartridge. He tossed the weapon and ammunition off the porch, sending them skittering across the packed snow of the clearing.

"Get up, Mr. Murchison," he said quietly.

Blaine scrambled to his feet, twisting his head from side to side as if to make sure that he was still in one piece after his tumble. As he straightened, his hand went to a holster concealed inside his jacket, and he came up with a revolver, leveling it at Raul. His eyes crackled with hatred.

Tally moved in front of Blaine, and he tried to shove her aside. She wouldn't budge.

"Whose side you on anyway, girl?" Blaine demanded.

"I'd like to think I'm on the right side," Tally replied evenly. "Put away the gun, Blaine."

He stared past her to Raul. "Tell your friend there to put his hands on top of his head," he growled. "He's under arrest."

Raul didn't move. "I've come for Federico Fuentes," he said calmly.

"You have, have you? Maybe Fuentes doesn't want to go with you." Blaine glanced at Tally, then lowered his gun. "Has he got another weapon on him?"

Tally hesitated. Raul had told her the moment of truth was at hand. She had to make a decision, had to choose sides. "I . . . I don't know,' she said.

"You know the drill, girl. Search him."

Tally turned and stepped over to Raul, avoiding his eyes. She patted at his legs and waist, and her fingertips grazed the thin, angular bulge of the Beretta in one pocket of his parka.

She turned back to Blaine. "He's clean."

Her decision had been made.

She prayed it was the right one. . . .

"How'd you find this place?" she asked.

"Same way you did, girl. Cordova was only too happy to talk to the Border Patrol."

"Yes, but . . ."

But how did he find Cordova? she wanted to ask. That was the real question.

Blaine motioned with his gun. "Let's all go inside and have us a talk. You first, Devlin."

Raul stepped through the doorway, and Tally started to follow him. Blaine caught her arm. "You all right, girl? He didn't hurt you, did he?"

"I'm fine," Tally said, shaking herself loose. She didn't want him to touch her. "Let's get this over with."

They passed through a darkened kitchen, past a dining room and into a long, pine-paneled gallery in the center of which stood a walk-around stone fireplace. The gallery was bordered on three sides by a loft broken into separate rooms. The only light in the gallery was that coming from the open fireplace and from a string of lanterns hanging from the supporting beams of the loft.

Federico Fuentes was slumped in a lounge chair on one side of the hearth, hands folded atop the fur robe that covered his legs. The firelight splashed deathly lines and shadows across the parchment of his face. He was gaunt and white-haired and looked very tired and very helpless.

Fuentes glanced up with hollow eyes as Raul walked across the room. He blinked. "Is that you, major?" he said in a weak voice.

"Yes, *maestre*," Raul said softly, squatting down at the side of the chair. "Have they been treating you all right?"

Fuentes nodded slowly, a wan smile upon his lips. "They have been...quite hospitable, major. I have no complaints. Only gratitude." He was having trouble forming the words.

"Your friends miss you, *maestre*."

"And I miss them." The smile was gone, and for a few seconds the voice seemed to strengthen, gain conviction. "I said I had no complaints, but it is not true, major. My one complaint is that I fear I shall never again see my friends—my friends or my homeland...." He closed his eyes.

"Maestre?" Raul touched the old man's shoulder.

"It won't do you any good trying to talk to him, Devlin," Blaine said from the doorway, where he had remained at Tally's side. "They've got him under sedation."

Raul stood up. "They?"

Blaine flicked his head to indicate the shadows at the far end of the room. "A couple of your old buddies from south of the border."

Simon Ybarra and Hans Uhlmann stepped out of the shadows. They were wearing hats and overcoats, and their hands were in their pockets.

Seeing them again, Tally remembered Raul's telling her
how the smuggler Guerrero had described Ybarra and Uhlmann—two men with the look of death about them.

Her hand tightened on the grip of the revolver at her side.

Raul looked at Ybarra and Uhlmann, then at Blaine. "I
assume you're working together—"

"Just doing my job," Blaine said quickly. "With Abrahamson out of action, somebody had to step in."

Tally stared at him. "But Abrahamson sold out to them—
don't you see? You can't turn Dr. Fuentes over to them!
They're killers!"

"Don't tell me, tell Abrahamson!" Blaine snapped.
"He's the one who brought them into this in the first place."

Simon Ybarra stepped forward. "It's a moot point," he
said impatiently. He looked at Raul. "Hans, your old com-
rade-in-arms, has taken care of the two guards upstairs, and
now all we need to do is dispose of you and the young lady.
I don't think that will be at all difficult."

"Hold on!" Blaine spoke up. "You can have Devlin and
the old man, but leave the girl alone—hear me, Ybarra?"

Raul edged away from the seated Fuentes. "Tell us what
you have in mind for us, Señor Ybarra."

"Of course, major. It seems only fair after you and Miss
Gordon located this place for us." He brought a gun from
the pocket of his overcoat, hefted it in both hands and then
put it away. "You know as well as I do that we cannot permit the good Dr. Fuentes to return to his native land. He is
a troublemaker—even more of a troublemaker than you,
major, if that's possible."

Raul took another step back, and Tally knew that he was
shifting to keep Fuentes out of the line of fire. She waited
for Raul to make his move.

Uhlmann was holding a strand of wire in his hands,
stretching it tight and grinning evilly ear to ear. He was obviously enjoying himself as he contemplated his vengeance
upon the man who'd had him court-martialed.

Ybarra glanced disapprovingly at Uhlmann. "Patience, my friend. Those who are about to die deserve the solace of truth." He turned his attention back to Raul. "We most certainly are not going to kill Dr. Fuentes just yet. We are going to take him with us, and nurse him back to health. And then, when he is up to it, we are going to videotape him making a speech that will be broadcast on the eve of the February elections. The whole world will be watching and listening, and Federico Fuentes will be at his most eloquent as he reads the words we shall prepare for him. Needless to say, this speech will destroy whatever credibility the Movement still has." He paused. "Only then will we permit him the comfort of death."

Blaine grabbed Tally's arm and started to pull her out of the gallery, back into the dining room. "This is none of our business," he announced. "We're getting out of here."

"Nobody's going anywhere!" Nate Abrahamson bellowed from the steps leading up to the loft. His left arm was in a sling, and in his right hand he carried a sawed-off shotgun.

Moving with surprising swiftness for a wounded man, Abrahamson relieved Ybarra of his gun, then slipped back into the shadows where he could watch everyone in the room.

"In a minute," he announced, "Dr. Fuentes and I will be leaving you." He glanced at Raul. "I'm going to borrow that Jeep you left down the road, Devlin. I'm not sure our friend Fuentes and I could make it up over the ridge the way I came. The blasted snowmobile kept bogging down on me."

"It's not an easy hike either way," Raul said. "I doubt Dr. Fuentes is up to it."

"He'll make it all right. You and Gordon will come along and help carry him."

Raul casually put his hands in his pockets, and Tally knew he was reaching for his Beretta. "I'm not sure I care for that idea," he said.

"You don't have any choice, Devlin." The dull blue barrel of his shotgun shifted in Raul's direction. "I suggest you take your hands out of your pockets—slowly. There's no need for a show of bravado. Except for the two men upstairs, who are quite dead thanks to our Protector friends, everyone here is going to walk away in one piece."

Raul brought his hands out of his pockets, empty. "For how long?"

Abrahamson laughed dryly. "You and Gordon have a very poor opinion of me, don't you?"

"I don't know what gave you that idea," Tally said. "Just what are you going to do with Dr. Fuentes?"

"He's going back to Central America—alive. That's my assignment, and I damn well intend to carry it out."

"Then why have you been hounding Raul? Why have you been trying to kill him?"

Raul spoke up. "I don't think he has been, Tally. I think he's been following us in the hopes we'd lead him here. He needed me to track down Dr. Fuentes, and he needed you to find me. We've both been used from the moment our paths crossed in El Paso."

Tally glanced across at the two Protectors. "What about them? Why have you been working with them?"

"It should be obvious," Abrahamson said. "I had to keep one eye on them at the same time, just in case they got lucky and found Fuentes before you did."

Tally stared at him incredulously. "But they've murdered at least five people—Olivera and the cabdriver, the smuggler Valdez and those two men upstairs."

Abrahamson shrugged. "Actually, they killed six people. Uhlmann went back to take care of Cordova just before I showed up. But Cordova was still alive, and he managed to tell me what happened—how he'd been tricked into telling you about this ranch." He paused. "But those are matters for the police to handle. I work for the State Department, and my job is to see that Fuentes gets home safely. He's still the best hope we have for peace in his part of the world."

"I'll see that he gets home," Raul said.

"Sorry," Abrahamson said curtly, "but you don't have any vote in this, Devlin. Now if you'll help Dr. Fuentes to the Jeep—"

"Just a minute," Tally said. "I want to know how you managed to follow us all the way through Colorado?"

"I didn't. I simply had my people keep an eye on your colleague—Murchison. He took Ybarra and Uhlmann with him when he when out to interview Cordova."

Tally wheeled to face Blaine. "*You* were the one who had us bugged all along, weren't you? You planted that tracking device on us!"

Blaine stared at her. "I don't know what you're talking about, girl. I just did some plain old, hard-nosed police work, that's all."

Tally nodded slowly. She'd begun to understand. "You were working all right, but for them—" she glanced at Ybarra and Uhlmann "—not the Border Patrol. How much did they pay you to help them get to Raul through me?"

"You're out of your mind, girl."

"Am I?" Tally raised the revolver she'd been holding at her side, and Blaine took a step back, uncertainty in his eyes. She tossed the revolver to Raul, who caught it by the barrel. "Take a look at it," she instructed him. "It's the only thing I've had with me constantly since I left my apartment in El Paso. I'll bet a month's pay if you unscrew the grips on the handle and look inside—"

"Dammit!" Blaine growled, taking a step toward Devlin. "I don't have to listen to this!"

The muzzle of Abrahamson's shotgun swung about to cover him. "You're wrong there, inspector. I think the young lady is on to something. Go ahead, Devlin. Check it out."

"I remember now," Tally said. "That night you found me handcuffed in my apartment, Blaine took the revolver out of the room—to have it checked for fingerprints, he said. That's when he planted the homing device in the butt.''

Using a coin as a screwdriver, Raul removed the handle grips and then held up a small, round bit of black plastic between thumb and forefinger. "And here it is," he said with an approving smile. "Speaking of fingerprints—''

"I just did it for her own good!" Blaine broke in, looking at Abrahamson and ignoring the others. "The damn girl's stubborn as a mule, and I knew she'd be hell-bent on catching up with Devlin to even the score. It was the only way I could keep track of her.''

Tally shook her head slowly as the truth sank in further. "It won't wash, Blaine. You weren't the one who followed me from Socorro and through Albuquerque the night Professor Olivera and the cabdriver were murdered. The Protectors were the ones on my tail every step of the way, thanks to you. You not only sold out to them, you were a party to murder.''

"Why deny it?" Ybarra spoke up. "The inspector saw an opportunity to pad his pockets and he seized it. The ten thousand dollars we paid him in El Paso was money well spent." He cocked his head and looked at Abrahamson. "You know, I never did trust you, *señor*. I thought it was wise to have someone else working for us on the inside, just for insurance.''

"Damn you, Ybarra!" Blaine growled, lunging at the Protector.

Uhlmann had dropped the wire and now had a gun in his hands. He fired at Blaine, dropping him in his tracks, then spun around to shoot Abrahamson.

Abrahamson's shotgun roared, and the Butcher of Buenos Aires toppled backward with a sharp scream. He was dead before he hit the floor.

Blaine sat up, holding his shoulder. Blood was oozing between his fingers, and he was still holding his gun.

Abrahamson took a step forward, working the slide action of his shotgun to reload. He trained the shotgun on

Blaine. "Relieve him of his weapon, Gordon," he said curtly.

Tally held out her hand. "Better do as he says, Blaine."

Blaine looked at her imploringly. "Look, girl, I tried to protect you. I told Ybarra that if anything happened to you, he'd have me to—"

"I don't want to hear it, Blaine." She took the gun from him, then backed off, his blood staining her fingers.

Abrahamson grunted. "Your story touches my heart, inspector. I wonder if I'll still be touched when we have the justice department run a check on your bank accounts." He glanced at Devlin. "Gather up the rest of the hardware and find a bag to carry it in. And no tricks."

"Dr. Fuentes is going with me," Raul said softly, hooking his thumbs in the pockets of his parka, his right hand only inches from his Beretta. "I still don't trust you, my friend."

"You don't have any choice!" Abrahamson snapped, moving out of the shadows and taking up a position behind Fuentes's chair.

Raul hesitated, and Tally knew exactly what he was thinking. He'd come so far only to have success snatched away at gunpoint.

His hands came away from his pockets. Empty.

"Come on now. Help me get this man out of here," Abrahamson ordered. He looked at Ybarra and Murchison. "You two stay here while Devlin and Gordon carry Fuentes out to the Jeep. Then I'm going to send them back here and you can sort the rest of it out among yourselves. Incidentally, I wouldn't recommend trying to leave. I've got people covering all routes and they'll be showing up here any time now."

Raul picked up the frail Fuentes in his arms and carried him to the front door. Tally held the door open and Raul stepped out onto the porch. Abrahamson backed out through the door, his shotgun cradled in his arm.

"Let's move it," the man from Washington said crisply as Tally closed the door behind them. "Those clowns aren't going to give up that easily."

"Why didn't you bring some backup when you came across the ridge?" Tally asked as they slogged through the snow toward the parked Jeep.

"I told you before, Gordon—the fewer people who know about this, the better. Besides, the minute Ybarra is booked, he'll be on the phone to his lawyers and we'll have one hell of a time getting Fuentes back safely. Ybarra has death squads staked out everywhere."

"But surely—"

"Just shut up and listen, both of you. Here's what we're going to do...."

TALLY WAS STILL SCREAMING, her clenched hands held to her cheeks in horror, as Ybarra came running out of the ranch house, followed by Blaine who was moving slowly, obviously in pain. Raul had one arm around Tally's shoulder, as if trying to comfort her. He'd recovered the submachine gun from the pile of confiscated weapons, and he waved it at the approaching men in a signal to stay back.

"They're dead!" Tally cried, tearing herself away from Raul and pointing to the edge of the road where the churned-up tire tracks told the story.

"What happened?" Blaine demanded from a distance, keeping a wary eye on Raul and his submachine gun.

Tally sobbed. "Abrahamson put Dr. Fuentes into the Jeep and started down the road. Suddenly he spun around and went over the edge, down into the canyon. Oh, God, it was awful!"

Raul was visibly moved. "The world has lost a great man," he said.

In the moonlight, they could see Ybarra's evil smile as he assessed the situation. "It is most unfortunate that Dr. Fuentes will be unable to perform for us on camera, but at least he will cause us no more trouble. If the truth be known,

Mr. Abrahamson has saved us a great deal of trouble." He turned and started back toward the ranch house. "Come, inspector, we may as well stay warm while we wait to be arrested." He took Blaine's arm to help steady him. "Cheer up. It will be only a temporary inconvenience, I assure you. My attorneys will have us out of jail in no time. After you serve a short prison sentence, perhaps we could find gainful employment for you in our organization."

Angrily Blaine shook free and took a tentative step forward. "Tally, I—"

"Keep away from me!" Tally shouted. "You're as bad as Ybarra!"

"Look, girl, you can't stay out here in the cold. Come on back to the ranch house with us."

"I'd rather freeze, Blaine Murchison!"

"Suit yourself." He glared at Raul. "What the hell, maybe the two of you deserve each other."

I should hope so, after all we've been through together, Tally thought.

Epilogue

"You won't have any problem," Nate Abrahamson said as he stood with Tally and Raul on the tarmac at the Grand Junction airport and gave a thumbs-up signal to the white-haired old man seated at the window of the twin-engine Beechcraft. "We've already filed a flight plan for you, Devlin. It will take you over the border west of Nogales, then across the Gulf of California and straight into La Paz—and with no static from the Mexican authorities. Your new identity papers will be waiting for you, and we'll have someone down there who can fix you up with disguises your own mother wouldn't see through. A month or so of warm sun and sandy beaches, and Fuentes will be ready to take on the world again, raring to go in time for the February elections."

Tally linked her arm with Raul's. "I don't know," she said teasingly. "Dr. Fuentes may be all right, but this man here certainly needs a keeper to help him stay out of trouble."

Raul squeezed her hand. "Are you volunteering to come along?"

Tally sighed. "I'd love to, but I don't think I could sell the Border Patrol on the idea. I'm turning in my resignation as soon as I get back to El Paso, and I want to leave them happy. Who knows? They might send business my way when I set up my law practice."

Abrahamson frowned. "I don't know why you want to waste your talents in the field of law, Gordon. The woods are full of young legal eagles trying to scratch out a living. We could use you back in Washington, doing security work in my office. Since the Protectors think I'm dead, I'm going to have to go into hiding for a while, too. But I'll be happy to pull some strings for you when I get back. It'd be quite a career move for you."

Tally shook her head. "Sorry, I already have my career mapped out."

Abrahamson winked at Raul. "Maybe she wants to try her hand at acting, Devlin. You'll have to admit that the performance she gave up at the ranch house after we shoved the Jeep off the cliff wasn't bad, even if she did have a captive audience."

Tally laughed. "No more government work, no more acting. I'm going to practice law in El Paso. I want to specialize in immigration work."

"As in illegal aliens?" Raul asked.

"As in undocumented aliens," she corrected.

He took her into his arms. "Then hang out your shingle, my love. I'll be back in February. Do I have to wade across the river to get your attention? Maybe I can be your first case."

"I'm counting on it," Tally said, kissing him.

If **YOU** enjoyed this book,
your daughter may enjoy

Romances from

Keepsake is a series of tender, funny, down-to-earth romances for younger teens.

The simple boy-meets-girl romances have lively and believable characters, lots of action and romantic situations with which teens can identify.

Available now wherever books are sold.

ADULT-1

Taylor House

by Leigh Anne Williams

Enter the lives of the Taylor women of Greensdale, Massachusetts, a town where tradition and family mean so much. A story of family, home and love in a New England village.

Don't miss the Taylor House trilogy, starting next month in Harlequin American Romance with #265 *Katherine's Dream*, in October 1988, and followed by #269 *Lydia's Hope* and #273 *Clarissa's Wish* in November and December of 1988.

One house . . . two sisters . . . three generations

TYLAG-1

ABANDON YOURSELF TO

Temptation ™

In September's Harlequin Temptation books you'll get more than just terrific sexy romance—you'll get $2 worth of **Jovan Musk** fragrance coupons **plus** an opportunity to get a very special, unique nightshirt.

Harlequin's most sensual series will also be featuring four of Temptation's favourite authors writing the Montclair Emeralds quartet.

Harlequin Temptation in September— too hot to miss!

JOVAN-1

ATTRACTIVE, SPACE SAVING BOOK RACK

Display your most prized novels on this handsome and sturdy book rack. The hand-rubbed walnut finish will blend into your library decor with quiet elegance, providing a practical organizer for your favorite hard-or soft-covered books.

Only $9.95

Approximately 16" x 8" when assembled

Assembles in seconds!

To order, rush your name, address and zip code, along with a check or money order for $10.70* ($9.95 plus 75¢ postage and handling) payable to *Harlequin Reader Service*:

Harlequin Reader Service
Book Rack Offer
901 Fuhrmann Blvd.
P.O. Box 1396
Buffalo, NY 14269-1396

Offer not available in Canada.

BKR-1A

*New York and Iowa residents add appropriate sales tax.

HARLEQUIN SIGNATURE EDITION

VIOLET WINSPEAR

HOUSE OF STORMS

Editorial secretary Debra Hartway travels to the Salvador family's rugged Cornish island home to work on Jack Salvador's latest book. Disturbing questions hang in the troubled air over Lovelis Island. What or who had caused the tragic death of Jack's young wife? Why did Jack stay away from the home and, more especially, the baby son he loved so well? And—why should Rodare, Jack's brother, who had proved himself a man of the highest integrity, constantly invade Debra's thoughts with such passionate, dark desires . . . ?

Violet Winspear, who has written more than 65 romance novels translated worldwide into 18 languages, is one of Harlequin's best-loved and bestselling authors. HOUSE OF STORMS, her second title in the Harlequin Signature Edition program, is a full-length novel rich in romantic tradition and intriguingly spiced with an atmosphere of danger and mystery.

Watch for HOUSE OF STORMS—coming in October!

HOFS-1